CELESTIAL SHADOWS

THE CELESTIAL MARKED SERIES: BOOK FOUR

EMMA L. ADAMS

I was quite possibly going to kill Fiona.

I stood uncomfortably in my four-inch heels, the lights of camera flashes wielded by balaclava-clad vampires dazzling my eyes. The vamps themselves were covered from head to toe to protect their sensitive skin from their own cameras. I wouldn't risk certain death to snap a picture of Devi Lawson, but then again, I *was* Devi Lawson, and being me wasn't as wonderfully inspiring as the awestruck vamps seemed to think.

After fighting a gruelling battle to the death a few weeks ago, I'd wanted the privacy of my old life back. Being in public made me enough of a target, considering the whole world had watched the battle… or part of it. But hours of listening to Fiona beg me to talk to the public had worn me down. People were still scared, there was a lot of misinformation out there, and it was on me to set the record straight. Or put up with a million new unflattering pictures of me appearing under ridiculous headlines. Unfortunately, my celestial magic only worked on demons and other preternaturals, not cameras.

The majority of the crowd was human, but the vampires I'd helped save from a massacre a few weeks ago occupied the front row. Since I'd stopped the demonic virus turning the vamps into bloodthirsty killers, I guess I understood their need to hero-worship me a bit, because the rest of the celestials had wanted them dead. With the virus gone, however, their sensitivity to the sunlight came back. Being surrounded by people wearing what amounted to snowsuits on a blisteringly warm summer's day made my own skin feel uncomfortably warm even in a skimpy dress. My palms were sweaty underneath my elbow-length gloves, but I didn't quite trust my celestial mark not to activate and burn someone's face off if I removed them. Grade Four celestial powers took some getting used to.

The interviewer, a twenty-something brunette with heels even taller than mine, took to the stage beside me, speaking into a microphone. "DivinityWatch welcomes the one and only Devi Lawson, hero of Haven City."

Cheering rose up from the crowd. Fiona waved from the back. I gritted my teeth, giving her a look that communicated that she'd be getting an earful as soon as this was over. She'd said a private interview to be uploaded to DivinityWatch's website would be enough. No stages and squealing vamps waving 'we love Devi' signs. If someone threw underwear at me, I was out.

"I'm Devina Lawson," I said into the microphone a vampire held out in a gloved hand. "You've probably heard of me by now."

Natural celebrity, I was not. The crowd gave another loud cheer as though I'd declared I'd found the cure for world hunger. Then the interviewer said, "What we'd all like to know, Devi, is how you worked out the celestial guild was corrupt."

Some of the anticipation died down. If I was being

honest, I'd have said, *a long time ago, but definitely when they started murdering vampires.*

"There's not much to say. I found a conspiracy within the celestial guild, and when nobody believed me, I took matters into my own hands."

Even as a member, I'd never really believed the guild were as competent as they pretended to be, but *evil* was another thing entirely. I'd actually found out by accident when a demon pretending to be the ex-celestial traitor Damian Greenwood tried to fool the vampires into thinking the celestials had a cure for the virus afflicting them. He'd roused my suspicions enough that I'd gone into the guild to spy on him, and instead found that he, not to mention Inspector Deacon, one of the most respected senior guild members, had been replaced by a demon. The result was that the celestial guild in Haven City had more or less imploded, or at least torched their own reputation in the eyes of the public. The vamps and other preternaturals, not to mention the humans, were keen to find someone new to worship. Meaning, me.

The DivinityWatch site was run by humans who thought there were angels hiding amongst us, and had once featured thousands of photos of what people thought were Divinities. It hadn't escaped my attention that most of said photos had been replaced by pictures of me. Also, a not insignificant proportion of their members were vampires who believed if they slept with a celestial, we'd save their immortal souls. But the owners of the site had saved lives when the guild had fallen, and played their part in protecting the public. This interview was the least I could do to repay them, but there were some things I didn't want the public to know. Like the fact that the one sure-fire way to kill a celestial was to use a demon-infected vampire bite, for instance.

"I heard you ascended to Grade Four," said the interviewer. "But you also work with the warlocks."

There was no point in denying it. Javos, my warlock employer, had let the other warlocks know not to touch me despite my celestial powers. A nice gesture, even if he was a bad-tempered prick most of the time.

"Yep. You might say my situation is a little unusual."

The vamps *oohed* and *aahed* and generally made tits of themselves in the front row.

The interviewer smiled broadly. "Of course it is. Do you know what the guild's next move is?"

Well, no. The public *did* need to know someone was handling the situation, and their perception of the celestials was at an all-time low. But I had zero clue what the celestials planned to do about the fact that an arch-demon had almost succeeded in creating a bridge between this realm and the two demon realms of Babylon and Pandemonium. Monsters had spawned in the streets, vampires infected by the demonic virus had attacked everyone within sight, and I'd helped lead the army to stop them.

That was the official version of the story. The unofficial one— involving deals with arch-demons and bargaining with fallen angels—remained strictly between me, Fiona, and a very small group of warlocks.

"The guild is, as far as I know, functioning as normal," I said. "They're killing demons. The ones who worked against the former Grade Fours did so at great personal risk. I'm not working for them because I prefer to work alone."

"Is it true you're a demon?" someone shouted.

"Nope. Human. Not divine, either." Or rather, all three at once.

"Show us your divine powers!" someone called out.

"I'd demonstrate, but I don't want to start a vampire

barbecue." I held up my left hand. The vamps backed slowly away.

"Is it true you're dating a warlock?" said another. "A shadow warlock?"

"My love life is nobody's business but my own." I dropped my polite facade. "I think that's enough questions."

"The interview is over!" said the brunette, thankfully picking up on the warning signs. Thank heavens for small mercies. I could hardly breathe for the heat, let alone the dress I'd squeezed myself into. Nikolas thought it looked hot. I thought the seams would split if I lifted my arms above my head. I was too athletic and muscular to be considered conventionally feminine or pretty, and had a fairly extensive scar collection courtesy of years of demons getting into my personal space. Under the gloves covering my celestial and demon marks, my hands were mostly scar tissue. Still, my skin had darkened into my summer tan and I no longer looked like a pasty vampire. I wore my hair down for once, my curls temporarily tamed. Good enough for Nikolas Castor, who stood apart from the crowd, his own magic deflecting him from attention.

Nikolas was a warlock—half human, half demon. Half *arch*-demon, which also made him a demigod, the most powerful class of warlock. He smiled at me from a distance as I wobbled off the stage. The preternatural grace I got from my celestial mark didn't extend to walking in spiked torture weapons.

As I drew closer, his attention-deflecting spell encompassed me, too. "Thanks," I said. "Too much?"

"Everyone knows we're together. It's not a well-kept secret."

I shrugged. "They have my whole life story online." Including my history with my former guild partner, Rory, who'd died two years ago. "I didn't want them to get yours, too. Anyway, let's get out of here. I'd rather wear Rachel's boots than these."

He grinned and took my hand, and the shadows of Babylon, the demon realm, rose to meet us.

———

"That is *not* how it happened." I watched the interview unfold on my phone, having to stop every so often to scroll past the sponsored "DivinityWatch's Warlock of the Week" feature (winner: The Wingless Warlock, for the twenty-fifth week running). "They cut down what I said to make me sound like I was the only one who won the battle and the celestials were totally incompetent."

"They *were* totally incompetent," said the very naked warlock in the bed beside me, an amused smirk on his face as the video played.

"Not all of them. Anyway, I thought you said the level of attention I'm getting was likely to result in bad consequences."

"We already saw the end of the world," said Nikolas. "At this point, I'd rather the public believe us than believe whatever nonsense the guild comes up with next."

"The guild's being pretty quiet, actually." Losing their leader—twice over—had hit the celestials hard. "I look like I'm going to burn the place to the ground at the end. If anything, I think I made them more frightened than before."

Nikolas said, "You're marked with demonic and celestial power, and you've outwitted both arch-demons and powerful warlocks—not to mention a fallen angel. I think they're justified in being a little afraid of you."

"You don't sound too worried."

"When you've defused as many potential wars as I have, dealing with volatile powers becomes second nature."

"So I'm a 'volatile power' now?"

He grinned and wrapped his legs around mine. "You're *my* volatile power."

"You sure know how to flatter a girl." I clicked off my phone as his strong hands massaged my shoulders. There were some—okay, a lot—of perks to dating a warlock, but having to wear a cuff over my wrist all the time to stop my celestial power accidentally burning a hole in him definitely wasn't one of them. Nikolas had said his regenerative healing power worked on almost anything, but it was a mood-killer to say the least. Nikolas himself wore his formidable warlock strength in every inch of his six-foot-something frame. He was built like a fighter, for speed, grace and power. His dark hair gleamed a reddish colour when it caught the light, which, combined with his golden eyes, served to make him look decidedly non-human. That, and the wings, but he rarely wore them in this realm. Like most warlocks, his magic gained a boost from being in his home dimension, and he'd spent most of the last week in this one.

I disentangled myself from Nikolas. "All right, I'm done with this crap. I'm going for a run."

He stood in a fluid movement. "Want company?"

"Only if I need a reminder how out of shape I am."

He grinned. "Think of me as a motivational coach."

"You're tough enough as a magic coach."

"Good. I wouldn't want Javos to steal that title."

———

My legs screamed in protest, and by the time I caught up to Nikolas on the third lap, I would have pledged my soul to the first demon to make the agonising stitch in my chest go away. I skidded to a halt before I crashed into him. "Enough."

His mouth curved into a smile. "I didn't even have the

chance to shout my words of encouragement at you. I even prepared a script."

"Dick." I caught my balance, clutching my side. "How is that fair? You and I have both done nothing but lie around in bed all week, but you can still outrun me." Bloody warlocks. He could run two laps in the time it took me to run one, at least. My demon mark had given me magic, but not the other perks of being a warlock.

He gave me another grin. "Now, as far as I remember, we spent most of the time in bed engaged in rigorous physical activity." His hand trailed down my back, and my skin heated in response to his touch.

"Did we? I might need a reminder." I pressed my lips to his, and his arms came around me, lifting me off my feet. There was a rapping noise. Probably the people whose garden we were making out in. Oops. At least Nikolas's wings hadn't come out. It'd been known to occur in times of sexual stimulation.

He set me down. "I think we've tormented these people enough. Want to go home?"

"Sure."

He took one step—and vanished. It still freaked me out a little when he disappeared into the shadow realm mid-conversation, though he didn't do it often. *Typical.* We'd been lucky to have a few weeks of relative peace, but it was impossible to entirely forget he was a shadow demon with ties in two worlds at once.

"Seriously?" I said, mostly to myself. That's what I got for not bringing a car. The city overlapped geographically with Babylon, his home realm, so if he was heading to the castle he spent most of his time in, he'd reappear somewhere entirely different when he came back to Earth. Unlike him, I didn't have wings.

I found a bus stop to sit in and skimmed through DivinityWatch's website on my phone. I was lucky, considering my newfound fame, that I hadn't run into too many crazies in real life, but the eyebrow-raising comments on the photos of me made me wish I'd used an alias. Weirdos on the internet were still weirdos in real life, after all.

Nikolas reappeared in a flash of black shadows, several feet away. Wings extended from his shoulder blades, shadowy and fairly noticeable in this mundane street. I shoved my phone in my pocket and walked away from the bus stop towards him.

"Hey. Use your magic. Nikolas." I waved my hand in front of his eyes, then gave up and activated my demon mark. He'd never outright forgotten himself in this dimension before. I drew his magic into the mark and directed it at the few people out on the street and peering from windows, telling them to go away and stop gawking at us. "Nikolas. What is it?"

When he spoke, he used the higher demon language, Malthric, and simply said, "Casthus."

"What?" I said.

His eyes opened, and they were a simmering red. This time, he spoke in English: "The arch-demon Casthus has announced his intention to return to Babylon."

2

Casthus—I guess his demon name was—was the absentee ruler of Babylon, the shadow realm where Nikolas ruled over a castle of warlocks in his place. Not someone I'd ever wanted to meet, considering I was dating his son, and the pair of us had both stolen the shadow demon's army *and* freed the fallen imprisoned underneath his castle.

"Now?" I asked, my voice dropping to a whisper.

"No, but word spreads like wildfire in the nether realms." He began to walk, and I hurried after him, the pain in my side forgotten. "We need to be ready."

"Ready to meet him?"

"Casthus strongly dislikes surprises. I think I should speak to him first. He'll find out about you in time, but I'm going to explain the situation with the fallen before he acts hastily."

So, before he smites me on the spot. I'd met three arch-demons in the last few months and they'd all scared the living hell out of me. But the shadow demon carried a reputation few could match. He'd ditched Babylon ages ago as it'd been a dead-end world where no demons could be summoned. "He found out, right? You know that probably means he knows about me anyway."

"Yes. I suspected he would find out eventually, but I was counting on him being preoccupied with other things."

"Like the war with heaven." I'd narrowly escaped being dragged into the war myself, and was still unsure of where I fit into the big picture. As a Grade Four celestial soldier with the powers and mark of an arch-demon, the fact that I had command over my own soul made me a valuable commodity to anyone who could get their hands on me. Which was nobody, as far as I was concerned. Two arch-demons had already tried to claim me and I had no intention of ending up at the mercy of another, whatever reputation he carried.

"Have you ever met him? I mean, in person?" I asked, my breath quickening as his pace increased faster than I could keep up with. His eyes had lost their freakishly red colour and returned to their usual golden tint, but they were a reminder that I'd never seen him lose control before. Most demigods—even Javos—kept the darker part of their nature under wraps. But if he had to go up against an arch-demon, he'd probably need to go full demon.

"Of course I have. He ruled Babylon up until I was fifteen. Then he abruptly disappeared, so I had to step in and take over or someone else would have."

"Seriously? Wait, who raised Zadok?"

"He left that task to another warlock."

And Nikolas himself had been raised in this realm. To say Zadok was resentful at being the unwanted sibling, left behind on a demon realm by his own mother, was an understatement. But I held little sympathy for him, considering he'd tried to kill me and my friends more than once. Not to mention let an arch-demon into his tower and nearly doomed us all. But *this* arch-demon was something else entirely. Heaven knew how he'd react to finding out I'd freed the fallen—immortal children of angels, left to ruin when their forefathers fell from grace—from where the shadow demon had callously imprisoned them underneath the castle.

And to think I'd thought that bloody interview was all I'd have to worry about today.

Celestials didn't exist on Babylon and humans were few and far between, since the demons had won the war with heaven and mostly died out themselves in the process. That meant the only so-called allies we had there were warlocks who barely respected Nikolas and didn't respect me in the slightest.

We entered the warlock's headquarters, a plain brick house with a pair of devil horns perched on the fence. While I now stayed at Nikolas's house more than I did my own flat, I usually spent my days here training my demon powers, supervising Fiona's magic lessons, and driving the leader of the warlocks into an early grave by causing controlled—and occasionally uncontrolled—explosions in the lab with Rachel, Nikolas's adoptive sister.

Rachel looked about eighteen or nineteen, with bubblegum-pink hair, and waved at me as we entered.

"You look like a demon crapped in your shoes," she said. "Did someone take a picture of you two and put it on the internet?"

"Nope. It's Babylon," I answered, jerking my head at Nikolas. "Specifically, its long-lost owner."

She winced. "Oh. Him."

"You could say that," Nikolas said. "This is going to stir things up, that's for certain. Where is Javos?"

"Strangling a client."

"Not Fiona?" I said, alarmed.

"No. She's hiding in the lab. He wouldn't hurt her on my watch, anyway."

I'd almost begun to think Javos was warming up to my best friend's constant presence. Fiona had been bitten by a vampire carrying a virus that attached part of a soul to a person—except in her case, that soul fragment had belonged to Azurial, a fire demon. While Clover had managed to detach his soul from Fiona's without damaging her, some of his magic had been left behind. Not enough to make her partially a demon, like me, but the photos that'd emerged of Fiona during the battle had been enough to get her fired from her call centre job. So now she was stuck assisting the warlocks until she got her newfound magic under control.

Javos shouldered his way into the hall, throwing a long-tailed warlock into the air. I moved wisely out of the line of fire as the warlock hit the wall with a bone-shaking thud.

"Get out," Javos rumbled.

The fork-tailed demon picked himself up, opened the door, and ran like hell. Good idea. You didn't want to get on the bad side of the warlocks' leader during a fight. Huge and muscled, Javos stood at seven feet tall and was built like a tank. He was also immune to celestial powers, even Grade Four, and had telekinetic abilities that put even his formidable strength to shame.

"Bloody incubi," he growled, yanking the door closed behind the fleeing warlock. "Making trouble at every corner. What did you do this time, Devi?"

"Actually, it wasn't me this time," I said. "Babylon's esteemed leader is apparently on his way back."

Javos turned on me with blazing eyes. And a blazing aura, too. It took a lot of self-control not to accidentally activate my celestial mark, which still spontaneously caught fire sometimes whenever I got too close to a warlock or vamp.

"I seem to remember you're the one who drew attention to that realm in the first place."

"Don't pin that one on me," I said to him. "You know

perfectly well the person who marked me in the first place was the orchestrator." Especially as the arch-demon in question had also marked the ex-celestial vampire king, setting things up so Babylon would turn into a battlefield between two angry arch-demons and the celestials.

The whole thing had been a setup for the gods' entertainment. One arch-demon, Abyss, had played along because she'd wanted the Divinities to help her. Lythocrax, I wasn't so sure about. He was the demon who'd marked me, and he hadn't wanted me to run around using the power of my own free will. We hadn't parted on pleasant terms, which left me with no guarantees of having his back if the shadow arch-demon decided I was an enemy.

I had a feeling the Divinities themselves only knew why he'd marked me in the first place—after all, he'd *been* a Divinity before he'd fallen. Like all the arch-demons. None of them were particularly keen to discuss their own history, obviously, and no mortal was foolish enough to ask.

Javos let out a long growl. "If any of you bring *anything* from the netherworld back to Earth—arch-demons included —you can consider me your enemy as well."

"Don't pretend you don't know the arch-demons could stride in and out of this world any time they wanted," I retaliated. "Pretty sure I'm the one who convinced Abyss *not* to do that. So if you don't mind, Nikolas and I need to come up with a plan."

I walked pointedly into the lab, our usual meeting spot. Fiona peered at me from behind the table where I kept my props, looking wary. I'd meant to confront her over the interview, but that could wait for later.

Besides, I wasn't really mad at her. More at Divinity-Watch's annoying admins for holding up someone like me as the paragon of amazingness. I barely remembered to do laundry, for the Divinities' sakes. I definitely wasn't a good example to follow. I'd prevented a war, but most of what I'd done had been down to sheer luck.

Nikolas and Javos briefly exchanged a few words in the demonic tongue of Malthric. How Javos had learnt it when he wasn't from the shadow realm, I had no idea. Probably, it was on the warlock curriculum. Along with ways to murder one's relatives. I knew next to nothing about Javos's own family—except that to be a demigod like Nikolas, he must have one arch-demon parent and one human one—and to be honest, I planned to keep it that way.

Fiona dropped her voice. "What is it? An emergency?"

"You might say that," I said. "A certain arch-demon of shadows is apparently coming back to claim his castle."

"I highly doubt he's planning to stay," Nikolas said. "He has no use for it at all. Babylon is a dead-end world. The only reason I can think of for his coming back is the situation on Pandemonium and the events surrounding it."

Nikolas had a gift for understatement. The 'events' included the death of an arch-demon and a war that had nearly swallowed Earth up and plunged the nether realms into chaos. Warlocks, like their demon kin, were rarely fazed by anything. Even irritable dickheads like Javos, who ranged from raging mad to a pretend calm that had almost fooled me when we first met. Nikolas, however, reacted to catastrophe as though it was merely an irritating fly buzzing in his ear. He was the type of person you wanted to have around in a crisis, that was for sure.

"It's been fifteen years," Nikolas added, seeing my not-quite-fooled expression. "I have a system in place. The other warlocks know what to do. Zadok certainly does. If it's a simple visit, it'll be no issue."

"No issue?" I echoed. "What in the seven hells do we tell him about the portals, the bridge...?"

"The truth," he said. "Arch-demons try to conquer worlds

all the time. He knew it was an inevitability. I rather think he'll be more concerned with Themedes's fate and how Abyss has taken his place."

"I can claim responsibility for that," I said. "But only if there's a guarantee he won't come here to Earth."

Dread coiled in my chest like a viper. I'd lay my life down to protect my world without a second's thought, and had done so. I should have known that my actions would bring a wave of new enemies after me, but I'd never guessed that the shadow demon would be the first.

"No guarantees, but I can promise I'll do everything in my power to stop him if he tries." Nikolas paused. "He'll certainly want to speak with you. I think the best bet is to tell him the truth. If he thinks you're Lythocrax's pawn, he might decide to go after him."

"He's welcome to," I said. "You know Lythocrax highly regrets ever marking me in the first place. I caused him so much trouble."

"Did the arch-demon set a date?" said Javos. "I need to inform the other warlocks on the council if there's any danger. Maybe the other preternaturals, too."

"No," said Nikolas. "Any day now is specific enough for me. I'll be ready."

Javos left the room, swearing in demonic languages under his breath, and Rachel entered in his place. "Nice," she said. "You really can't catch a break. That's one trip I won't be signing up for."

"Believe me, I wish I didn't have to either," I said. "Just one perk of being the most famous non-demon in the netherworld."

Fiona winced. "Shit. Did the interview cause it?"

"Nope," I said. "I doubt they have internet in the depths of hell. They wouldn't know DivinityWatch if they were elected Arch-Demon of the Week. Don't get any ideas."

"I wasn't," said Fiona. "You know I'm not actually an admin on the site. Anyway, what are you going to do?"

"Same as usual. Fuck things up, accidentally or deliberately. Nikolas wants to speak to him before bringing me in."

"Only if I'm certain he's not going to make a power play," growled Nikolas. "I did not go to the trouble of establishing my control over Babylon for him to snatch it from in front of me. He doesn't *need* that realm. I think he's more curious about Abyss's new position as ruler of Pandemonium."

"Good. Those two can fight it out. But the fallen…"

"Exactly," he said. "He gave me specific instructions not to let the fallen roam free. They're harmless, which is excuse enough, but I've had enough grief from the warlocks about it. I need to find somewhere else for them to stay during the arch-demon's visit."

"Not to rain on your parade," said Rachel, "but I distinctly heard Javos just say *'If any of you bring* anything *from the netherworld back to Earth—arch-demons included—you can consider me your enemy as well'.*"

"Wonderful," I said. "I helped look after displaced vamps for weeks, but they can at least hold a conversation. The fallen only speak Malthric, so everyone's going to think they're demons if we bring them here. There's no way they'd survive Earth. Also, to be honest, knowing they exist would crush what's left of the celestials' spirits."

Because the fallen were the closest the nether realms got to actual celestials, in that they bore the gods' powers… kind of. And they were immortal, so the warlocks couldn't kill them off even if they weren't too scared to. Did the arch-demon share that fear? I didn't know, but subjecting them to any more torture didn't appeal in the slightest.

"I'm thinking." Nikolas paused. "Returning them to the dungeon seems the only option. It'll be distressing for them, but the arch-demon would slaughter them in any other circumstances. Unless we found another dimension, which would come with its own set of problems."

"Then I'll tell them," I said. "They trust me." Which meant I was about to betray them in a major way, but I was sure they preferred imprisonment to being maimed and tortured by an arch-demon. "Were you heading there now? I can do that while you break the news to the other warlocks."

"They know," he said. "That's the problem."

I looked down at my running clothes. "I'll change and get some weapons. We should deal with this before Javos kicks up a fuss again."

My weapons were mostly for show these days. After all, I *was* a weapon. But I fixed twin knives to my arms as well as one of my trademark full-body-blister attack spells around my neck. Finally, I pocketed a number of shards of demon-glass, the substance I used to hop between dimensions. Demonglass itself remained a mystery. It was a reflective type of glass found on demon dimensions, and it absorbed power. Like me. Nikolas could bring me with him into the shadow realm without me using the demonglass, but he carried some so I could find him if we got separated.

Nikolas wore dark clothes in the style of army fatigues, custom made for wear and tear—not so much for demigod regeneration. His weapons came in the form of his three demigod powers: zapping his enemies with lightning, hitting them with his lure power, and using a subtle type of mind control. As an added bonus, he could fly and hop through dimensions to Babylon from anywhere he chose. His aura was shadowy black. My Grade Four celestial upgrade had afforded me the ability to see any warlock's aura, but his was familiar enough for me to forget what gave me that power. And what I'd paid to get it.

The main route we used was down the road from the former celestial guild. I drove, in case Nikolas took an unceremonious trip into another dimension again and accidentally caused us to crash.

"You're expecting this to go badly, aren't you?" I asked. "You never know. Maybe this arch-demon will be the first I've met who doesn't try to kill me on sight."

Nikolas glanced sideways at me, his jaw tight. "Lythocrax did, too?"

"I thought I mentioned it. I know his true name, which protected me from harm." Wait a second. "Do you know your father's true name? I know you said Themedes summoned you once using the name…"

"Yes, I do. But if I told it to you, he'd find another way to punish both of us."

So that's why he was confident his father wouldn't smite *him* on the spot. "And Zadok?"

"The same with him." His aura darkened so much that it blanked out my vision on his side. He wasn't as calm as he'd pretended to be to begin with. He expected a fight.

"Tone it down, can't you?" I slowed the car down. "I'm a great driver, but not when your shadow magic is blocking the view."

The shadows receded a little. "I want to protect you in any way I can, but you had a unique advantage over Lythocrax because you wore his mark."

"With both Themedes and Abyss, I worked out their weaknesses."

He shook his head. "That won't be the case this time, Devi."

I didn't know Nikolas's own weakness. It was an intrusive question to ask and I didn't want to violate his trust in that way. Not when I already carried a weapon that could burn him to cinders, and while my soul was my own, there were still forces on opposite sides of the war acting against us.

Was Casthus's arrival part of the gods' plan? Maybe. No

matter how much I professed to being in total control of my own destiny, the powers that be remained all-powerful, and my knowledge was entirely too lacking. Even the celestials' was, as far as I knew, though they'd lost a lot of their files when the guild had been destroyed—a fact I couldn't forget as I parked my car within view of the charred remains of the collapsed building that had once housed the celestial guild's main headquarters. The second to be destroyed in the city in five years.

Nikolas took my hand, and a moment later, the ruined guild was replaced by a huge forbidding castle, its turrets and towers dark against the violet sky. It was always night time here, with stars gleaming around a huge luminous moon that darkened the shadows and created an eerie kind of beauty not seen on Earth.

Zadok's tower, the fallen's new home, was separated from the rest of the castle by a bridge that had been destroyed during the battle. The tower itself was made of gleaming demonglass, and a familiar tingling ran up my palm at the sight of it. Cold air bit through my thin jacket, making me shiver. If the arch-demon was here, I'd definitely know, so I walked quickly alongside Nikolas towards the castle.

Ahead of us, a small group of warlocks froze at the sight of Nikolas and me.

"Castor!" one of them yelped. "I didn't know you were coming."

"What exactly are you doing?" Nikolas said.

"What else?" said the warlock. "We're leaving."

Oh, seven hells. "You know you can't run from an arch-demon, right?"

"What's it to you, human?" he said.

Warlock logic. There were no other demigods in the castle. Nobody else whose skills even came close to an arch-demon. They'd lose the battle before they started, and they probably knew it.

"Look, I don't know if arch-demons are generally nicer to you guys than they are to humans, but if not, you'd better get back in that palace. He'll catch you."

"He won't. Get out of the way, human."

Bloody warlocks. "I'm protecting you from certain death."

"There's no point in staging a mutiny," Nikolas said. "He'll come whether you like it or not. Will he find obedient servants, or traitors to the shadows? Feel free to choose your side."

The fork-tailed warlock I'd met a few times approached us. His chest was bare and covered in tattoos. He'd be a catch amongst humans, in spite of his tail. "I told them it's their own fault if the Great One smites their sorry arses, but they refuse to listen to reason. Leave them for the demons, I'd say."

"Maybe you're right," Nikolas growled. "If you'd like to live, get back inside," he added to the others.

He didn't wait to see if any of them listened. We passed through the open doors of the castle, where dark flagstones formed an austere entrance hall and staircases and corridors branched off in all directions. I never had figured out where they all led, though Nikolas had finally kept his word and showed me his quarters here. The castle was nice—modern, by demon standards, but said standards weren't high, and I preferred working showers and central heating to bathing in the river and shivering next to a fireplace too much to give up Earth for here.

I looked around the entrance hall, not seeing many of the other warlocks about. "Let's hope the others had more sense."

"I'll address them," Nikolas said. "Are you okay talking to Zadok on your own? We need to clear this up fast."

I nodded. "Yeah, sure. The fallen should understand why they need to hide, and I can deal with Zadok."

I hope. The path across to the tower was bare and scorched, even more so than before, since the battle for the realms had taken place directly here. The river raged past, its waters free of blood, but I could still smell it on the air along with the stench of brimstone. The tower door was closed, probably locked. I rapped on it with my knuckles, my nerves spiking a little. Zadok and I weren't on great terms. He'd tried to kill me the first time we'd met. He'd also helped me—saved my life, even, not to mention loaning his magic. And then he'd betrayed us, so Nikolas had ordered him to take care of the fallen as penance. I hadn't heard too many updates on how he was coping with that position, but if he blamed me, things would get ugly fast.

The door opened, and one of the fallen looked at me. Pale and skeletal, man-shaped and naked, with clawed hands, they walked at a crawl, spoke the demonic language haltingly, and their auras glowed as brightly yellow as a demon-infected wound. Thanks to my Grade Four abilities, I couldn't switch off the second sight, much as I tried to quell the instinctive reaction of revulsion and fear. Maybe it was the celestial side of me, the half-buried part of me that had almost believed the guild's lies about damnation. I'd walked through hellfire itself and come out unscathed, but having had propaganda thrown at me for years, sometimes it stuck despite my best efforts.

"What is it this time?" said a voice from the shadowy corner.

"Hiding again." I stepped into the room, past the fallen. "If you don't mind, I'd like to speak to the fallen alone. You'll only distress them."

"Distress them?" Zadok repeated. "You were singing a

different song when you put me in charge of looking after them."

They certainly looked much more alert than before, though they still cringed away from the light and seemed to have no intention of putting clothes on.

"Fine, you can listen in. It's not like you didn't know it anyway."

"Know what?" he said, the shadows lightening to reveal his tall frame standing in a corner of the room. "That my brother has no intention of relieving me of this indignity? Or does he plan on handing these abominations to someone else?"

"You're all best friends now, then?" I asked. "I suppose you've heard the arch-demon is coming back."

Shadows blasted outwards, knocking several fallen off their feet. Zadok swore in a voice like thunder, and I stepped aside in case he decided to blast me, next. "Excuse me?" he growled. "What are you talking about?"

"You seriously didn't know?"

He stepped out of the shadows, his golden eyes aglow. "Now, why would my dear brother do anything that might spare me a great deal of pain?"

It was disturbing how much like Nikolas he looked. They were both tall and broad with dark red-tinted hair and golden eyes. Zadok was a little paler than his brother and his features were sharper, as though he'd lost weight recently. But the shadowy aura at his back was as dark and menacing as ever.

"The other warlocks know," I said to him. "If you weren't a dick to them, they'd probably have told you."

"Some of them would have gladly sided with me over my brother if he hadn't blackmailed them," he said. "They fear the fallen, and won't come near."

"Oh." Crap. Now I knew where those warlocks had been

running to. Zadok himself clearly hadn't known, though, and unless he was messing with me again, he didn't plan a mutiny. What a mess. I didn't fault Nikolas for taking his eyes off this realm for a moment—mostly because I'd been the one who'd distracted him in the first place. "Look, you must know he'll be unhappy with all of us for letting the fallen out of the dungeon. In the interests of safety—"

"Is my brother still treating you like a fragile human?" He laughed. "Dear Devi, if our father wants anything, no dungeon walls are going to get in his way. And if he wants the truth, he'll tear me open to get it."

"I have no idea if you meant that in a literal sense or not, but your attitude isn't helping." I stepped back. "Help me get the fallen into the dungeon before your father shows up, or you'll be the one he smites."

"How thoughtful you are to give me such a tempting choice." His voice was flat. "Clear the path. You'll have to forgive me if I retaliate should any of them strike me. I defend myself. Force of habit."

"Except when Abyss is involved," I muttered.

He stiffened. Then the tower trembled, the remaining light fading out. *Tell me it isn't—*

Zadok's aura surged jet black. "Now you've done it."

Warning the fallen to stay back, I opened the door and ran outside the tower. A shadow blotted out the moon and stars entirely, rendering the castle almost invisible. Icy air blasted me in the spine and my demon mark snapped to attention. *Nope. You can't feed on an arch-demon.*

Then he appeared, a darker shape etched against the shadows… almost human-like, with a pair of huge, spiked wings.

My mouth went dry. The Earth trembled. Blades of shadow punched down at the warlocks who'd been fleeing. Severed warlock limbs flew left and right, leaving a trail of dark blood, and I was suddenly very glad it hadn't been Zadok who'd staged the mutiny. And too stunned by the sudden explosion of violence to wonder when I'd begun to care in the slightest about the fate of Nikolas's brother.

I stood in front of the door, blocking the fallen from view and hoping to hell that the demonglass was sturdy enough to stand up to an arch-demon. Abyss hadn't needed to knock the door down when Zadok had invited her in. If he did the same now, at the expense of the fallen—

The shadow descended directly in front of me.

Oh... seven hells.

The being inside the darkness was huge enough to defy comprehension, a winged creature with no pity or remorse in his gaze. His furnace-like eyes surged with fury. His aura… was oblivion. There was no other word for the raging darkness beyond him. The sky had disappeared entirely, and the whole world might as well be blanketed in unforgiving darkness.

"DEVI LAWSON."

How… how did he know my name?

"I guess you spoke to Lythocrax," I said. My voice sounded steady enough to my own ears. I nearly called Lythocrax 'Altheare', his true name, but handing that name over to another arch-demon would ignite a war. If his presence didn't mean the exact same. "Just a hello would do, not that yelling thing. If you're wondering."

Casthus raised a hand. Shadows burst to life around me, and my demon mark ignited. The demonglass in my pocket fell free, and an inferno rose to blot out the midnight sky.

3

The flames disappeared, and within a few seconds, I became aware that I lay on my back in the lab at the warlocks' headquarters. The world swam around above my head, and the uncomfortable sensation of sharp objects digging into my spine told me I'd landed in the lab's store of demonglass.

"Did he just bitch-slap me into another world?" I asked of the ceiling.

"I'm guessing yes," said Rachel, looking down at me.

"Ow." I shook my head, dislodging shards of glass. "Dick. That was unnecessary."

"The good news is that he let you live," said Rachel. "And Nikolas, too, I'm guessing."

"I'm not leaving him to handle that maniac alone." I lurched to my feet, my body shaking. I was fairly certain the demonglass had just saved my life. *Nikolas. The fallen.* Seven hells. That power—there was no comparing. Apparently, Casthus didn't want me as an ally after all.

"Whoa." She stared at me. "You're... what's the opposite of glowing? Shadowing?"

I looked at my demon mark, which had turned jet black, streaming trails of smoke. "Oops. I think I took some of his power. In fairness, he kind of threw it at me."

"Damn." Rachel shook her head. "Don't go using that against the other warlocks."

"Wasn't planning to. I'm going after Nikolas."

"He's a demigod," she said. "He's built more resilient than a tank."

"I can absorb the same power," I said, folding my arms to stop the shadowy magic leaking any further into the room. "Besides, arch-demons are stronger than demigods. They destroy whole worlds on a whim and slaughter armies." *Of celestials.* Damn. If he came *here...*

I'd done that. I'd caused it, directly or not. Never mind that the gods had manipulated events so it'd turn out this way: I'd played along because I'd had no choice, and now yet another bloody arch-demon had decided to start breaking things.

And to think I'd once thought Themedes was the most terrifying being I'd ever meet.

I grabbed a handful of demonglass and fiercely concentrated on the fragments, picturing the dark castle of Babylon reflected within. But no castle nor tower appeared.

"Oh no you don't," I muttered. "I don't care if he thinks I'm scum—I need to know if he's planning to go after the fallen."

Casthus wanted me dead. But I needed to make sure he didn't also want a war on Earth. I swore at the glass, which continued to look maddeningly blank, reflecting my own pissed-off stare at me several times over.

"Great." I threw down the handful of glass. "The bastard locked me out."

How, I didn't know, but he'd known my name, which, if Zadok hadn't been lying, must have come from Abyss or

Lythocrax. Or even the Divinities. I didn't know how the shadow arch-demon spent his time, aside from waging war.

The Divinities… *they'd* caused this, indirectly. And I had contact with one of their representatives.

Clover, retired celestial soldier and my only ally at the guild, was an actual angel, reincarnated into a human body. As far as celestials went, she was ranked on Grade Three level and weakened after a long life as an active celestial in human form, especially after she'd given a portion of her life force to remove the demonic influence from Fiona. I hadn't asked her to do it, but being an angel gave her some perks. I didn't know how far those perks extended, but I was willing to try anything at this point.

I pulled my phone out of my pocket and dialled her number. After a couple of rings, she picked up.

"Hey," I said. "Have you heard?"

I had zero clue how her channels of communication worked, to be honest. Whether she had Heaven's number saved in her phone contacts or friends in high—ha—places. Whatever the reason, she seemed to be on top of all things Divinity-related, so I figured the latest on Babylon surely couldn't have escaped her attention.

"Have I heard the arch-demon is back?" she said, in her brittle voice. "Yes."

"A warning might have been nice," I told her.

"I found out at the same time Nikolas did."

He wasn't even on this realm when he found out. I really needed to ask how her divine magic worked, but my priority was getting back to Babylon.

"He didn't want to stick around for a chat. He would have killed me if I hadn't absorbed some of his magic and used my demonglass power to escape. If he's aiming to attack Earth, I have to know."

"He wouldn't have warned you if he was. He'd have struck, fast and brutal."

"Figures." I rolled my eyes, my hands still shaking. "Might he have run into Lythocrax at all? He found my name out somehow."

"Possibly, but it's unlikely that the two would have reached a mutual understanding. What Lythocrax did—putting his mark on a human—is not an action the other arch-demons would accept. They would demand answers, and wouldn't brush the matter aside."

"He literally did brush me aside. Or slapped me. Whichever. If he wants to underestimate me, he can feel free to."

"You're not wrong there, but I doubt the mark went unnoticed. He'll have doubtless heard about it via the netherworld routes before his return."

I frowned, recalling our last conversation. "You said *you* died and were reborn on Babylon. Did the shadow demon have something to do with it?"

"I told you my memories of my previous life were erased. It'd have been before Nikolas was born. Maybe before his father settled on that realm…"

"He got bored and abandoned the place. I know that much. But that was only fifteen years ago. I guess he could have conquered half a dozen dimensions in that time…"

Maybe he and Clover had even met before. Clover had already told me she didn't remember her previous life, but she'd said that the celestials had made a deal with the Divinities to protect Earth by sealing Babylon off from the rest of the netherworld. So the Divinities must have been on that realm before Casthus arrived. Babylon hadn't always been a dead zone between this realm and the rest of the netherworld.

"Clover," I said, when she didn't respond to my comment.

"I'm not a celestial anymore. If he is a threat to Earth, I need to know."

"He isn't. That is, he wasn't, the last I heard. I'm not privy to the whims of the netherworld's rulers."

"Dammit." I got it, though. Even the angels didn't know the impulses of arch-demons, and certainly weren't as omniscient as the stories said. Or impartial, come to that.

"Devi," Clover said. "I said before that I felt the events of the other week were the start of something bigger."

I dragged my free hand through my hair, feeling shards of demonglass bite into my fingers. The sharp pain brought my focus back. "Yeah, got it. Doesn't mean I like running around in the dark. *Or* being bitch-slapped by an arch-demon. You can't go to heaven and ask? Can the heavenly beings only interact with humans if they fall or get reincarnated as human?"

"If I knew, I'd know what had led me to come back here in the first place," Clover said. "Do you really think I'd have suffered the indignities of low-level celestial training if I remembered my previous life?"

"If the inspector was in charge, then he could probably bully even an angel into training gormless buffoons like Sammy. Wait, the inspector is younger than you are. So you were reincarnated how many years ago?"

"That's a polite way to ask my age, Devi."

"That's not why I'm asking. I wanted to know how long Babylon has been cut off."

"I'm seventy, give or take a couple of years. I never had a family in this realm, and I don't recall much of my earlier life. As far as I knew for a long time, the guild was all I had."

That sounded familiar. Too much so. I'd assumed, since she was an angel, that she'd always been immune to the guild's brainwashing. She'd certainly hung around long enough to subtly push me into my continued rebellion against the guild's rules, anyway. But maybe even she'd fostered a lingering connection to the guild as it was—or more accurately, the guild as they wanted it to be. Like her comrades in heaven, not a collection of terrified humans led by other humans who were far from infallible.

Clover said, "The heavenly beings remain out of reach. I'd suggest looking closer to home, Devi. Your home, not Babylon. The realm of your power."

"Earth is my home. Look, I need definite answers, Clover. Not more of your cryptic nonsense." It'd been less difficult than I'd expected to reconcile the image of Clover the retired celestial with Clover the angel when I considered all the times she'd said things that made a weird kind of sense in hindsight.

"I wish I had definite answers. My memory isn't as reliable as it once was, and I'm no longer in contact with heaven."

"Then if you hear anything useful, tell me," I said. Then I hung up before she told me not to go back to Babylon. If the fallen died, it'd mean bad news for heaven *and* the nether realms.

I stuck my hand in my pocket and it came out empty. The demonglass I'd used must have burned out. *All right, then.* I headed down the corridor to the storeroom, pushed the door open, and stared at the box-filled but otherwise empty room in disbelief. "Where's the demonglass?"

Nobody answered.

"Hey!" I shouted. "Where's the bloody demonglass?"

Javos ambled down the corridor, wearing a barely concealed smirk. "Gone."

"That's not funny, Javos. I need that demonglass."

"Let me elaborate." He bared his teeth. "I was instructed to prevent you from returning in the event that you were forcibly ejected from Babylon, on the grounds that in those circumstances, the arch-demon has indicated that he'd prefer not to have you there. And *I'd* prefer not to have to deal with the consequences if Nikolas is forced to witness your demise."

"That's the closest you've come to admitting you care for my well-being, but it's not helpful. I have to be there. Nikolas—"

"—can handle the arch-demon himself."

"I'm aware of that. The fallen—"

"Will die, as they should have. You did this, Devina. Now you reap the rewards of bargaining with hell."

His words rang somewhere deep inside me, with a pain buried but never entirely forgotten.

Bargaining with hell.

"You know who you sound like?" I said. "A celestial who wants to terrify the living daylights out of someone. I'm not a novice anymore, Javos. I didn't bargain with hell alone."

"I heard you talking to the angel. She's nothing, too."

"Look, I know the bare minimum about this situation and even I know that the fallen were part of a bargain between heaven and hell. If you can't conjure up any sympathy for their lives, you know what their deaths will mean for the war. It'll mean the conflict parks itself in this dimension again."

"Then you'd better trust Casthus and his son to work out an arrangement."

He turned and walked away.

My hand flared to life, white light igniting at my fingertips.

"I wouldn't," he said. "I've given you the benefit of the doubt, but don't mistake me for someone who will happily sit by and let you stride in and out of the demon realms when there are negotiations with hell going on. Last time you were the target. This time it's none of your business."

"The hell it isn't. You think he won't notice the holes between that realm and Earth? If you're going to place the blame on me, then you have to accept that gives me the right to take responsibility for the decisions that led us here. So it's my job to do everything I can to fix the damage."

He didn't answer. Just kept walking. My celestial light died out. He was immune to it anyway, and I wasn't yet desperate enough to piss off the warlocks' leader.

I took in a calming breath and marched back to the lab.

"No luck?" said Rachel.

"Nope. Javos stole the demonglass."

"It could be worse," said Rachel. "Niko can deal with it. I'm not welcome over there either. We should have a sleep-over party."

"Rachel, you're not five."

She pouted. "I didn't get to have a normal childhood."

She hadn't talked much about her early years, but her life had not been a happy one before Javos had taken her in. Nikolas had rescued her from enslavement to a monstrous demon known as the Mother in the palace of Pandemonium, and brought her to Earth. That ought to be proof Javos was less of a dick than I'd thought, but he was indifferent at best to most humans and he'd never lay his life down for the fallen. Or me. I could hardly believe he'd taken away my props. Babylon meant nothing to him, but I'd thought he and Nikolas were allies.

"I'm not caving," I said to Rachel. "Any ideas where he might have hidden the demonglass? Or do you have any more samples?"

She sighed. "I can't say I didn't see this coming."

"You know why this is important," I told her. "He just killed three warlocks in the space of a second. I can't let him do it to Nikolas or the fallen."

She pursed her lips. "I think he has at least some of the

old superstitions about the fallen. Enough not to kill them on the spot, anyway. There must be a reason the other warlocks think killing them is a bad omen."

"I thought they couldn't permanently die. Anyway, I'm Earth's representative. I need to talk to him, to make sure he's not plotting an attack on this realm."

"I think he just unambiguously told you he has no interest in making an alliance with you."

"No shit. Doesn't mean I have nothing to say myself."

Rachel sighed. "I'm not going to stand in your way, but I'll toss you a friendly reminder that he nearly killed you just then."

I shrugged, dislodging more broken demonglass from my coat. "Every arch-demon I've met has tried to do the same. I had a contingency plan. What do you know of him? Have you ever met?"

"Nope," said Rachel. "Come on. You know I can't even go near Zadok without him trying to throw me out of windows and generally act like a dick. His father is worse. Niko wanted to keep me safe. It took him long enough to actually tell me about him."

"So how old were you when you came to Earth?"

"Eight. Niko was eighteen."

"Holy crap. I didn't realise he was that young when Themedes summoned him..." Not to mention being left in charge of the castle at fifteen. No wonder he seemed infinitely more adult than I was.

Rachel nodded, her expression unusually solemn. "Yeah. You might say he wants to stop me from ending up in the same position. I'm the one he locked out. Not you."

"He specifically locked the demonglass." I squashed my rage down and prodded the remaining fragments with my foot. "Might have told me how he did that, so I can try it myself."

My left hand lit up so suddenly that Rachel yelped and jumped sideways. "Seven hells, Devi. You singed my hair."

"Crap. Sorry. It keeps doing that without my permission." I shook my wrist to switch off the light, and shadows appeared at my right hand, like my demon mark wanted to join in the fun, too.

One light on each hand. Demon and celestial. One for each of heaven and hell. I might not be demon or angel in the usual sense. I might have been shoved into this fight through no choice of my own. But Earth was my home, and I'd protect it with everything I had.

I crouched down, seeing something flash into the discarded glass fragments. A building I knew well. The guild… the celestial guild. *Huh? That's not right. There's no demonglass there.*

"Devi?" said Rachel.

"There's—" I brushed the glass with my fingertips, and without warning, light enveloped me.

I fell out of the glass onto crumpled brick and other debris. Grimacing as the impact bruised my knees, I crawled upright, staring around at the ruins of the former celestial guild. Beneath me were a handful of demonglass fragments. So there had been some left behind after all, probably from one of my own ill-advised spying attempts.

Why bring me here?

I glanced around, and my gaze caught on a body half-buried under the ruins. A fresh body—he'd smell worse if he wasn't.

Oh, boy.

Gritting my teeth, I shifted the debris, revealing the body as a warlock's. His mouth was half open, his eyes wide and terrified, and handprints marked his skin. Handprints the colour of blood. No other visible injury.

The handprints had burned right through his clothes. I

released a breath, slowly, pushing aside a familiar panic. I didn't know the man—or warlock. But who'd buried him in the ruins of the old guild?

I climbed over him, breaking into to a run, then skidded to a halt. The portal inside the former tower was long gone, the bridge to Earth long-since collapsed. He wore modern clothing, so he couldn't have come from Babylon. *Calm it, Devi. You know he can't have.* But who—or what—killed with lethal handprints?

"Anyone lost a dead warlock?" I asked of thin air. Nobody responded.

Oh, come on. I thought I was done with being found next to dead bodies on celestial property. Calling the police wasn't an option in this case, not with a potentially magical cause of death. This wasn't the demon realm. People asked questions. And I could think of several unwelcome questions that would arise when someone got wind of a dead warlock on celestial territory, abandoned or not.

Why me?

I called the warlocks' guild. There wasn't anyone else to report the murder to.

"Hey, Javos," I said.

"What?" he growled.

"I just found a dead warlock."

"Of course you did. Where?"

"The celestials' old headquarters."

"Those bastards."

"Wait, there aren't any celestials here. They haven't come back since before the battle." Since the inspector's traitorous demon replacement had doomed them. "I already looked, but I'm pretty sure I'd sense if there was a portal nearby."

The building had been the site of the bridge between the realms, but I'd thought nobody had set foot in the place since. The body was fresh, too. *Is someone setting me up?* It wasn't like even *I* had known I was coming here. Unless someone had seen me park my car before crossing to Babylon.

"What was the murder weapon?" Javos demanded.

"Burning handprints, apparently." Could a celestial do that? Theoretically, our celestial light burned anything demonic, but I'd never known a celestial to get close to a warlock for long enough to touch his skin. Most of us applied our weapons from a distance, and when the light came on, the whole demon disintegrated. I'd never seen a wound like this inflicted by a celestial, but I hadn't seen it from a demon, either. And there was no denying that our weapons were designed to burn out evil and sin. The odds of us explaining away this one without a viable alternative were slim to none.

"I assume you found that Babylon has locked you out," he said. "So you decided to stir up more trouble."

"I don't go around looking for dead bodies, Javos. Want me to bring it back to headquarters, or would you rather look at the crime scene yourself?"

There were no bloodstains on the ground. Either he'd been killed on the spot, or someone had transported him here by other means, with the intention of catching the eye of, say, a hot-headed warlock who hated the celestials. Seven hells.

"I'll send some of my people… in a bit. But I think I'll let you stay there and stew in your mistakes for a while, Devi," he said.

"If you weren't already hell-bound, Javos, I'd send you there myself."

And with that, I hung up the phone.

4

After two minutes of scouring the crime scene for clues, I stopped when a car pulled up outside and two warlocks who worked for Javos got out. *Nice of him to make an effort, considering it's one of his own people.* I was certain the celestials hadn't done it, but both warlocks gave me suspicious looks as they removed the body. Arguing that celestials didn't have the ability to burn bloody handprints into people would be ineffective, so once they'd taken the body away, I found my car where I'd parked it before I'd been to Babylon and drove straight to the celestials' new guild.

With Nikolas occupied and Javos unreliable, it was up to me to deal with the latest imminent shitstorm. I didn't even know who might have been responsible for the murder, but the positioning of the body carried a clear message. Someone wanted to inflame tensions between the celestials and the warlocks. I needed to forewarn the celestials first, then worry about the specifics later. At least driving distracted me from worrying about what might be going down on Babylon.

I parked outside the celestial guild, which was now

housed in their academy for celestials-in-training. With the school still running as usual, the place was twice as crowded as before. Most celestials developed their gift in their teens, and it was compulsory to complete several levels of education before qualifying as a full-fledged celestial soldier. I'd spent the bare minimum of time in education and got out into the field as soon as humanly possible, so I'd never been able to relate to people like, say, Lydia, who'd ranked at the top of every class and seemed genuinely disappointed to graduate.

I faltered, my hand on the buzzer. Lydia was one of the celestials listed as missing after the battle, presumed dead thanks to the vampires' venom. The celestials were used to dealing with loss, but it'd take months to come to terms with a battle on this scale. They didn't need to deal with paranoid warlocks on top of that.

The door slid open and a novice shyly peeked out. "You're Devi, right?"

"Yep." They'd probably known it was me before opening the door. The foliage on the wall didn't quite disguise the new addition of a security camera. The celestials' anti-demon defences used to be enough to deter threats. Me included, since my demonic magic prevented me from walking inside unless someone let me in. "I'm just paying a friendly visit. Who's in charge here now?"

"That would be me," said a female voice with a Welsh accent. A woman stepped out into the corridor, her dark hair falling over her shoulder and a pair of spectacles perched on her nose. She was tall and tanned and had definitely come from outside the city, because I'd met every authority figure in Haven City's guild at some point or other. "You're Devi Lawson."

"That's me."

"Your reputation precedes you."

"It usually does. Are you working with demons?" I didn't expect her to admit it if she did, but after Inspector Deacon, I'd take no chances.

"No. Are you?"

I raised an eyebrow. "If the warlocks fit that definition, yes. Otherwise, no. You're…" Think, Devi. "Mrs Battle-Axe. I mean, Mrs Barrow."

"Did you come up with that nickname?"

"Me? Nope. We've never met. I'm not the only one with a reputation." 'Mrs Battle-Axe' was one of the leaders of Swansea's celestial guild, and had been known to terrorise scores of novices. Some of my more long-suffering teachers had used her as a warning and threatened to pack me off to Wales if I didn't stop misbehaving, to which I'd responded that I'd have liked the challenge. Those were the days.

I'd take Battle-Axe over Inspector Deacon, but only if she wasn't a demon in disguise, and let's face it, I'd had less than encouraging experiences in that department lately.

"I wasn't misinformed on your honesty," she said.

"Glad someone filled you in." It sounded like her reputation wasn't unfounded, but the last thing the guild needed was someone indecisive or inept when they'd suffered enough from poor leadership already. "I don't want to cause any alarm, but the body of a warlock was just discovered beside your old headquarters. I'm assuming nobody on your side has been back there since, but I just wanted to forewarn you."

"A body? No one has been into that place since the battle."

"I thought not," I said. "I don't expect the warlocks to show up on the doorstep just yet, but in case you're asked for a statement, it might be an idea to come up with one. Has anyone left the guild in the last twelve hours?" I'd guessed the body was that fresh, at least.

"Yes. Two patrols." She frowned at me. "None of my people would murder a warlock."

"Er… where is the former inspector? In jail?"

"Not in jail, but he's stayed here since the battle."

Figures. They should have locked him up. The celestials had run from one extreme to the other. Instead of executing everyone who might be a traitor without asking questions, they'd pardoned everyone instead, including him, since he'd been rescued from his prison on Pandemonium. He was disgraced in the eyes of the guild, but they'd also ruled that he had never betrayed them. He had, technically, but I didn't have enough clout to argue the point. What if he'd killed the warlock, or ordered someone else to? I might be having trouble disentangling his actions from those of his demonic impersonator, but the fact that I hadn't the faintest idea when the switch had taken place pretty much said it all.

"I'd like to speak with him," I said, thought I'd rather pull off my own toenails. "Are any of the patrolling celestials from today Grade Four?"

"No, of course not. There aren't currently any Grade Fours known to be stationed within the city."

Meaning: if there were any survivors, they worked outside of the guild's laws.

"And has anyone here had contact with the Grade Fours?"

She eyed me over the top of her glasses. "The only active Grade Four celestials are spread worldwide dealing with the ongoing demonic crisis."

That figured. "Grade Three? What about them?"

"They're spread thin, too. We only sent out smaller patrols."

That warlock hadn't looked like a pushover, but if a group had ganged up on him, they might have been able to over-power him. Still, those handprints on the body were plain weird. Not like a regular celestial kill. We rarely had to kill warlocks—they took care of their own crimes—but the guild didn't hesitate to take action on the rare occasion that one of them went rogue.

"Right. Can I speak to the inspector?"

With no other clues, my best bet was starting with the most evil person in the building and working my way down from there.

Inspector Deacon, disgraced former guild leader, had betrayed his former hunting partner, Inspector Kenneth Angler, kicking him out of the guild after the headquarters was destroyed in a demonic attack four years ago. The official story said that the ex-celestial Faye Carruthers had summoned a demon that started the attack, but since few had survived to tell the story, accounts were murky. And if the former inspector Angler had actually been alive, it was possible others had survived, too, and that Faye was innocent. Inspector Deacon, despite being jailed and disgraced, refused to tell me what had really gone on, and I'd been out of the country on a mission at the time. He himself hadn't been working with the netherworld, but the whole thing stank of a demon's manipulation. After all, the guild's rejection had sent ex-Inspector Angler running straight to the netherworld. At least *he* was dead, permanently so.

The one person who might give me the answers looked up and glared at me as I entered the office Mrs Barrow had pointed me to. Inspector Deacon was fifty-something, as athletic as a man twenty years younger, and looked as though he'd never smiled in his life. The room itself was small and bare—and, thank the Divinities, did not contain the guild's valuable old pentagram. Probably because said pentagram had been destroyed. However, the sight of the guild's resources so close to the man who'd been impersonated by a demonic clone for days before anyone had noticed made a familiar anger stir within me.

"Devi Lawson," he said, in his robot-like voice. If anything, the demon clone might even have had more personality than he did.

"That's a nice way to speak to the person who saved your sorry neck from a demon realm. You actually got them to give you back your old office?"

"My office," he said, through gritted teeth, "is currently lying in ruins, thanks to you."

"You mean, thanks to the demon you let replace you," I said. "Don't try to pin this one on me. If I were in charge of anything, I wouldn't let you out of the jail. I take it you're at least on probation?"

"You're lucky I haven't put out an arrest warrant for you."

"You don't even have the authority to give people detention," I told him. "You know that. I'd like a favour."

"Haven't you taken enough from the guild?"

My jaw twitched. "What, aside from your dignity?" Ticking him off was in no way satisfying, considering the list of deaths he'd directly or indirectly caused made my own demon-killing record look miniscule.

"You're a liar and a deceiver," he said. "Why should I give you anything?"

"Four years ago," I said. "You know what you did."

He scowled and said nothing.

"Look, you know perfectly well that I was catching demons in Auckland with Rory when the old guild burned down," I said. "I didn't even hear about the attack until a day afterwards, thanks to the time difference, which was probably what you intended. Right?"

"What are you trying to blame me for this time?" he said.

"You sent me on the mission," I responded. "You sent me on a *lot* of missions." Including the fatal one which had resulted in Rory's death. "There's no point in trying to paint over the truth. I know your partner got dragged into a demon realm and you told everyone he was dead. Then when he came back, you decided to send him away again because you'd lose your shiny new promotion, right?"

He couldn't deny it. Everyone knew he'd screwed over the former Inspector Angler, sending him on the inevitable path to demonhood. What bothered me the most was that if this office was anything to go by, the powers that be were willing to forgive him for that oversight. And if that was the case—what else might he have got away with?

"What's your point?"

"My point is that you were replaced by a demon without anyone noticing," I said. "Similarly, a demon orchestrated the attack on the guild four years ago and was never caught."

"A *celestial* instigated the attack, and has been top of our wanted list for four years."

"Faye Carruthers," I said. "Yeah, I'm not buying it. I don't know her, but I think the demons wanted you to blame one of your own. They used the opportunity to recruit Inspector Angler. If I'm to believe the story you told the celestials, that was all coincidence."

His face reddened. "I have never bargained with hell, Devi. Unlike you."

"That would sound more impressive if you were the first person to say that to me today."

"Is that so?" He narrowed his eyes. "You might have good reason to accuse me of plotting against my colleagues, but Kenneth was the demons' all along. When he came to me following his disappearance, I knew him for a demon in an instant. He was theirs the moment his Divinity fell."

"What?" I stared at him. "How did you know that? You do have connections in heaven?"

More to the point—the demon who'd claimed him had been the same one who'd marked *me.* Lythocrax. Arch-demon, most recent fallen Divinity...

Oh. My own demon mark had remained inactive until I'd set foot in a demon realm. So obviously, at some point during the attack on the guild, a portal into a demon realm had opened, and the moment the former Inspector had passed through… he'd upgraded.

"We wouldn't have half the resources we do if we didn't," said Inspector Deacon, yanking me back from my thoughts. "And we certainly wouldn't have worked with the likes of you if heaven hadn't thought you'd stay on their side."

I gave a short laugh. "Yeah, right. I know the person who runs your tests for Grade Fours is a fallen angel. I'm beginning to think there was a miscommunication. Someone from heaven orchestrated the attack on Earth."

"What nonsense are you speaking now?"

Maybe he doesn't know. He was no spectacular actor. It'd likely been a long while since his own Grade Four test, and I'd had the impression that the fallen angel who'd tested me didn't reveal his true appearance to everyone. "Never mind. Have you talked to anyone outside this building lately?"

"Is there a reason for this interrogation?"

"Someone decided to kill a warlock and throw his body into a place where you and the other celestials would get blamed for it," I said. "I'm here to talk to all the people who'd have reason to kick off another war."

"If you think I wanted to bring the demons' conflict to Earth, you're mistaken. The warlocks kill one another all the time. They probably trespassed on purpose."

"You're making it really difficult for me to defend you. If I didn't know you for a coward, I'd pin the blame on you. Did you send Sammy instead?"

"What? The novice?"

Ah. It was his demonic counterpart who'd worked with Sammy—or Demon-Sammy anyway.

"I'm disappointed," I said to him. "I hoped you'd have

more to tell me. But if you had anything to do with that warlock's death, the consequences will be on both of us. Not to mention the whole guild. I suppose you swore never to turn your back on them again and begged for forgiveness?"

"If they let you in, they are not the guild I knew. Your soul will go to hell in the end."

"My soul is my own. The arch-demons themselves said so. And I made sure of it."

With that, I left him to stew in his own misery. Now what? Someone in this building *might* be the killer, but I really thought they had bigger problems to worry about. While the inspector wasn't allowed to play Mad Scientist like his replacement had, I knew the guild would be looking for ways to ensure the incident with the vampire virus could never happen again. Since there was no cure except for my demon mark, the majority of day-walking vampires had died before I'd been able to save them, burned in celestial fire or driven out of the city altogether. As for the celestials who'd been bitten by those vampires, using their own celestial fire caused them to die horribly as their divine magic clashed with the demonic virus in their veins. The handful who survived had the best of both worlds. Or worst. At least until I'd robbed them of that power by using my demon mark to absorb the demonic virus from everyone it'd infected.

Unfortunately, some people weren't taking that news well.

And as luck would have it, I ran into the second most evil person in the building on the way out—my old enemy, Bad Haircut Sammy. Since a demon had wandered around impersonating him for weeks, I didn't actually know when he'd been bitten or if he'd been complicit in helping the arch-demons. The guild had given him the benefit of the doubt, which meant he was still ambling around annoying everyone. He seemed to be missing his usual group of hangers-on, a requirement of school bullies across the globe. I supposed being impersonated by a demon had made them avoid him as though he carried a contagious disease. More's the pity.

Sammy scowled, folding his arms across his chest. "You took away my powers."

"You'd have died if you tried to use them," I said. "Horribly."

"What do you know? Just because you have a demon mark doesn't make you better than the rest of us."

"You're jealous of this?" I held up my right hand. "If you want an arch-demon to bitch-slap you, I can hook you up right away."

He took a step backwards. *"You're* a bitch."

"Wow." I rolled my eyes. "You never stopped to question, did you? Not once. Would an innocent man have put you in charge of observing a bunch of comatose celestial-vampires?"

"So I made a mistake. And?"

Like killing the warlock? No… he was only Grade Two, since he kept failing classes and had never been promoted. Most warlocks could trounce him. Generally, he tried to suck up to every available authority figure and had fallen hook, line and sinker for the false inspector's act. Warlock killer, though… somehow I doubted it.

My phone started buzzing in my pocket. "As much as I'd like to stop for a chat, I have places to be."

I exited the building and answered the call: "Javos."

"There's been a complication," Javos growled into the phone. "The traces on the body matched celestial fire. Your level. They were also all *left* handprints."

My mouth dropped open. "What—Grade Four?"

"Apparently so."

Well, damn. Despite my questions to the inspector, I hadn't actually expected that. The Grade Four rogues were supposed to be dead, after they'd turned on the vampires and warlocks during the battle. If any had survived, though, they'd certainly have reason to take out the warlocks.

"Let me see the body," I said to him. "I'll know if it's definitely a celestial-related injury."

He made a low growling noise. "I think you'll find any demon would know better than you do. You've never been burned by your own fire."

The call ended.

I got back into my car and drove to Javos's place. Never a dull moment. The warlocks ruled by hierarchy and didn't generally get along, but they stuck up for one another and they wouldn't let the death of one of their own go unpunished, especially if they suspected the guild might be involved. Craptastic.

5

The warlock's body was laid out on a table in the lab. Rachel hovered beside it, bouncing on the balls of her feet. "Javos wouldn't let me start cutting him open to see what his insides look like."

I shuddered. "I think I can guess."

Up close, I could see clearly that all the handprints were of someone's left hand—the same someone, judging by the size and shape—and had burned right into the skin. Not a pleasant way to die, but not typical of a celestial death, either. Celestial flames left little trace behind, but we'd run into a demon who sowed confusion by mimicking the celestial mark on his victims before and causing them to burst into flames. This guy looked more like someone had turned their celestial power onto its lowest setting and carefully tortured him to death. Torture wasn't the celestials' style either, not even the most dedicated to taking down the demons. We weren't supposed to actually enjoy the job—or anything else, for that matter.

Javos strode into the room, his huge body filling the available space. "That's your people's handiwork, Devi."

"It's not Grade Four," I said. "The control level is too high. Grade Four power would turn him to ashes even on the lowest setting."

"You're not exactly making an effort to tone it down, though, are you?" Rachel remarked.

I scowled and removed the cuff on my left wrist. With two warlocks in the room, its desire to switch on was like having ants crawling up my arm. Sweat beaded on my forehead as I attempted to turn it onto a low setting. A beam of light shot out and hit the wall, leaving no mark but making Javos snarl. "You've made your point, Devi. You're officially off the suspect list."

"Why the hell did you put me on the list in the first place? I wouldn't have called you to report the body if it was me who did it. Bloody cheek."

Rachel let out a laugh. "Guilty until proven innocent is how the warlocks do things."

"Hope the guild knows that." I replaced my cuff. "I'd have to deliberately dampen my power somehow, if it's possible, to kill someone in that way. And there's no way to dampen a Grade Four's power."

"No," he said, "but there are no official guild Grade Threes *or* Fours in the city according to my resources. That leaves the rogues."

"They died," I said. "I seem to remember you were thorough in taking care of it." I returned to the desk where I kept my lab equipment, wishing I could concoct a spell to identify a murderer. But there wasn't a spell equivalent to a DNA test. If the killer had been a demon, I could call on Dienes, the magical sniffer demon who could detect any demon type. But I didn't even smell brimstone on the body.

Still, I wasn't entirely convinced that this wasn't some netherworld plot. It usually was. They'd just got a little more creative this time.

"Hang on." Rachel reached for my arm, holding her hand inches from the cuff. She winced and pulled it back. "The cuff… doesn't it dampen your power?"

Javos wheeled to face me, his eyes narrowing.

"There are hand prints on the body, not cuff-prints," I pointed out. "Stop looking at me like that, Javos. The cuffs are all the guild's property, besides. I'm the only non-guild person who wears one." Because the alternative was accidentally burning every warlock I went near. I'd gone without a cuff for two years after I'd quit and got along just fine as a Grade Three, but Grade Four was a step too far. Unless someone had created a glove to slap demons around with, which I sincerely doubted. The celestial mark on its own did the job just fine.

I yanked my cuff off and tossed it into the cauldron on the desk.

"What the hell are you doing now?" Javos asked.

"I'd get out of the way of the fumes," I said. "Best move the body, too."

"You, Devi Lawson, are a bloody menace."

"Happy to be of service." I laughed over the cauldron like an evil witch as he grunted and wheeled the body out of the room, out of range of what was likely to turn into another explosion.

Rachel said, "You have the weirdest hobbies."

"Yep. Might need to visit the guild for a spare cuff—"

I broke off as shadows filled the room, abruptly smothering everything. Nikolas appeared, staggering under the weight of a demon the same size as him—a winged demon covered in burn marks so vicious, I couldn't even make out his features.

Wait…

"No," I said. "Tell me he didn't."

Nikolas deposited his brother's mangled body on the floor. "He's alive. Just."

My mouth dropped open. "He… I thought you said you'd never bring him here."

Was Zadok *dead?* There were ways to kill demigods, but few, and certainly not widely known. Apparently, the shadow arch-demon knew all about his son's weaknesses. His skin had burned clean off, and his wings were little more than stumps.

Fiona ran into the room and screamed loudly. "Holy *shit.* What's that?"

"That's Zadok," I told her. "Or what's left of him. I don't think Casthus was happy about what took place on Babylon in his absence."

"You might say that," said Nikolas. Only then did I notice that some of the blood was his own. Burn marks marred his own right arm, but considering I'd once seen him regenerate an entire hand from scratch, I couldn't help but look back at Zadok's mangled body, even as bile crept up my throat. He'd been utterly brutalised.

"What happened?" I whispered.

"I told Casthus to get the fuck out of my castle. It went about as well as expected." Nikolas shook himself, crouching over his brother. "He's breathing."

"Will he live?" I asked uncertainly.

"No idea," said Nikolas harshly.

Whoa. Nikolas had been known to zap his brother in the face with demon lightning and throw him off buildings. Both of them could regrow limbs, and I'd even seen Zadok walk away after having his neck snapped. But fire was his one weakness, and it had damaged him beyond recognition. "Javos went out of the lab about a minute ago. I'd hide him quickly if you're not planning to let anyone find out."

Golden light flared in Nikolas's eyes, and his expression

was positively menacing. "If we fight, I'll win, but he'd finish Zadok off without a second's thought. I'm taking him to my house."

"You're sure?" My throat closed up, but I refused to let myself feel guilty. None of this was my fault. Zadok had brought most of it on himself.

"I'm sure," he growled.

"I'll drive." Hang on a minute. "The fallen?"

"He left them alive."

That did not sound promising. "Are they in the dungeon? We never did get them there… is it because of them that he…?" I indicated Zadok.

"I'll tell you more later. Where exactly is Javos?"

"Dealing with a dead warlock that showed up at the old celestial HQ. I'm the one who found the body, by total accident. Yes, I know."

He shook his hand once more, and the burn marks entirely disappeared. "You haven't lost your touch."

"Nope, she hasn't," Rachel said. "But you don't want to tick off Javos, Niko. He's pissed."

"He can fucking deal with it." For a moment his wings appeared, and I gasped. One was torn and bloody, not unlike Zadok's.

Rage burned inside me. How dare Casthus stride into Nikolas's castle like he was entitled to take over the place? Sure, it was typical demon behaviour, but Nikolas had earned his position. My hands curled into fists. "This isn't on."

Nikolas crouched beside his brother. "Casthus has asked to speak with you, Devi. In two days."

My stomach lurched. "Now he's changed his tone? I take it he's not planning to murder me?"

"If you keep your tongue."

"I guess Zadok didn't." I cast a look at him. "You know

this will put us on Javos's hit list forever. And he just removed me from a murder suspect list a minute ago."

"Believe me, this isn't ideal for me, either."

No kidding. "All right. Let's get him out of here."

———

Two days passed, and Javos didn't discover Zadok. Probably because he was up to his neck in the ongoing murder investigation. Nikolas had locked Zadok in a guest room in his own house, covered in wards, which seemed a little unnecessary considering the warlock hadn't woken up yet and wouldn't be able to walk when he did, let alone fly. Nikolas went to check on him every few hours and returned looking grimmer each time. Javos didn't seem to have suspected what Nikolas had done yet, but the weight of keeping that secret on top of the lack of answers from the warlocks on the murder maintained a very tense atmosphere. My upcoming audience with the shadow demon only added fuel to the fire.

As for the murder, I remained as clueless as ever. I wouldn't have thought any celestial would have murdered a warlock for no reason, but Javos refused to believe me, and I sensed that he was aware of my fraying nerves. By the time the evening of my meeting with the shadow demon arrived, I'd reached my limit.

I paced around the house for most of the day—avoiding the room where Zadok remained confined—and ended up in the smaller lab I kept at Nikolas's house, concocting magical traps to give me something to do with my hands. With ten minutes to go, I jumped when a rattling noise came from Zadok's room overhead, at the same moment as Nikolas himself entered the room. He wore dark clothes, made to withstand wear and tear, like mine, and the shadows of wings appeared behind his shoulders.

"Are you sure you want to do this, Devi?" he asked me.

Another bout of rattling from upstairs accompanied his words. "What's that?"

"In case my brother wakes up in my absence."

Has he chained him up? Never mind Zadok. The person who scared me most was on the other side of the shadows. He'd completely torn apart a demigod who was supposed to be indestructible, and nearly killed me once already. But what choice did I have? The fallen were stuck on Babylon with no allies, and if I turned Casthus down, he'd assume Earth was undefended and weak. My friends were counting on me.

"I'm ready." My voice sounded slightly unsteady, and my palms were damp with sweat when Nikolas took my hand. "Let's do this."

He squeezed my hand, and shadowy power stroked my palm. It would normally provoke an intense reaction, but all my attention was on the upcoming confrontation. From the steely expression on Nikolas's face, so was his.

"Are you two done?" said Rachel. "Because I deserve compensation for keeping an eye on your brother."

"I don't think he's going anywhere." I took in a steadying breath. Playing nice with arch-demons was a necessary evil. As long as I didn't tick him off like Zadok had...

"I hope not," said Rachel. "But if Javos shows up, I won't be able to stop him from breaking the doors down."

"I set up a few spells," Nikolas said. "I know my brother can't stay here permanently. He's as good as dead now everyone on Babylon knows his weakness, even if he survives."

I frowned. "Doesn't every warlock in the city know Javos's weakness?"

"Earth is different. Besides, what self-respecting demon would carry a radio to a battle?"

Rachel snorted. "Exactly."

"This is why you're all going extinct. That and the fact that you can't stop murdering one another." I grimaced. "You know Zadok can't stay here. And I don't think he'd have hung on this long if he wasn't going to make it. Doesn't his regenerating power help?"

"Against injuries like that, every bit of magic he has is consumed in healing him," Nikolas explained. "He'd fare better on Babylon itself, but that isn't an option."

"Then let's get this done."

"Good luck," Rachel said, as Nikolas took my hand again.

The world disappeared when I gripped a handful of demonglass pieces in my pocket, transporting us to the fragments I'd left beside the old celestial guild. I'd checked to make sure nobody was around first—dead bodies included. It'd be quicker to transport ourselves directly into Babylon's castle, but it was supposedly bad manners to hop into an arch-demon's castle without knocking on the door first.

Once Nikolas and I were a respectable enough distance from the guild, he crossed us over in a heartbeat.

Cold air blasted me in the face, and ahead of us, the huge doors of the castle opened. A massive winged beast exited the castle, flanked by two smaller demons. Either demigods or other higher demons, judging by their flaming auras.

He had fire demons working for him. That's how he'd hurt Zadok.

The air itself shook with the arch-demon's steps. A familiar primal terror took root inside me, locking my limbs to the spot. His form was wreathed in darkness so complete, the castle behind him was completely blocked out. I suppose he resembled a man, a particularly tall one, but the wings made him look twice the size of a regular person, and the darkness cloaking his frame appeared infinite.

It'd been a very long time since this beast might have been

considered divine. And he was looking directly into my eyes. Into my soul, half dark and half light.

"Hey," I said. "Glad you invited me back to chat."

The arch-demon looked me over. "So it's true." Even when he wasn't yelling, his voice was resonant, impossible to miss. He spoke Malthric, the favoured tongue of this world, and walked as though he expected the universe itself to kneel and worship him. "You're truly an entire human."

"Technically, yes. What's your point?" To my intense relief, my voice didn't shake. You had to be direct and demanding when dealing with demons, and arch-demons were no exception. Hell had no place for weakness. Luckily, I had years of experience in defying authority.

"You bear a demon's mark," he said, remaining where he stood. Not going to invite me inside, then.

"Tell me something I don't know." I shivered under the intensity of his stare. Beneath the shadow, his eyes were golden. Like Nikolas's, but devoid of any warmth.

"You won't survive. You're not made to. You're born to die, nothing more."

"Speak for yourself. Just because you're a little more indestructible than the rest of us, it doesn't mean you can't die."

He'd have some kind of weakness, as all arch-demons did. Not that I had any way of knowing what it was. For Abyss, it was sunlight. I wondered if he knew.

"They say you were involved in passing on Themedes's territory to a new master," he said. "They say you gave Abyss his palace."

"Technically, the doors were already open. I just showed her the way." I figured I'd violated some kind of demon protocol when I'd done that, but I had no regrets. "I assumed you'd object if I let her stay here, so I'd have thought you'd be grateful I got her out of your way."

The arch-demon laughed. It was a booming, terrible

sound. "You speak of gratitude? You trespassed onto the land of the gods, human."

"The gods provoked a war," I said. "I didn't have the luxury of waiting around for someone else to deal with the problem. She wanted Earth: I wouldn't let her take it."

"She's remarkable, isn't she?" He addressed Nikolas, who stood unflinchingly at my side. "Has she claimed a true name yet, if she is truly one of us?"

The honest answer was, *well, no.* According to Nikolas, claiming a name would enable the demons to use it against me. Not that I actually knew how to go about getting a demon's name when I wasn't one, despite my mark and my magic.

"She doesn't have to answer your questions," Nikolas said, his voice clipped. "Nor does she deserve your scorn. She defended her realm, as you yourself have on more than one occasion."

"Perhaps you need a reminder of your brother's fate."

His demon servants inched forwards. I glared at them. "If any one of you touches Nikolas or me, I'll ram your own eyeballs down your throat."

The demon on the left raised his hands. Fire surged towards me. I dove to the side, my enhanced celestial speed guiding my steps. My demon mark tingled as I pulled the fire towards me, reminiscent of the power I'd once been gifted by the arch-demon Themedes. The fiery light mingled with the celestial force in my other hand, and the demon hissed.

"Give me fire and I'll pay it back to you, twice over," I said.

The demon roared in anger and expelled a jet of flame, looking not unlike a dragon minus the scales. Wings spread wide, he dived at me with a rattling growl. I dodged another whirl of flames and conjured my celestial blade. Formed of white fire and etched in flames, it gleamed in my hands as I held it in a defensive stance.

His own flames continued to burn, blocking Nikolas from view. The message was clear—he'd burn me in the same way. I doubted it mattered to the arch-demon that I didn't have the same regenerative power. He wanted me dead, one way or another.

Light and darkness blended in my hands, forming a blade which gleamed with a blue aura, like my own appeared in the warlocks' eyes. *I'll teach him a lesson, then.*

Lava burst from the fire demon's hands, bouncing off the ground around me and leaving sizzling holes in its wake. I dodged and ducked, blade singing, trailing white fire. The part of me reborn to kill demons thrived in fiery fury, while the demon mark longed to bathe him in his own flames. I lunged towards him and the blade impaled him in the chest, pinning him to the ground.

His companion roared in fury, advancing on me—only to run into a wall of shadow, thrown up by Casthus's hand. "That's enough."

"Why?" I looked down at my sword protruding from the demon's chest. "He can regenerate."

My right hand tingled as I let go of the blade. Shadowy power fed into my demon mark as though of its own accord. I hesitated, then drew on that cold dark depth of simmering power. Ice slid over my skin, drawing goosebumps to the surface. The arch-demon narrowed his eyes, recognising what I was doing. "You cannot use my power against me, fool."

"Then tell me what you did with the fallen."

All the cards were on the table. It wasn't like there was a way to prevent him from knowing, if he wanted to.

"The fallen?" he repeated. "What are they to you?"

"Does heaven know you left their people trapped here?"

"The Divinities were the ones who abandoned those monsters to the shadows." He tilted his head, examining me. "Imagine that. No true name, but such raw power. You wear one's mark, yet I smell another on you. Abyss. Maybe... yes, I'll speak with her myself and get her version of events."

Well, crap. She wouldn't be happy to see him—from what I'd seen, she'd seemed scared of her fellow arch-demons when she'd been hiding on this realm. But she wouldn't have taken the palace if she hadn't expected to have to entertain demonic guests.

"Go right ahead," I said. Apparently, I was destined to spend the rest of my life sandwiched between two angry arch-demons.

The demon I'd stabbed spat out blood. "Scum."

"One of us is bleeding, and it's not me." I smiled at the arch-demon. "I hope you're ready for a reckoning."

6

Nikolas transported us back to Earth the moment the arch-demon dismissed us. My hands shook so much, it took me several attempts to find the demonglass in my pocket, and the wrecked guild behind me didn't help. Nikolas's hand rested reassuringly on my arm, and we disappeared, landing in the middle of the living room of his house.

I released a shuddering breath, only now aware of how tightly wound I was. "Holy shit."

"Was he what you expected?" Nikolas looked sideways at me. I wished I had his natural ability to stay calm, but being brought up anywhere *near* that demon would either break you or turn you into, well, a demon.

"Nah. I expected him to have better taste in servants."

"They're likely temporary ones," he said. "He gets bored easily. The same goes for his offspring. We're far from the only ones he's abandoned."

"Gods. Sorry."

"Don't be. We're not human, Devi," he said calmly. "Some

demons eat their young. I rather think I got the best of a dozen fates, when it comes down to it."

"Not human. Right." He knew how to act like one of us, enough to make me forget where he'd come from, but…

Did it matter? Demons had feelings. Just look at all the temper tantrums the arch-demons threw. And he cared about me. That was abundantly clear. If anything, I was the one who was the most messed up, because I *was* still human, despite what I'd done. I hadn't grown up in this world. I was proof of just how adaptable humans could be, but no role model, despite whatever DivinityWatch's creators might think.

There was another rattling noise from the room above, and plaster dust rained down. I looked up. "Uh. I think Zadok—"

Rachel ran into the room. "Thank the seven hells you're back. Zadok woke up."

"Did he break the chains?" asked Nikolas.

"No," said Rachel. "He broke the floor instead."

Oh boy.

"I'll speak to him." He was halfway to the stairs in a blink, and I hurried after him, against my better judgement. "Wait here, Devi. I'll see if he's in a reasonable mood first."

"There's a hole in the floor," Rachel said. "He wouldn't talk to me, but I don't think he's up for attempted murder either."

"No kidding." I let Nikolas walk ahead of me, while I sank onto the sofa. My body still trembled with the aftershocks from my conversation with Casthus. Zadok had entirely rejected the discipline required for a warlock to live amongst humans without breaking the law, and if he was alive, I was more worried for his potential victims than anyone else. I hoped Nikolas had been prepared for this eventuality, because I sure as hell wasn't.

Nikolas returned to the living room within a few moments. "He wants to speak with you. If you're sure."

"I already dealt with an arch-demon. This is child's play."

I hoped.

In the room upstairs, there was indeed a splintered hole in the floor, exposing the floorboards. Not that Zadok seemed to be paying particular attention to it. He sat in a hunched position, his head bowed, hands and ankles chained in front of him. He wore clothes that Nikolas must have loaned him, and what I could see of his face, he was scarred beyond all recognition. His hair had been scorched clean off. When he looked up, his formerly golden eyes had faded to pale white. Only his aura remained the same—jet black as his brother's.

"I thought my father threw you out." His voice was raspy, and threw me for a moment. Then it hit me—he thought he was still on Babylon. Nikolas had purposefully set things up that way. The dark room, the chains…

"He changed his mind," I said to him. "Decided he wanted to chat after all."

He laughed, the sound painful. "I thought by now you would have learnt the perils of bargaining with us."

"Looks like you needed to remember that yourself."

He grinned. "Oh, I provoked him on purpose, dear Devi."

Okay… maybe he'd lost it before Casthus had set his demon on him. I looked uneasily at the hole in the floor, then back at him. "Maybe you should have done that with Abyss rather than letting her take over your tower, stealing Nikolas's army, then hiding like a coward."

When Abyss had sneaked into Babylon via a portal set up by the vampire king when he rose from the dead, she'd tossed Zadok out into the dirt, and he'd seized temporary power over the other warlocks before she claimed them, too. His actions had been cowardly, if in his own self-interest, and I'd thought he had more sense than to provoke an arch-demon.

He gave a soft laugh. "I allowed her to take over to prevent this very turn of events, but don't fool yourself into thinking I am a simple coward."

"I don't know, what you did looked pretty cowardly from where I'm standing. You didn't tick off the shadow demon for any noble reasons, did you?"

"My reasons are my own. Do you know how it feels to have your skin peeled off inch by inch?"

"Thankfully not."

"Be thankful, Devi. It sounds like my father was merciful to you."

"Guess he didn't want to kill off the only celestial demon."

Which was more than I could say for his son. Kind of harsh even for demon standards. There was a reason celestials didn't use torture. It wasn't effective. The person who did this had wanted to inflict suffering and a lot of it.

"Kill or enslave." He shrugged. "Those are the two options most arch-demons have. If you'd picked a side, you might not be in this position."

"What, free and in control of my own soul? Is that such a terrible fate?"

"The demons are quite capable of making you regret that decision. I did offer to help you."

"We're enemies," I told him. "No matter how many times you've helped us."

He sat up straighter. "You still see things in black and white. You're just predisposed to hate warlocks from the nether realms because you know no better. I would rather you were informed on the matters you blundered into."

"Are you kidding? You lorded it over me about how you knew so much more than I did from the moment I met you.

You tried to trick me into claiming a demon name while knowing anyone could use it against me."

His face twitched. "Excuse me? I mentioned nothing about demon names."

"They'll call your name and you'll be powerless to resist, you said."

His chains rattled as he attempted to raise a hand. "I meant they'll call for you, fool. And they did. Frankly, I think a demon name would have provided an advantage, but I can't say I know whether that option is available to humans. You might have noticed none live on Babylon."

Curiosity rose, despite my best efforts. "Was I the first human you met?"

He gave a grim smile. "My brother still hasn't told you all of our history. His time with you might be shorter than he thinks."

"I don't know, we're both resilient. More than Casthus thinks, anyway."

"It could have as easily been my brother in my place. He might think himself superior, but we're equals."

"It wouldn't have been him," I said, "because I would have stopped him first."

"And again, you fail to understand that you're still human. The arch-demons have laid waste to worlds and burned the ashes."

"They clearly didn't do that to every world," I said. "They have limits. I don't suppose you know Casthus's weakness?"

This time he burst into harsh laughter. "You think I wouldn't have used it if I did?"

"You just lectured me a moment ago about getting cocky about standing up to the arch-demons. Sounds like you're just bitter because you couldn't even control the fallen."

"My realm was cut off from heaven and hell," he said.

"The fallen were our penance, and my dear father's property, so he can do whatever he likes with them."

"So the fallen deserve to be tortured just for being in the wrong place at the wrong time?"

"They deserve the mercy of death," he rasped. "It's a punishment that they continue to exist at all."

I swallowed. "That's not your call to make. The Divinities—"

"The divine ones are as good as dead, celestial."

They wouldn't be able to screw with me if they weren't alive. Of course, Nikolas wouldn't have told him what Clover had implied—that the Divinities had been the ones to set things up so the arch-demons would go head to head with one another for their own entertainment. It was entirely likely that Casthus had come back to Babylon for similar reasons. Though the events themselves had seemed the precursor to something worse, it was hard to tell how much of it was manipulated by outside forces, and how much was just the arch-demons conveniently seizing control of the opportunity to make a nuisance of themselves.

"If you say so," I said. "You did a terrible job keeping an eye on the fallen, so I'd be glad they *aren't* here."

"Devi, dearest, there is nothing the divine might do to me which would even come close to the torture that monster inflicted on my brother and me."

My stomach twisted. "He tortured Nikolas, too?"

Did Casthus know his other son's weakness? Even I didn't.

"He's saving it," said Zadok, his gaze dropping to the floor. "The fool will continue to lie in front of our father in the hope of gaining his favour. I'd suggest that you don't do the same, Devi. You're more breakable than we are."

He looked pretty damn broken to me. I couldn't look at him any longer. I backed out of the room and found Nikolas standing in the dark, his eyes glowing faintly. He closed the door behind me, sealing it shut. The outside of the wood was covered in interlocking chains which snapped back into place when he moved them. Not a trapping spell I was familiar with. Ordinarily I'd have studied the chains in fascination to see how they worked, but not now.

"He said…" I swallowed hard, moving out of earshot of the room. "He said you were tortured, too."

"I wouldn't call it torture," Nikolas said. "Zadok provoked him. I tried to intervene, so he had his demon pin me down while the other burned Zadok."

"You probably shouldn't have told me that. Because I'm going to have a lot of trouble facing Casthus next time he summons me without attempting to burn his eyes out."

"He's immune to celestial fire. All arch-demons are."

"Of course. Wouldn't want to give us any advantages in this war. Our enemies are invincible and our allies are indifferent bastards." I gave a bitter smile. "Zadok knows that, at least."

Yet he didn't seem to feel any regret over what he'd done, which made his offers of advice seem suspicious to say the least. But I couldn't afford to let him distract me.

"Where in hell is Javos?" I asked Nikolas. "He might not need to know Zadok's here, but I think he'll want to hear about Abyss at the very least."

"He'll be at the Harpy's Nest."

Right. He would be. The most popular warlock haunt, the Harpy's Nest, shouldn't be my top choice of destination considering that I'd been the one who'd found the warlock's dead body, but Javos needed to know the latest developments in the nether realms. And I needed a few drinks after the day I'd had. "Then let's go."

7

My master plan lasted less than a minute, because Nikolas disappeared into Babylon again before we reached the bar. Very luckily, I was the one driving. One second he was in the passenger seat, and the next, he'd disappeared into shadows.

"Great," I muttered. "Wonderful timing there."

There was little point in following him after the shadow arch-demon had thoroughly dismissed me, so I parked a couple of streets away and walked to the Harpy's Nest alone.

The pub was packed out with warlocks, and there were forked tails and horns everywhere I looked. I crossed to the bar, where the punky haired vampire owner regarded me over the blood-red glass he was polishing. "I haven't seen you for a while, Devi."

"No blood cocktails, thanks," I said before he could make his usual offer. "I'm looking for Javos."

"He just left."

You might know it. It was getting on for midnight. Shadow demons kept antisocial hours. Maybe it was for the best that Javos hadn't got suspicious enough to go investigating Nikolas's house for missing warlocks and found Zadok instead, but you'd think he'd be interested in the situation on Babylon.

"Devi!" Fiona pushed her way through the crowd, her eyes wide. "I heard you were here. You have to leave. The warlocks—"

Two warlocks shoved their way in behind her. Both were more human-like than the average warlock, forked tails aside. Muscled frames, rugged features, and oozing sensuality from every pore. *Oh, crap.* Incubi. Similar to Nikolas's lure power, their magic overwhelmed their victims and turned them into drooling idiots. Even my celestial power gave me no defence.

"Is there a problem?" I asked, ignoring the tingling sensation in my fingertips as their magic caressed my demon mark. In any other scenario, I'd knock their heads together and toss them outside, but there were at least a hundred other warlocks in the bar, all of them likely to jump to their kin's defence.

"You killed him," growled the incubus on the left.

Oh no. They'd heard I'd found the body. I should have guessed, since word of the murder had ripped through the warlock community. "I didn't kill anyone. Turn your magic off and nobody gets hurt."

The incubus on the right bared his teeth. "Your demigod won't save you now."

Magic poured from his hands, sliding over my skin like silk. My mind blanked as sensual thoughts caressed every inch of me—and Fiona smashed into me, knocking me into the bar. Stars exploded before my eyes, and sparks literally flew as the magic of the incubi clashed into one another, hitting the bartender and several patrons, too.

"Ow." I groaned, shaking off X-rated images. "Fiona. Speak to me." Crap. She was human, which likely made her more vulnerable, but even the warlocks weren't immune to the lure of an incubus. Several of them had fallen to the floor, crawling towards the incubi wearing slack-jawed expressions, including the bartender.

Oh no. Anyone in the room with any level of attraction towards sexy male warlocks would start stripping at any moment, and I could live a long and happy life without that kind of mental scarring, thanks.

My celestial mark chose that moment to kick into action. Light blazed to the ceiling, and the warlocks scattered, yelling. So they did have a sense of self-preservation after all. Rubbing the growing lump on the back of my head, I detached myself from the bar. My back was sticky with the residue of spilled warlock cocktails and Divinity-knew what else. One of the incubi was surrounded by pawing patrons, but the second detached himself from the crowd with a murderous glint in his eyes.

"I knew it." His eyes glowed with menace. "That magic of yours killed him."

He lunged in a blur of light. I took back my thought about self-preservation and grabbed his arm with my demon-marked hand, throwing him over my shoulder. He landed on his back, hard, and I punched him in the jaw. My fist smoked with residual energy, and his eyes rolled back in his skull. As he fell back, half-conscious, I swayed a little. "Look in the mirror," I told him. "Your face is what happens when I tone down my power. Plainly, it doesn't match the killer's mark."

Muttering rose up, making me aware that the crowd hadn't actually left. The ones who hadn't been hit by the warlocks' spell had backed to the edges of the room, and swiftly got out of the way when Javos shoved his way through, his expression murderous.

"Devi Lawson. Why am I not surprised to find you surrounded by bodies?"

"I just saved you from a major lawsuit, dickhead."

Fiona poked her head up from behind the bar and said, "Those incubi were seconds from using their magic on the saviour of Haven City."

"What in damnation did you bring the human here for?" Javos glared at me.

"She didn't. I came to warn her," Fiona said. She didn't seem to have suffered any effects from the incubus lures, thank the Divinities. "I was with Rachel until a second ago."

"And *I* came looking for you," I added.

"You picked a bad moment," she said. "That's what I was going to tell you—they found another body."

Brilliant.

"This way," growled Javos, beckoning me outside. "Both of you. Now."

"Chill out." I gave up trying to wipe cocktail residue onto my jeans and went after him before the other warlocks recovered from their shock. "Who? An incubus, by any chance?"

"Yes. Same marks on the body," Javos said harshly, shouldering his way through the door. "What were you thinking, coming here?"

"I came to find you," I said. "I thought you'd want to know what Casthus said to me in our meeting."

"I assume you didn't aggravate him, since you're still alive," he growled. "You aren't even capable of dealing diplomatically with the warlocks in this city, let alone the rest of the nether realms."

"Not when they try to kill me, no." I dug my hands in my pockets and walked on. "Nice of you to intervene," I added to Rachel when she sidled up alongside me.

"I really hate incubi. Besides, you had it covered, and I didn't want you to set my head on fire."

"Fair enough. I'm driving back, but Javos, you'll have to lie down in the back seat if you want to ride in my car."

He grunted. "Drive back to the guild. No detours."

"Yes, sir," I said, with a mock salute, and ran back to my vehicle before he changed his mind. "Seriously? Another dead warlock? Surely they know I wasn't even here."

"They're edgy, Devi," Fiona said. "Something about a public fight in that bar a while ago…"

"Against demon-infected vampires," I corrected. "Pretty sure I helped everyone, actually. Some gratitude."

When we got back to the warlocks' guild, Javos beckoned me into his office.

"Skip the lecture," I said to him. "I know I shouldn't have been in that bar, but since they apparently all think I'm guilty, they'd have come looking for me anyway. You know perfectly well that I'm not the killer. There aren't even any Grade Fours at the guild at the moment, and none of the others are trained on their level."

Not until they replenished their forces, anyway. I didn't like that every preternatural in the city knew that the guild was greatly weakened following the battle. The celestial guild had been a long way from perfect, but it'd been at the centre of the fight against the demons in everyone's eyes, including their own. It wouldn't surprise me if the murderer knew, too, and was taking advantage on purpose.

"You're free to pursue your own leads against your fellow celestials," said Javos. "But I don't need to tell you that you're not to keep any information from me, even if it implicates your friends."

"The celestials aren't my friends. And you'd better believe I'm planning to get to the bottom of this. I'm not fond of murder accusations, believe me."

"If you stopped finding your way to murder sites, you wouldn't have any," he said. "I'll take your request into consideration, but if I see evidence of the killer myself, I will take action."

Translation: he'd rip them to pieces. "So what was this second murder?"

"I'm still waiting for the details, but it sounds like the death was the same as the first one. The same… handprints."

Oh boy. "It's a setup," I said. "Someone's trying to inflame old tensions. It's obvious."

"Would you bet your life on that?"

I exhaled in a sigh. "Javos, I've had a day of it already. The shadow demon tried to scare me to death, his fiery friend tried to kill me, I got thrown into a bar by a horny incubus and I have some unidentifiable crap all over my jacket and probably a concussion, too. Let me know about the body when you have the details. Okay?"

I got out of his office before he started another lecture, finding Rachel and Fiona waiting in the corridor.

"That went well," I muttered. "You'd think he assumes I set myself up as a murder suspect because I obviously don't have anything else going on in my life. Which is complete bullshit."

"Ignore him." Rachel shrugged. "You're more qualified than him to deal with this investigation. That's why he's pissed at you. It's supposed to be *his* job."

"He's welcome to it," I said. "What possessed you to bring Fiona to the Harpy's Nest? You know she hasn't had the best experiences with preternatural bars."

"Precisely," said Rachel. "I wanted to show her it's not all violence and murder. Her abilities mean she's going to be part of this world one way or another, so she decided to come with me."

I wasn't convinced. Fiona might not be as naive about all things netherworld as she used to be, but it'd be a long time before she ever trusted a warlock. She was still incredibly wary around Javos, though she seemed to get on fine with Nikolas and Rachel. Her human life had been snatched away suddenly enough that she still needed to adjust.

"Ask me first next time," I said.

"I'm right here, you know," Fiona said wryly. "Where's Nikolas, anyway?"

"Babylon. Again." Worry squirmed inside me. Casthus hadn't made a move against either of us earlier, but maybe he wanted to speak to his son alone. My presence wouldn't help, besides, and I hadn't the faintest idea how to stop him and Abyss from wrecking both realms if they started a war with one another. "What a day. Hang on… who's watching Zadok?"

Rachel gave me an alarmed look. "Nobody. I thought Niko was with him."

"I thought he asked *you* to watch him."

She pulled out her phone. "Ah. Missed call. The bar was noisy."

"I swear, if he gets out…"

"He won't," she said confidently. "I'll check up on him. You should probably sort your friend out—she's bleeding."

I spun around to see Fiona tugging her sleeve down.

"You didn't say," I said accusingly to Fiona.

"I'm fine. You should probably stop that demigod from breaking out. I can hang on until we reach the house."

I resigned myself to driving to Nikolas's house without having the chance to ask Javos for more details on the latest murder. I doubted any demons wanted to talk to me after the debacle in the bar, and Javos himself was in such a foul mood that stopping Zadok from breaking out was the priority. The second murder could come later.

When we reached the house, Rachel immediately ran upstairs. "It's okay," she called down to me. "He's still there. I'll redo the wards."

"Good." I flopped back onto the sofa, suddenly exhausted. Constant adrenaline spikes did that to you. "Fiona. The first aid kit's on the second shelf."

"Got it." She walked over to the mini lab I'd constructed in the corner of the living room. "I'm glad you're okay. And Zadok. I didn't want to stay here alone with him. He was screaming and rattling the chains, so Rachel offered to take me out. She didn't leave me alone, not like last time."

"You deserve to have some fun. Just maybe hold off on the warlock bars until you have more control over your magic. And until I'm absolved of the murders I never committed." I shrugged off my jacket. Sure enough, it'd turned neon blue-green from whatever cocktail I'd landed on when I'd been thrown into the bar. Since my vision wasn't blurry, I assumed I didn't have a concussion after all, but it probably helped that I still had some of Nikolas's regenerative magic rattling around my demon mark somewhere.

Fiona picked up the bottle containing the warlock-made healing potion and squeezed some onto her hand. "Of course you're not the killer. Javos should know better."

"You're handling this well," I added to her. "I'm glad you didn't end up as incubus bait. I thought their lure hit you."

"It did." She paused in the middle of applying the potion to her injured arm. "The lure... their power is based on attraction, right?"

I frowned. "Yes..."

"I'm asexual. The lure doesn't work on me because I'm not inclined to be attracted to the person using it in the first place."

"Oh," I said. "When the vamps lured you into going into that nightclub—"

"That was him. Azurial." She grimaced. "He was controlling me at the time. I didn't know, obviously. It's not like 'there's a fire demon possessing me' was my first thought. I thought I was developing an addiction to vampire venom, and maybe I was."

"No, it makes sense," I said. Demons dealt in lust, but love and sexual attraction weren't the same thing, however much some incubi might have you believe they were. "You once said you were saving yourself for the Wingless Warlock, but I guess that was a joke? Just wondering."

"Ah." She chewed on her lower lip. "My parents didn't really get it. They wanted me to meet a nice boy and move back home away from the vampire-invested demon city. I figured they'd let it go if I confessed to a crush on the biggest demonic celebrity in all the realms."

"They didn't see the pictures, did they?" I knew Fiona had had issues explaining her friendship with me to her entirely normal-human and straight-laced parents after photos of the pair of us standing on a battlefield strewn with dead demons had shown up online. I thought the Wingless Warlock's images from the web would probably cause even more of a horrified reaction from her family.

"Divinities, no," said Fiona. "I can think he's cute without wanting to jump him, and for the record, if he showed up naked in my bed, I'd probably throw a shoe at him."

Fiona had mostly been uninterested in dating during the time we'd known one another, but I'd put it down to her devoting all her free time to DivinityWatch. That'd teach me to make assumptions. "Well, I'm glad I didn't have to wrestle you off a horny incubus."

"I'm pretty sure our friendship would have survived." She grinned. "You knew when to duck, though. You don't need the lure when it comes to Nikolas. You have the same look on your face whenever you meet his eyes anyway."

"Thanks," I said. "It's not the lure that's the problem, it's that my demon mark amplifies every kind of demonic power it comes into contact with. The last time he accidentally used it on me, I lost all reason, all memory—everything. Those incubi didn't actually know that, but if they'd got any closer, my celestial power would have burned them, and probably everyone else in the bar, too."

"Whoa. You never mentioned his lure hit you." She pulled a face. "Do I even want to know this story?"

"Probably not. We were standing in an alley full of dead bodies at the time."

"You know, since it's you two, that doesn't surprise me in the slightest."

"It was… the night the vamps took you."

"Oh." Her expression sobered.

"It wasn't his fault," I said. "He was aiming at the vampires so we could get away and come back to you." I released a breath. "I was terrified we'd be too late. I can't afford to let our relationship get in the way of the fact that—well, he's a demigod."

"Star-crossed lovers." She wore the same dreamy expression as she did when she looked at DivinityWatch. "You two have 'life partners' written all over you."

Something wrenched in my chest at those words. "I thought I had a life partner once. Didn't quite work out that way."

"Oh. God, Devi." She looked stricken. "I'm sorry—I'm so sorry that ended up online. I swear I don't know how they found out."

Oh. The information on Rory that had wound up on DivinityWatch. To be honest, I'd forgotten all about it, considering everything that'd happened since.

"It's okay. Price you pay for being a minor internet celebrity." It wasn't Fiona's fault, and heaven knew we had a billion more urgent matters to contend ourselves with.

"It wasn't cool of them. I told them to leave you alone, but…"

I gave another head-shake. "I don't care what they say about me. The cat is out of the bag: I'm a celestial demon. And Rory's family is dead, not to mention he'd probably roll his eyes at the comments about us if he could see them."

Including the ones which said I'd made a deal with a demon to kill him in favour of Nikolas the warlock.

Fiona bit her lip. "I really am sorry. About the interview, too. It wasn't supposed to go the way it did. They said the event would be in a small venue, but those vamps insisted on paying for the big one and it all snowballed from there."

I shrugged. "Believe me, I've had worse experiences in the last week alone than vamps cheering my name."

"Yeah." Fiona nodded. "I—I think you and Nikolas will be fine. You will."

"Just forget the angry arch-demon and we might all make it out alive."

And then? Who knew. I was highly attracted to Nikolas. But was I in love with him? Let's face it, I didn't even know what love was. My relationship with Rory had been completely different, and it was too loaded a question to face with an angry arch-demon's threat hanging over our heads.

"Is he okay?" Fiona asked tentatively. "Do you know?"

"More than Zadok. I think." I heaved out a breath. "Gods above, this is a mess, isn't it?"

"You're telling me."

8

Nikolas returned at midnight. I stayed up, nerves frayed with worry, and leapt from my seat when he appeared in the living room.

"Thank the Divinities."

He didn't look hurt this time, to my intense relief, though his expression was grim and tired. "He's dead set on meeting with Abyss. I had to talk him out of opening a portal there and then."

"Given that there aren't demons materialising in here at this very moment, I guess you succeeded?"

"Just about." He crossed the room to me and wrapped his arms tight around me.

I yelped. "You're as cold as the ninth circle of hell."

"He never did take my attempts to install central heating in the castle seriously."

"In that department, this realm's winning," I mumbled into his shoulder.

He stroked my hair. "This realm also doesn't have an angry arch-demon in it."

"Better hope we keep it that way," I said lightly, though

something inside me broke a little at the thought of Casthus smashing through this realm and destroying everything we had. Even today, at the very least, I could have lost him.

Fiona was right. I was in deep. Way deep.

———

The following morning brought no updates from Javos on the second murder. Knowing him, he was keeping the details under wraps just to annoy me, but stopping the arch-demon's rampage through the nether realms took first place on my list.

"He didn't even say *when* he wanted to speak to Abyss," I told Nikolas over breakfast. "He never said I couldn't speak to her first. Just to forewarn her."

He gave me an assessing look. "No, I suppose not. Is that what you want to do?"

I took a bite of toast. "It seems to me she'll be pissed off if he springs this meeting on her without warning. Maybe pissed enough to drag Earth into the conflict again. If I warn her he's coming, maybe she'll play nice."

"Perhaps," he said. "I can't imagine she'll react violently to the revelation. She must have expected the other arch-demons to seek her out sooner or later."

"I haven't checked on Pandemonium for a while," I said. "Also, I'm kind of wondering if this is all connected. The murders, even. The demons know Earth is weakened, and they probably know some of the celestials turned on one another or died in the fighting, too. The killer is definitely taking advantage of the situation, whichever realm they're from."

He nodded slowly. "It's worth looking around, since you already have contacts. If you're sure."

"Seriously. I really should get paid more for this."

Despite the lack of monetary compensation and the constant threat to my life, my fortunes had improved substantially since I'd joined up with the warlocks, in more than one way. My time as a celestial soldier seemed like someone else's life, and the two years of civilian life after I'd quit were a blur. Only in the last few weeks had I begun to let go of the guilt, the notion that Rory should have been spared, not me, and that I deserved a real shot at happiness. Now, I had so much more to fight for.

I walked into the living room to set up the pentagram to contact Abyss's realm. Warning Nikolas to stay out of range in case my arm caught fire again, I held my hand steady, burning five points of light into the wall which connected with glowing lines. Then I tossed in some brimstone and said, "I summon you, Dienes."

A little horned demon appeared with a popping noise. He sank into a bow. "How may I help you, Devi?"

"You can stop being a hypocrite, for a start." The traitorous little worm had screwed me over when he'd set me up for the demons to reel me in, and I'd only kept him alive because I'd never met another low-grade demon with the ability to sniff out almost any other demon I asked him to. He was also terrified of me, so he'd tell me anything Abyss said or did if I asked. One could never have enough allies, even treacherous demons.

"I'm coming to talk to Abyss," I said. "I'd like you to warn her so she doesn't flay me alive. Tell her I'll be over soon."

He squeaked, his eyes widening. Telling her would probably put him at the mercy of her temper, but I was running low on fucks to give. "For you, Devi? Absolutely. Pleasure to be of service."

"I bet you are." I let the five lights of the circle die out. "I'll give him a few minutes. How's Zadok? He didn't break any more holes in the floor?"

Nikolas shook his head. "No. I think he burned himself out. What Casthus did to him drained almost all his power."

"At least that means he shouldn't have any schemes to make mischief here on Earth, if he even realises where he is yet." I rocked back on my heels. I wore Rachel's gravity-defying boots and was armed to the teeth, yet dealing with Abyss brought more apprehension than I'd anticipated. It'd be just my luck to find out she was behind the warlock attacks—and then I'd have to take responsibility, because I was the one who'd handed Pandemonium over to her. Not that it'd been mine to begin with… but she'd accepted my bargain easily. Maybe too much so.

"I wouldn't put anything past him," Nikolas said. "Are you sure you want to do this?"

"I have to do something. Anything."

He leaned over and kissed me, his hands gently caressing my face. "This isn't all your responsibility, Devi. I promise it isn't."

I didn't entirely agree, but I hadn't volunteered to play nice with arch-demons in the first place. They'd picked me, so now they had to deal with the consequences. "Time to see what our delightful demonic overlord has to say about meeting her fellow arch-demon."

Probably nothing pleasant. They likely knew one another already. They'd both been *Divinities*, once. Thousands of years ago. I couldn't imagine the shadow demon ever being merciful or kind, but the Divinities were neither of those things. They left bodies of celestial soldiers strewn on their battlefield. And just look at the fallen.

"I'll wait here," Nikolas said. "And I'll check on Babylon, too, to make sure my father hasn't done anything too heinous since my last visit."

"How are the other warlocks coping?"

"He killed five of them. So, not well. I've fooled him into

thinking we're allies and hiding my emotional ties to you, but if he feels that either of us has displeased him, he'll use one of us to hurt the other. He'd do the same with Zadok, but I told him he died."

"Shit, really?" I'd known my connection to Nikolas would likely prove problematic at the very least, but having to fake his own brother's death... "What a colossal twat. And the fallen?"

"Still imprisoned."

My fists clenched. "I don't care if he owns the place or not, you can't own *people.* Maybe I can break them out when he and Abyss are fighting."

"I wouldn't advise it," he said.

"Worth a shot." I kissed him once again before activating the demonglass, hoping Dienes had kept his word.

Fire rose from the fragments in my hand. Even now, I had to resist the urge to shrink away from the flames, but they were gone before I knew it. And Pandemonium...

I stared around. Where there had once been a huge demonglass palace with countless towers was a narrow room filled with endless mirrors. My reflection stared back, my aura half dark and half glowing white. It looked like that in every mirror now, not just demonglass, but it was still weird to be pursued by a dozen Devis.

"Is there a door in here?" I asked, aloud. Nobody responded. I stepped forwards and reached out, running my fingers along the glass. Theoretically I could transport myself anywhere I'd already been, but did that apply when the palace had been changed beyond all recognition? Abyss couldn't look at the sunlight, so she'd either moved all the demonglass underground or rebuilt it into a windowless and possibly door-less palace of her own creation.

I stepped in the other direction and then almost fell head-first into a wall that wasn't there. The demonglass didn't comprise four walls but two, and what had appeared to be two more walls were actually opposite ends of a corridor. Thanks to the demonglass's dizzying reflections, there was no way to tell how long it went on for.

"Wow," I said. "This must have taken days."

I doubted it, though. The arch-demons could easily rearrange the whole world in a heartbeat if they liked, and the demonglass corridors looked suspiciously like the tunnels which had once filled the area beneath the palace. There was no real way to see an enemy coming in a place like this. My body tensed, my celestial hand switching on and off as I kept walking, pursued by endless reflections all along the way. This was probably her idea of a game—

A demon jumped at me, and I immediately summoned my celestial blade. Luckily for the demon, the blade glanced off the demonglass and just missed skewering it in the chest.

"What are you?" I asked the cowering demon. "Sent to welcome me or sent to kill me? Because I'd hate to damage my relationship with your master by accidentally killing one of her trusted servants."

"Mistress would be honoured to welcome you," he squeaked, several arrows falling out of the quiver strapped to his back.

"Poisoned arrows?" I rolled my eyes. "You're a god-awful assassin. Just so you know."

"Not poison!" He glanced around in a panic.

"I know demon poison when I see it."

The blade flashed as I brought it down, and the demon exploded into ashes. Celestial light bounced off the mirror-like walls, momentarily blinding me, and several screeches told me that the assassin hadn't been alone.

"Is there anyone up there who *doesn't* want me dead?" I called through the tunnel.

No response.

"Can't say I didn't warn you," I said, and my hand lit up with flames once more.

By the time I reached the fourth room of demons, my temper was frayed to say the least. "Did you send them here like lambs to the slaughter on purpose, Abyss? I could do this all day, but I think you're going to want to hear what I have to say."

I let the last demon's ashes blow away. Fine, then. I faced the wall and thought, *take me to Abyss.* The visualising method wasn't the most reliable, especially when my surroundings were unfamiliar, but there was no harm in trying.

The glass's reflection didn't change, and still showed the corridor. "Helpful." I pressed my fingers to the glass. Surely if my demon power evolved like my celestial abilities did, then I should be able to learn to control the destination, but it wasn't like I could take lessons from the demon who'd marked me. I was fairly certain he was glad to see the back of me, and the feeling was mutual.

"Take me to Abyss. Or summon someone who will. I command you."

My demon mark made no impact on the glass, but as my rage peaked, I accidentally let the shadowy magic in my palm leak out. Instead of dissipating without a target, it remained floating there, a piece of disconnected shadow. Oops.

"Shoo." I waved a hand at the shadow. It didn't move.

Great. I wouldn't shed a tear if one of those demons walked into it and got a limb chopped off, but usually I instinctively knew how to use the magic I stole. I had with Themedes, though throwing fire around was straightfor-ward. Both Nikolas and Zadok had a different variant of the same shadow magic, so it stood to reason that their father's was different, too. Didn't give me much to work with. I'd only seen him use it to kill.

I waved at the magic, calling it back to the demon mark. To my surprise, it obeyed. Now that was more like it.

All right, then.

Calling the shadows to the surface of my right palm, I aimed deliberately at the glass at the corridor's end. Then I released the magic.

Shadows burst from my fingertips in a manner not unlike Nikolas's lightning magic, and the glass shattered like I'd thrown a heavy object at it.

Whoa. I'd never encountered anything that could shatter demonglass before, but it figured that the arch-demon's power could do it. There was apparently nothing they couldn't do.

When the glass had ceased falling, I carefully picked my way forward. Another corridor waited ahead, this one with walls of stone.

"Anyone there?" I shouted.

"How dare you use that magic in here!"

The world sped past as a blast of air hit me from behind, sending me flying forwards. My feet left the ground, the tunnel flew past, and I hit the ground so abruptly that if not for Rachel's boots, I'd have face-planted in front of the arch-demon looking down on me. She wore her human-like form, clad in the same golden armour she'd worn the last time I'd seen her. Her youthful face almost hid the dark intelligence simmering in her golden eyes. Bat-like wings extended from her shoulder blades. Her aura shimmered like spun gold— ironic, for someone whose major weakness was sunlight.

"You carry his magic," Abyss hissed. "The tainted one is not welcome here."

I smiled up at her. "Funny you should say that. I'm here to—"

"My answer is no."

"Did someone warn you first or are you just guessing?"

"If you carry his magic, you carry his word. I will not speak with him."

I kept my gaze on her face to keep the impulse to step back out of range of her blazing aura under control. Its reflections from the demonglass pillars were starting to give me a headache. "You're mistaken if you think he's giving you the option. I thought I'd be nice and warn you first."

It'd be nice if you acknowledged I got you this place to begin with. I'd been a little concerned about forcing her presence on the demons here, but it didn't sound like Themedes had been a particularly pleasant ruler either. When it came to the demons, their only two options were deferring to an arch-demon or breaking out into utter anarchy until the next one showed up. The gods wanted to watch Abyss and me murder one another for their own entertainment, so I refused to give them the satisfaction of watching our epic showdown. Abyss had chosen to take this realm instead, but apparently her disdain for me was undiminished.

Two horned roak demons appeared on either side of her. "Leave," she said. "Now."

I sighed and summoned my celestial blade. "Look, the arch-demon insists on a meeting, and if the two of you get into it, you're welcome to. But don't come crying to me when he barges in here and breaks your demonglass walls until the sun scorches your skin off."

She hissed out a furious breath. Magic exploded from her hands, and her pet demons died in shrieking fire. "Do not speak of that again."

"You don't want me telling *him* your weakness, do you? Deal with him. He's coming here either way."

Her aura simmered. "I will speak with him on one condition. Your friend contains some of the magic of one of this realm's demons."

"Nope," I said.

"You have yet to hear my offer. She will be kept comfortable and won't be harmed."

"She's human, from a non-demon world, and isn't interested in having anything to do with you."

Why wouldn't they leave Fiona the hell alone? It wasn't like she had the powers of an arch-demon. Azurial hadn't been that special. They just wanted her as a curiosity and a toy. I wasn't having any of it.

"It's not her choice to make, if she wields our magic."

"Forget it," I said, conjuring shadowy power to my hand. "I don't know how far this demonglass goes, but this power can blast straight through to the sunlight. I have no interest in getting my skin burned off by the shadow demon's little pet because you refused to honour his request for a meeting."

"He still employs those beasts?"

So she did know him. I'd be a fool to assume otherwise, considering both of them were thousands of years old. Maybe she had a reason to throw a temper tantrum over his insistence on meeting with her, but dragging Fiona into it was *not* cool.

"Yes. They tore the skin off a demigod the other day. And you know that I could give away your weakness if I wanted to. I owe you no loyalty just because we had a bargain once. And I won't be handing over Fiona."

I stepped backwards, through the demonglass wall, back to Earth.

9

I landed on my feet in the pile of demonglass I'd left in Nikolas's living room.

"How'd it go?" asked Nikolas, who sat on the sofa, for all the world like he'd waited for me the whole time I'd been gone.

"Apparently she and the arch-demon have a history," I said. "She's being stubborn and refusing to let him in, but I doubt he'll take no for an answer. I found out his magic can destroy demonglass, too."

"That doesn't surprise me," he said. "I imagine he'll just walk right in."

I crossed the room to join him on the sofa. "What do arch-demons talk about, murder and conquests and destruction? Or is he going to try to claim Pandemonium, too?"

"He hasn't mentioned it," Nikolas said slowly. "He hasn't yet told me why he came back, either, aside from you."

"I'm so honoured." I rolled my eyes. "I guess he wanted to see who got the best of Abyss. And she seemed to know his servants..." I trailed off. "Wait a moment. Did we ever confirm for definite that her demigods didn't survive the battle?"

"I highly doubt they lived."

"But they can mimic anyone. Celestials included. The murders…"

"Her servants can't mimic their magic."

I slapped a hand to my forehead. "Right, right. I should have thought of that. Panic over. I doubt Abyss would bother killing random warlocks on Earth."

"No, it's a valid theory," he said. "It *is* likely that the rogue celestial killer might have demonic help, like the former Grade Fours."

"So you do think it's them." I had to admit, there weren't many other people who could burn handprints into warlocks.

"It's more likely to be them than anyone else. Unless the Grade Fours maintain their divine vows even in exile, there must be a reason they've evaded the celestials' attention."

"Working with the demons deliberately, though? They were so convinced they were in the right that they saw murdering innocent vampires as collateral damage. Maybe they've been tricked into believing they're following the Divinities, but I don't see what they think they're accomplishing." I rested my head against the back of the sofa beside him. "No, maybe it's an angry rogue. I haven't a clue. Has Javos come up with any more answers? I never did see the second body."

"He hasn't yet found a theory," he said. "The incubi were apprehended. Apparently he knocked their heads together. Did they really… threaten you?" His usually golden eyes were dark. "You should have told me."

Oh, right. Sex demons. "They didn't get close," I told him. "My celestial power activated and nearly burned the place down."

"Good," he said. "I don't think you should walk into warlock-only places until your innocence is proved. The risk of someone getting hurt is too high."

He didn't just mean me. He was walking a tightrope trying to keep everyone safe, and my latest jaunt probably hadn't helped a bit. But the power burning in my demon mark, the shadowy magic that could even destroy demon-glass, was a glaring reminder that the fallen remained imprisoned in Casthus's home. We had to get them out.

The murmur of voices came from upstairs. "Is Rachel here?"

"No, she went to help Javos."

I jumped to my feet. "Wait. Fiona—"

"She was asleep upstairs. She didn't want to go back to the guild without you."

"Oh no." I knew the other voice. *He didn't. He'd better not—*

I took the stairs two at a time, towards the room which definitely shouldn't have voices coming out of it, and kicked the door open.

Fiona jumped up from where she'd been sitting on the floor. "Hey, Devi."

I scowled at Zadok. "What were you saying to her? If you even think about corrupting Fiona, you're going back to the arch-demon."

"Do I look in any fit state to be corrupting anyone?" His voice was low and raspy.

"I'm pretty sure you corrupt people in your sleep."

"Ouch." He twitched one mangled wing, while Fiona herself ducked around me and left the room. Probably a good idea. Casthus's magic burned beneath my demon mark —and now I looked closer, shadows filled the room at the edges, too.

"What's that?" I pointed, half expecting his army of

shadow clones to appear. But though the light was dim, the points of a pentagram were etched on the wall behind him.

"Babylon," he said. "Oh, don't look so shocked. I knew this wasn't my home the moment I woke up here. My magic knows it."

Darkness filled the entire space behind his shoulders. The portal... ah, now I understood. Warlocks were dependent on their own realm's essence to fuel their magic. Nikolas must have opened a portal to keep Zadok's regenerative power running.

"So you got your magic back. Want a medal? What the hell did you want to talk to Fiona about?"

"Would you believe it gets lonely in here? I haven't spoken to any humans in a long while, except you, Devi."

"Spare me," I said. "If you think I'm letting you out of this room, you're mistaken. You're heading back to Babylon as soon as Nikolas says so."

"You think I want to stay in this shithole dimension?" His sharp teeth curled over his lip. "I want my home back."

I folded my arms across my chest. "I thought you wanted to get away because the warlocks hate you and you're stuck babysitting the fallen."

"I'm a demon. I belong in the nether realms." He sat more upright. "I'm not interested in this realm, Devi."

"Then why tell Nikolas you were?"

"Because it annoys him." He grinned. "He'd lose his shit if I insinuated I wanted to come after you. Of course he's not attached to this realm. He's just highly attached to *you*. Damnation knows why."

"I will literally never understand the two of you as long as I live. But keep Fiona out of this. What did you do, wail and rattle your chains until she came to tell you to shove off?"

"Actually, she came here of her own free will. Which you're both extremely lucky to still have. How was Pandemonium? I smell it on you. Brimstone and demonglass. And the merest hint of poison. Still at odds with Abyss? I thought you came to an understanding."

I shrugged. "She knows your father. I don't suppose you could enlighten me on the history there?"

"Now you want to make a bargain?"

"No, I want you to give me answers. You obviously want to talk to someone and you're not getting to Fiona, so tell me instead. I don't pity you in the slightest."

He scowled. "You can't deal out torture. You don't have it in you."

"Plenty of humans have tortured one another. A lot of them invented methods that would rival your demon ones. Also, I don't need to torture you to get you to answer me when you're like that."

I reached out a foot and lightly kicked at his leg. He hissed and pulled back. "Abyss once stole our father's possessions," he snarled. "If you must know. It's uninteresting. There was a scheme involving one of her demigod mimics and a lot of stolen treasure. My father didn't even need what was stolen, but he declared war on her on principle."

"Nice. So who won?"

"Stalemate. She sent her people to keep thwarting him at every turn and he gave up to avoid losing more of his army when she got another arch-demon involved."

"Right, I forgot she doesn't actually participate in any of her wars or conquests in person." I dropped my arms to my sides. "She's not much of a war goddess considering how long she spent locked up in your tower instead of actually going out onto the battlefield."

"She's a manipulator. She'll plan to meet him, but on her own terms and when she's certain she'll be able to gain something from that scenario."

"I somehow doubt he'll wait for her to be ready."

"You'd be surprised," Zadok said. "You shouldn't underestimate her. She caved to you because she wanted Pandemonium all along."

"And she was terrified of the sunlight," I added. "Torture *does* work in *that* scenario…" I trailed off at his expression of stunned disbelief. "What? How did you not know that?"

"Do you *really* think she'd have told me her weakness?"

"She didn't tell me. She was hiding in a tower on a world with no sunlight. A child could have guessed the same." Oh, damn. I'd genuinely thought he knew. She'd overpowered him so easily, though—that was a stupid assumption to make. "You seriously let her push you around without even trying to figure out her weakness?"

A smile slid onto his face. "No, Devi, but I will never be in that position again. I owe you a favour."

Crap. "You can start by staying the hell away from Fiona."

His eyes gleamed. "Why, you're afraid your friend can't make her own decisions? That's an interesting and useful power she possesses…"

"Drop it, dickhead. I thought you were terrified of fire."

His grin slid away. "I'm not terrified of anything."

I narrowed my eyes. "Yeah right. You spent the last battle letting your dimension turn into Abyss's stronghold because you were afraid of getting burned. And she knows your weakness, too."

The chains rattled as he straightened up. "That's not why I stayed out of the conflict until I had no choice. I knew from the moment you showed up that he would come back to Babylon one way or another. I hoped *he* would kill Abyss, if nobody else would."

"You wanted him to come and rescue you and would happily put Earth in the line of fire in the process? That's both cowardly and despicable."

An ugly expression twisted his mouth and a golden glint

appeared in his eyes as he climbed to his feet. Shadows leaked from his fingertips. *Don't poke the demigod, Devi.*

"You have no fucking clue about any of this, do you?" he rasped. "I've tried reasoning with you—*helped* you, even, and you repay me with rudeness and ingratitude."

I stepped forwards, so we stood nose to nose. "You threw me off a bridge and never apologised for it. You tried to kill Rachel and nearly handed Earth over to the enemy. If you're expecting me to grovel at your feet, I'd rather eat dirt."

Shadows slapped at me. I stepped out of the way. While my celestial hand itched to ignite, I let shadows leak out of my right hand. His eyes narrowed. "His power. You're in over your head."

"Heaven forbid I bruise a warlock's ego."

"Zadok!" Nikolas said warningly. I hadn't heard him slip into the room behind me. Had he witnessed the whole thing? Surely he would have told me if he thought his brother had no designs on Earth after all. It sure would make my life easier, anyway.

"You can stay out of this, brother."

Zadok's body leaked shadows, climbing up the walls. His eyes glowed golden, and the pentagram glowed, too.

"Terrifying," I told him.

He called me something unmentionable in the demon tongue.

"I'm wounded," I told him. "Niko, a word, please."

Zadok laughed a humourless laugh that followed us from the room as Nikolas firmly locked the door behind us.

"Are the defences secure?" I asked Nikolas. "I'm sorry. I didn't know he had no idea of Abyss's weakness. I shouldn't have—"

"I thought he knew." Nikolas gave the locked door a glare. "I thought that's why he let the bridge to Earth open. He certainly hinted he did. He often pretends to know more than he already does. It's not your fault."

I groaned. "Maybe he did pretend not to know just to play with my head. Like he tried to play with Fiona's. Does she seem okay?"

"Yes. Zadok can't influence thoughts via magic, and we don't share the lure ability."

"I'm more concerned that he's trying to persuade her to get close to him so he can use her power for his own ends."

"Possibly," said Nikolas. "Either that, or he wants to make sure she won't act against him using her powers. That's equally likely. After he nearly died… I've never seen him like that before. He survived, against the odds. And when a demigod is humiliated in the way that he was, there's nothing he won't do to revenge himself on the perpetrators."

I nodded, pretending to be less frazzled than I was. Dealing with Zadok was unpredictable on a good day. "Also, he said he's actually not interested in this dimension in the slightest, and he was just trying to piss you off by pretending he wanted to come here. So that might be a consideration."

"I've no doubt he doesn't *want* to stay," Nikolas said, making for the stairs. "I was considering dumping him on some other world, but he'd probably cause more damage if he tried to tear his way through to Babylon from there. And he would try."

I followed closely behind him, back into the living room. "You seem certain he'd survive it."

"We're made to survive," he said.

I exhaled in a sigh. "No offence, but your demon drama is going to drive me into an early grave."

"Does my demon drama bother you?" he said. "You've had to give up your peace of mind, your security, from the moment we met."

"My peace of mind and security jumped ship when I

signed up to the celestials, and again after I lost Rory. I know how to roll with the punches."

"I'm sorry, Devi." His voice was raw sincerity, and not at all demonic.

"Not your fault. I'm impressed that Javos was a good enough influence on you that you didn't turn out like that." I pointed up at the ceiling.

"Oh, he never raised me. My mother's parents did. They were human. Javos was more of a mentor."

"And Rachel?"

"I took care of her."

"Maybe that's why Zadok feels so bitter. He knows we're on Earth, by the way. What do you plan to do with him if your father decides to stay on Babylon long-term? If you use Javos's resources, he'll ask questions, won't he?"

"Zadok will have to live with the vampires we rescued, I imagine," he said. "In their safe house. But it would be a security nightmare if he escaped."

"And the fallen?"

"Even worse," he said. "Zadok can pass—reluctantly—as human. The fallen can't. The costs of keeping them alive wouldn't go unnoticed by Javos. He pays well enough, but his resources aren't infinite, and the war has caused damage to our relations with the celestials. A lot of the warlocks who used to sell pentagrams and the like have mentioned the guild's more reluctant to make such purchases."

"Guess that's not a surprise. Do they buy most of the props? I thought they were restricted."

"For us, they are," he said. "The celestials make the rules, but don't necessarily follow them. While they're undeniably hypocritical, they're also a major source of income for the city's warlocks."

"Figures." Bringing things from the netherworld to Earth was technically not allowed, let alone *people*. Zadok being here was breaking multiple laws both on the demons' side and the celestials'. And that wasn't getting into what might happen if he decided to make a bid for freedom.

Damn. What would it take for Casthus to leave Babylon?

I blew out a frustrated breath. "And now Abyss and Casthus have brought their old grudges right to Earth's doorstep. Were they ever allies? You'd think the shadow realm would be perfect for her."

He tilted his head thoughtfully. "You've come to conclusions it took me years to reach. I think they were likely allies at one point in the past, before the more recent events that made them enemies. I heard what Zadok told you, but I know little more than he does. That's just the last thirty years of history. Our father has been alive for much longer."

"I can't even comprehend that time frame," I said. "And he was a Divinity before that—right?"

"Long enough ago that he retains none of his divine powers," Nikolas said. "Abyss fell more recently, as far as I'm aware."

"And she wanted to be reborn as someone who can walk into the sunlight," I added. "The Divinities... if they're orchestrating this, what could they possibly gain from pitting those two arch-demons against one another? Entertainment? That's why they brought Lythocrax and Abyss together—"

The world trembled as though an earthquake's first rumblings stirred the ground below my feet. I grabbed Nikolas's arm for balance, while Fiona let out a startled yell from the guest room. My celestial light activated, narrowly missing Nikolas's face, but I didn't sense or smell anything demonic. "What in the world—?"

Nikolas's eyes had darkened to black. "He opened a portal. On Babylon."

"What?"

He vanished into shadow. I swore at full volume, my left

hand glowing with white light, my right bleeding shadowy power. Zadok shouted from upstairs, and my heart lurched.

"What the—?"

Cracks appeared in the ceiling, and there came the distinct sound of a lock snapping.

"Stop that!" I yelled, running for the stairs and bounding up to Zadok's room.

Cracks covered the entire door, and had begun to spread across the floor, too, shadowy magic spilling into the gaps.

I shoved the door inwards, my hand bleeding celestial light. Zadok stood at his full height, straining to break the chains. "Let me out of here."

"No," I said. "You can't—"

He lunged, and I blasted my celestial light towards him. He roared in pain as it seared his already raw skin, burning a hole in the floor. Then another. Swiftly, I burned five connecting lights into the floor. A pentagram, charged up at the highest level. Spitting out curses in the demon tongue, he rattled the chains, but the pentagram held him captive. "You bitch."

"I'm not letting you out." I backed out of the room and ran down the landing. "Fiona?"

"I'm okay," she said, running out of her room. "I—your hand's on fire!"

I looked down at the white flame encasing my palm. "So it is. Whatever happened must have been on Babylon, not Earth, but—"

Nikolas reappeared at the foot of the stairs in a shadowy blur. "He's gone through the portal."

"What—Casthus? Where? Not the guild?" I ran downstairs to join him, Fiona on my heels.

"No. We would have felt it. He crossed into Pandemonium, and that was the echo resulting from the former link between our dimensions. It's still recent enough for us to feel it when those two realms interact."

Holy shit. "What would happen if they fought one another?"

"I'd rather not contemplate it."

"And there I was thinking I'd get an invite." I released a breath, willing my celestial light to calm down. "I put Zadok in a pentagram and accidentally burned him in the process."

"A Grade Four pentagram?" he said. "I should have done that from the beginning, but I was a little too thorough when I deactivated the one we borrowed beforehand."

I dragged a hand through my hair. "Want to go to the former celestial guild in case the arch-demons start a fight?"

"If they start a fight, it's more likely to cause trouble across the whole city, not just there."

"That's not reassuring, Nikolas." The slightest movement in the arch-demon's power might send a wave of Abyss's assassins through into Haven City. Or worse, reopen the bridge. Babylon wasn't a neutral realm any longer, and maybe even the arch-demon wouldn't be able to fix the damage. If he had any intention of doing so, which I strongly doubted.

"It's not supposed to be," he said. "This isn't the time to downplay the danger all the realms are in."

"Then I'll go after them." I looked into his faintly glowing eyes. "Please. Maybe I can't stop them fighting if they get into it, but I can steal enough of their power to be a nuisance and distract them."

"It'll only cause them to target you instead, or provoke them into outright conflict. I don't believe that was Abyss's intention."

"Considering she never fights her own battles? Yeah, you're probably right. But I still think the guild should know."

The celestials' resources would surely tell them about the current movements in the nether realms, if they even had anything set up after the destruction of the old guild. And even the inspectors had never any direct contact with any actual Divinities. There was an international council board which operated at the very peak, and little was known about its members except that they received trustworthy information about netherworld activity direct from someone who knew. Considering the administrator of the Grade Four Celestial tests was a fallen angel, I had my sincere doubts that there were any actual divine ambassadors anywhere nearby.

I had to do something. Telling the celestials exactly what was going on between the arch-demons was out of the question, but...

Nikolas said, "I'm going into Babylon again to make sure he didn't leave any traces behind. I imagine he'll have taken his demonic servants with him."

"Why not—"

"Please stay here," he said. "Rachel's with Javos, and Zadok... I need someone to stop him from getting dangerous ideas. I can cover the ground quickly if I fly. You call the guild."

"You—" I broke off. "You're right, but dammit, if you get stuck over there, I'm not responsible for what I do to those bloody arch-demons. And what if he comes back?"

"I have every right to be in that castle. And it *will* be mine again."

He disappeared. I swore after him. "You know, I take back what I said about Zadok. They're *both* going to get themselves killed trying to outdo that bloody arch-demon."

"He's not actually on Babylon, right?" Fiona asked hesitantly.

"Nope. He won't let Abyss meet him there, so he's gone to

confront her on her own territory." I heaved out a breath. "Zadok didn't try anything, did he?"

She gave a shrug. "He's harmless. You forget I spent hours with Azurial." Her tone was flippant, but her gaze was shadowed. She'd never told me the extent of her terrifying experience on Pandemonium the first time.

"Point taken, but I wouldn't say he's harmless. He's an unhinged version of Nikolas with no empathy and a penchant for throwing people out of windows."

"I heard the story," she said. "I'll be fine."

"Don't take this the wrong way, Fiona, but he's trying to get on your good side because he knows you can shoot fire from your fingertips. Fire's his major weakness. It's not that he necessarily feels threatened by you, but he probably wants you as an ally for that reason."

"It's fine. Lesson learnt from last time. No trusting demigods. Except Nikolas. What a family. Who was his mother?"

"A human… I've no clue who." My phone vibrated in my pocket. "Oh… damn. Javos." He'd doubtless felt the aftershocks from Babylon, too.

Javos growled into the phone, "They've arrested one of your lot."

Celestials? "Who?"

"Get over here," he growled. "Or she dies."

10

I left the house and ran to my car.

"For crying out loud." I threw myself behind the wheel. "First Zadok loses the plot, now Javos. Is there something in the water turning every demigod into this realm into a raging maniac?"

"Maybe it's whatever happened in Babylon," Fiona said, climbing into the passenger seat next to me. "Ah—crap. Shouldn't I stay to watch Zadok?"

"He won't get out of that pentagram," I said. "Oh, for god's sake… I don't want to ask you to do this. And I meant it when I said he'll try to manipulate you."

"I'm not that naive. You forget this." Her hand glowed. "Firepower. I can bring it out if necessary."

The light became an orange flame. She'd been working hard to get her magic under control, and it showed. "If you're sure. I'll be back as soon as I stop Javos from committing murder."

After she'd climbed out of the car, I drove off as quickly as possible. Warlock territory was riddled with speed cameras, but they kept breaking for some mysterious reason, so I didn't slow down until I reached the warlocks' headquarters. The pair of devil horns usually perched on the fence had been knocked into the road, which was a warning sign if I ever saw one. Behind the gate, Javos's huge form loomed, clad in an oversized shirt, jeans and boots. His aura blazed like a furnace and would have caused traffic accidents if everyone could see it like I did. His eyes glowed the same colour.

"What the hell is wrong with you?" I marched up to him and replaced the devil horns on the date. "Are you certain the person you have is the killer?"

"This *celestial* was found skulking around the place where the second murder took place, and claims to no longer be affiliated with the guild."

Oh no. "Let me speak to her."

He grunted and beckoned me inside. Rachel stood in front of the locked door to the old storeroom, looking distinctly like she'd planted herself in front of the door to stop Javos from killing the person inside it. Rachel was the one person Javos wouldn't hurt. Nodding to me, she stepped aside to let me enter.

The prisoner was a blond woman around my own age. My mouth fell open. Of all the celestials I'd pin the murder on, Lydia was bottom of the list, not least because she'd been marked as dead in the battle. Her usually immaculate blond hair was caked with dirt and grime, and her clothes—ordinary jeans and T-shirt, not celestial gear—were ragged and stained with mud and what looked like human blood.

Seeing Lydia in a mess was like seeing Javos hugging a baby kitten. She was *the* model celestial soldier, the one all of us had been compared to. Top grades, perfect demon killing record, friendly manner. My gaze dropped to her cuffed wrists. Her hands were bloody, but surely she couldn't be the killer. Surely...

"Hey. Lydia."

Her gaze snapped up. Her pupils looked oddly dilated… and darker than before. But my newest Grade Four power showed me the truth of what a person was. If she'd been a demon in disguise, I'd have known instantly. Her aura had a slightly dark patch, but not like a demon, nor even a human with demonic magic. Since she'd survived the virus, maybe it'd left a mark on her soul after all. I hadn't seen enough of the other survivors to know for sure.

She picked a bloodstained nail. "Devi. So it's true… you're with the warlocks. Your… your aura."

She could see my aura? I'd thought she was only Grade Three.

"There's a demigod outside who wants you dead," I told her. "Were you really found at a murder scene? Why were you on the warlocks' territory?"

"I didn't kill anyone," she said, a tremor in her voice. "I was there by accident."

"I'm inclined to believe you… if you're who you say you are." My Grade Four power didn't lie, though. "Why leave the guild?"

She shook her head. "I never left."

"You were a celestial vampire," I said. "Do you not remember?"

"I can't forget if I tried." Her eyes grew wide and haunted. "I wanted to stop. I didn't want to hurt them."

Oh boy. When the venom had kicked in, every celestial who survived the transformation had lost all reason. All of them had run into battle against their former comrades, driven by the vampire bloodlust.

"Do you remember I removed the virus?"

Her wide eyes blinked. "You? That was you?"

"Yep. Do you remember attacking any warlocks?"

She shook her head. "During the battle—maybe. But not now."

"Two warlocks are dead. Both were killed by a celestial. The guild claims to have nothing to do with it, so a rogue is the only other explanation. Why would you go to the warlocks' district alone, especially at night?"

"I can't… I can't tell you."

I frowned. "Lydia, what in the world have you got mixed up in?"

She hadn't returned to the other celestials, an uncharacteristic decision. She'd lived and breathed the guild, and was the quintessential example we were all supposed to aspire to be like. She was likeable enough that I hadn't hated her for it, but the way she was acting now was more akin to an amateur rule-breaker who'd been caught in the act. Murder, though? Unless the virus was somehow still inside her… no way.

"I was… I was told to find you." She looked down, rubbing her arms. "The Grade Fours sent me to find you. They asked you to meet them at the fourth house on Bolt Street."

"What? The Grade Fours?"

They'd survived. Of course some of them had survived. Who else must be the killer?

When she didn't respond, I said, "You seriously think I'm going to a random address given to me by someone who isn't in her right mind, to meet with people who might want to kill me?"

"It's the sort of thing you'd do, Devi." She pursed her lips, looking more like the Lydia I knew. "Trust me, you'll know exactly what I mean when you see them. You can tell the guild you're going if you like. I tried to get through to them before, but—well. That was after I turned."

Oh boy. "I'll take it under consideration."

"Also," she added, "please don't tell the warlocks."

———

Fifteen minutes later, I was on my way to a random address given to me by someone who wasn't in her right mind, to meet with people who might want to kill me.

Okay, technically, I was on the way to the guild first, since I now had an innocent woman's innocence to prove. I'd made Javos promise not to touch Lydia while I checked with the guild about their wayward Grade Fours. I'd seen zero signs of them when I'd been spying, but I hadn't exactly walked in there with a plan.

Now I did have one—tell the guild there was a rogue, get backup if need be, then drive to the designated address. I didn't even recognise it, and I'd been to a *lot* of seedy corners of the city when I'd worked as a freelancer. Since I was on the same level as the Grade Fours, I could handle a couple of the bastards. I'd handled Farrell just fine even when I was a Grade Three.

I pulled up outside the academy yet again, got out of my car and headed for the security doors. As luck would have it, Bad Haircut Sammy entered the lobby as I strode in.

"Why do you keep coming back here?" He wore his best attempt at a menacing stare, which only made him look more gormless than usual.

"Why do you keep hanging about waiting for me? Have you nothing better to do with your time?" I wasn't the slightest bit interested in how he spent his days, but judging by his breathless state, he'd spotted me on the security cameras and ran in here to accost me. It was kind of reassuring in a way, that no matter how badly I screwed up, Sammy was there to remind me it *was* possible to sink lower.

"Nobody else seems to think you're a threat, but I know better," he said.

I walked past him into the main corridor. "You're the one

who followed the inspector when he was replaced by an actual demon. It's lucky the guild gave you the benefit of the doubt. Did you kill any warlocks lately?"

"What're you talking about?"

"I'm investigating a series of murders. Since you keep ambushing me for no good reason, I might have to elevate you on the suspect list."

He gave me a clueless blink. "What?"

Honestly. He still had his celestial mark on the safety settings because of how much destruction he'd wreak otherwise. He wasn't capable of killing a warlock. But he *was* certainly capable of colluding with hell, and was an easy mark due to his immense stupidity.

"No, I'm not a killer. Aren't you the one who keeps killing demons?"

"I said warlocks, not demons. Killing demons is supposed to be *your* job, if you ever get past the novice rank."

Antagonising him didn't feel particularly good. I just wished my celestial mark would illuminate the real villains as easily as it tried it scorch out demons' souls. I left him muttering insults, turned left down the corridor, and nearly walked headlong into the man I'd hoped *not* to find.

"What are you doing here?" demanded Inspector Deacon.

"Looking for Mrs Barrow. Are you allowed to leave your office?"

"I am *not* a criminal," he growled. "I'll thank you to show me respect, Devi Lawson. What do you want?"

"The warlocks' guild arrested Lydia. If you know anything about the real culprit, now is the time to tell me."

No recognition flared in his expression. "Lydia?"

"Your former celestial soldier? One of your people? Top grades, the person Mr Roth used to compare me to all the time… ring any bells?"

His eyes narrowed. "She's listed as dead. We did a thorough search of the city for survivors."

"Not through enough. Seen your Grade Fours lately?"

"What? They're dead."

"Not dead enough, evidently. Another warlock was murdered last night, and the marks on his body matched Grade Four celestial magic. I have no idea if you can fake that, but I'm leaning towards no. So if you have anything to say—"

He strode up to me, so his face was inches from mine, washing me in the stench of one of his foul cigarettes. "Devi Lawson, you have made a disaster of my entire life in the space of a few weeks. Do not push me, and don't try to sway me with your lies. There is nowhere in the city that's not under watch. The Grade Fours are *dead.* The guild watches everything, Devi."

I took a step backwards in an attempt to regain some personal space. "What, you have access to the city's security cameras? You're not watching..." Warlock district? Probably not, given the broken cameras. But everywhere else was likely fair game. And they'd given *him* access to that information, even after what he'd done?

"There is nowhere we aren't watching," he growled. "Because the demons will *not* attack this city again. No second chances."

"You should speak to the warlocks' leader if you want Lydia back," I told him. "If not, you're the biggest hypocrite I've ever encountered."

And a close second was whoever had reinstated his former position. I did *not* need him to be in the way when Lydia's life hung in the balance. Of course, that was assuming she was innocent.

"Get out," he said. "Mrs Barrow doesn't need to be concerned with your nonsense."

"Just pass the message on," I said. "Even if you don't believe me about the Grade Fours, Lydia is in jail for a crime she likely never committed. And if I get a hint you're in any way involved, Inspector, I don't care what protected status you have. I'll take care of you myself."

I left the guild, pulling out my phone to run a search on the address Lydia had given me. If I went ahead with this reckless decision, I should probably at least run a few searches to check the address was real. I climbed into my car, frowning at my phone. The address was in the older outskirts of the city, before the celestials had improved the infrastructure and built on top of it. That meant it'd be out of reach of cameras. Not ideal, but if I was going to go up against one of my former allies again, maybe it was for the best that there'd be no witnesses.

I drove quickly, playing my radio at full volume to drown out the thoughts telling me this wasn't my best plan. There was little traffic once I'd left the suburbs, where the houses were more spread out until fields replaced the spread of tower blocks and houses. I'd hardly left the city in years, not since I'd given up my celestial status and walked away from the guild without any money. I was pretty sure the last time I'd driven this way was when Rory and I had had to drive down to Cornwall for that last, devastating mission. The familiarity carried a bitter taste, and I cranked up the radio to shut the memories out. Bolt Street... there it was.

The smell of brimstone blew in through the open window, and the car rocked, tilting onto its side, and then slammed down with enough force to give me whiplash.

My left hand lit up, momentarily blinding me, and I killed the engine before my demon mark chimed in and destroyed my vehicle.

I shoved the door open and rolled out, coming upright with my hand blazing. I'd driven right into a pentagram someone had drawn on the ground, and flames outlined the car.

"What the—?"

The flames dropped, revealing my car—a little singed, but in one piece. A demonic spell, not one I'd seen before. An illusion.

"Oh wow," I said. "Terrifying. You can explain the damage to my insurance company."

Several people dressed in dark clothes stepped out of the house on my right. As one, they uncovered their left wrists, exposing their celestial marks in a blaze of light. Too bright to be a standard celestial. They were the same level as I was.

Bloody hell. Grade Fours—and not two of them. More like a dozen. Too many to fight all at once. "What in damnation is this?"

A fair-haired man with broad shoulders stepped forwards. "Lydia did give you our message. Excellent."

"Who the hell are you?" He looked vaguely familiar, but he wasn't one of the small group of Grade Fours who'd been involved in the fighting. Which meant he was likely an out-of-town celestial. Of course the survivors had allies. Idiotic move there, Devi.

My demon mark glowed, joining my celestial hand as my dual blade—half light, half dark, sprang into existence. "Stay back," I warned.

The blond man eyed the blade with interest. "So it's true," he said. "The powers of heaven and hell serves you equally."

"You're not from here, are you? You didn't take part in the battle." What the hell was his name? I was sure I knew him.

"I was told you were ignorant of the truth," he said. "Despite what you've done, you are unaware that there is another side to this war of heaven and hell. I think you're going to want to hear what we have to say."

The others moved to surround me. My blade flickered,

then went out. Even I couldn't take down a dozen Grade Fours at once. I gave one of them a warning whack when he tried to grab my arm, but otherwise, I walked without protest. I could probably fight my way out of whatever situation I ended up in, and I was curious as hell as to what they were doing out here in the first place.

"Who even are you?" I asked him.

"My name is Harvey," he said. "I've been very interested to meet you, Devi."

"All I want from you is a murder confession," I said. When he merely blinked at me, I added, "I take it one of you is killing warlocks?"

"Warlocks?" said the blond man. "No. We're not killers."

I snorted. "You're trained soldiers, same as me, and you just declared yourselves vigilantes. Someone with Grade Four celestial power is murdering warlocks in the city. Unless one of you has defected."

"From the guild?" He halted outside the unassuming brick house as one of the others unlocked the door. "We don't want to be independent of the guild. We plan to replace them."

Whoa. "On whose orders?"

He walked into the narrow hallway, the others parting to let me walk in first. I'd possibly rather walk into the depths of hell, but no way was I leaving this place without answers.

"Our own," he said. "The demons are too powerful and cunning for the current guild to deal with. They need new leadership, and they shouldn't have let that incompetent inspector stay in his position."

"I agree with that one, but it's better than the alternative," I responded. "If they'd punished him, they'd have inflicted the same punishment on every person who contracted the demon virus. They would all have been executed." *Including you.* No… he hadn't been a victim. But who in the seven hells *was* he?

Harvey entered a room set up like an office. Computer, printer, shelves filled with documents. Copies of the guild's files? I peered at the topmost paper of a stack on the desk. The answer was yes, apparently. His name rocketed around my head, searching for a memory to connect to.

Harvey sat down in the desk chair, rotating to face me. Like some watered-down Bond villain. "The guild is weak. They need stronger leadership. If not, hell will win."

I glanced over my shoulder. "What was the deal with the pentagram back there? Sure looked like hell's handiwork to me."

"Merely a tripwire in case of trespassers," he said. "We already use hell's handiwork in our pentagrams and other concoctions. Why not utilise our knowledge to get closer and learn their weaknesses?"

"I was under the impression that's what the guild already did." They also had a list of the warlocks' weaknesses which I assume had been destroyed, but the fact that it had existed in the first place pointed at the possibility that someone was obtaining that information through less than sincere means. And he looked *way* too familiar. I racked my brain, but came up blank.

"The guild is limited in its reach," he said.

"Er, no," I said. "The celestial guild is the biggest anti-demon organisation in the world. You're a weird little cult nobody has ever heard of."

"Actually, we were hoping to recruit you."

My mouth fell open. "Excuse me?"

"You fit in better with us than you do with the guild."

"You're seriously barking up the wrong tree here. I'm not interested in being a vigilante."

He tilted his head on one side. "Isn't that exactly what you are, according to all reports?"

"According to the guild, I'm annoying. Also, the guild is being blamed for a string of murders you people committed, so add 'no fucking chance' to my answer."

"Murders?"

"Warlocks," I said. "Like I said. A Grade Four did it. That's why I came here in the first place."

"None of us have any argument with the warlocks. We have need of their resources."

So a warlock was involved in this? Yikes. "If you want to recruit me, I need to know exactly what I'd be getting into. Where exactly are you getting your supplies? Not Javos?"

"We use one of the guild's back doors to get supplies. An outsider warlock collective."

"That's illegal."

"So are most of your antics, Devi."

"You're celestials, so you're still susceptible to being arrested by the guild. I'm not a celestial, certainly not by the original definition anyway. And I don't want to lead anyone. I have no leadership experience or any interest in running up against the guild, which is bound to happen if you keep this up. There's no way they'll just let this slide."

He learned forwards in his seat, his gaze intent. "You represent heaven and hell, and balance. You can spy on the demons for us."

I folded my arms. "If you mean the warlocks, it's not happening. And I'm not looking for another employer. Did you reel Lydia in with lies, too? Did you know the warlocks have arrested her thinking she's killing them? Was that the plan?"

"She's innocent. They wouldn't punish a human who has done no wrong."

In an ideal world, they wouldn't. His tone was matter-of-fact. Rational. How could he so easily believe what weird little vigilante setup he'd concocted was superior to the organisation which for all its flaws, still possessed the most clout when it came to resisting demons in this realm?

Maybe because there *were* no other Grade Fours in the city aside from me. If he attacked the guild with the others behind him, it'd be a bloodbath. Most celestials wouldn't want to fight their own comrades, demon involvement or none, and none were strong enough to fight multiple Grade Fours. Not even the inspector.

"Will you consider our offer?" Harvey asked.

Plainly, I wasn't getting out of here without making a vaguely satisfactory statement. "I'll think about it. I work for the warlocks, and joining with you would go against my contract. It'd also alienate the guild. Is this where you're operating from? The middle of nowhere?"

"Until we take the guild—yes."

Take the guild? Whoa. "And you think the guild would just lie down and accept that? You're putting an awful lot of faith in me deciding I won't report you for treason."

"I know you won't, Devi. You're the same as we are."

"Not even close."

His gaze was on my face, but his attention was elsewhere, like my words didn't even register.

"By the way," I said, "you owe me compensation for scratching my car."

And with that, I about-turned and left, my mind spinning. I could take out one or two Grade Fours individually, but not all at once, and if Harvey told the truth, one of them was going against their own orders by killing warlocks. A betrayer betraying the betrayers. I was fairly sure they *all* needed to be locked up, but the guild didn't have the resources. Where had they even come from? Somewhere else in England... and that was all I had.

My phone buzzed as I passed by the other vigilantes on my way out. Their gazes followed me, but they'd clearly been given orders not to stop me. Better than strong-arming me into helping, but suspicious. Did this Harvey really have so much influence over them?

I got into my car, and my phone buzzed again. I put it on speakerphone. "Hey, Fiona. Javos hasn't hurt Lydia, has he? She's not the killer, but I have some info he's going to want to know. If you're at the guild?"

"I am," she said. "Rachel's watching Zadok. I wondered where you disappeared to."

I filled her in as I drove back. "Wow," she said. "You handled those weirdos better than I would."

"I've spent the last ten years handling demons. You pick up a few methods. Those guys are a little more reasonable and well-spoken than the demons are, but the same principle applies."

"Meaning they're batshit."

"Yeah. They are. They're Grade Fours. They met an angel, got right to the top level of the guild, and *then* rejected their calling. Nobody with any sense of self-preservation would ever do that."

"The guild doesn't exactly seem like a stable career option at the moment," said Fiona.

"It's never been a choice. You're alone when they pick you."

"It does sound like a cult when you put it like that."

I gripped the wheel tighter. "Yeah, well. It's not like I ever planned to be in a position to make meaningful changes to the way they run things. That's not an option unless you stay for twenty years and then get recommended by the inspectors. They'd never do that for me."

"Nope," said Fiona. "So... what're you telling the warlocks?"

"I have no idea." There'd be casualties on both sides if anyone tried to arrest the whole group of outcasts at once. Javos was immune to their powers and so was I, but any other warlock who got close to any of the Grade Fours would burst into flames—without even considering what other magical tripwire spells they'd obtained through the guild's back doors. And they far outnumbered the other celestials in the city. Was there even a contingency plan to deal with a whole group of rogues?

I hit the brakes as a giant scorpion-shaped creature careened in front of the car, its venom splattering the windscreen.

Just what I needed to brighten up my day—a venos demon.

11

I leapt out the car, my hand blazing. White light coalesced into a blade as I drew on my celestial speed to catch them. Light burst from the blade, leaving everything intact except for the demons. They'd picked a human district, miles off from the warlocks' usual hangouts —which meant there must be a portal nearby, if only a temporary one.

I skidded to a halt, looking wildly around for any signs of a portal. Wait a moment—the demons might be a side effect of Casthus crossing realms. It'd happened before. Nothing remained of the venos demons except dust, brimstone, and venom stains on the roadside. No portal in sight. I searched the three neighbouring streets, ignoring the humans staring from their windows and probably snapping pictures of me to upload online, and returned to my car.

"Bastards." I examined my wrecked paint job, used my celestial hand to burn the venom off the road and the windscreen of my car, then got back behind the wheel and drove back to warlock territory, picking up speed as the sound of screaming echoed from the road ahead. I parked haphazardly and conjured up my weapon again. *What the hell now?*

I got back behind the wheel and drove back to warlock territory, picking up speed as the sound of screaming echoed from the road ahead. I parked haphazardly and conjured up my weapon again. *What the hell now?*

Answer: more venos demons, bearing down on a crowd of fleeing humans. Celestial light flared from my palm, forming a whip and dragging the nearest demon away from his victim without a thought. *Whoa. Hey there, new power.* I lashed two more of them, severing their stingers from a distance.

"Don't touch the venom!" I yelled to the humans. The panicked humans were completely blocking the road, so I'd have to run for backup on foot. I blasted the remaining demons into ashes, then dived back into my car to grab my phone. I'd forgotten to disconnect the call to Fiona—and I heard screaming in the background.

"Fiona! Are you okay!"

A series of crashing noises answered. Swearing, I jumped out of the car once again and broke into a run, ignoring the startled yells of the humans I zipped past at full-on celestial speed. I screeched to a halt at the end of the road around the corner from the warlocks' headquarters, where Rachel's teeth were buried in a venos demon's neck. I ran up to the nearest demon, blade swinging. Its stinger went first, my celestial blade slicing into its head. Rachel shot me a grin, her jaw unhinged in her slightly terrifying demonic true form. Several other warlocks fought the invading demons with teeth and claws, not seeming to care how much damage they left behind.

I used my celestial blade to scour the venom stains from the road so no unsuspecting humans walked into them. Rachel spat out a hunk of scorpion flesh and casually slipped back into her human guise. Only the blood streaming down her chin betrayed the sharp teeth she'd worn moments before.

"If this is happening all over, the guild will be stretched thin," I said. "Is it a side effect from the netherworld?"

"I'd guess it is," said Rachel. "Where have you been, anyway?"

"Confronting a cult of celestial outcasts."

A scream. *Fiona.*

I broke into a run. With my celestial blade still active, I easily kept pace with Rachel. We careened around the corner into the street housing the warlocks' guild, right into another group of venos demons. My celestial blade skewered them on the spot, radiating wrath, and revealing Fiona standing behind them.

Fiona's hands streamed orange flames. For a heartbeat I expected to see Azurial's fiery gaze staring back, but it was Fiona's disbelieving stare that met mine when the flames died down. "Wow."

"No kidding. You're amazing." I glanced suspiciously behind her. "Please tell me Javos didn't throw you out here in person."

"No. My power switched on by itself. I…" She trailed off, looking down at her palm. "What *is* that?"

I looked, and my heart leapt into my throat. An unfamiliar mark stood out on her pale wrist. Not an arrowhead like mine, but a pyramid-like shape.

"Holy crap." Fiona stood rigid. "Tell me that's not Azurial's mark."

"It shouldn't be." I moved in closer, lowering my voice. "He wasn't an arch-demon, so he's not important enough to have had his own mark. If it's any arch-demon's, it'd be Themedes… which is fine, because he's dead. He can't claim you."

"I should bloody well hope not." She shuddered, dropping her arm to her side.

"I'll ask Clover." I also should have asked her about the rogue celestials, because I had to tell someone, and the guild had flat-out refused to listen earlier. But if they sent inexperienced novices up against the highest rank of celestial soldier, the conflict could only end badly.

Not as badly as it would if Javos got wind of my little rogue problem. I'd just single-handedly obliterated close to thirty demons with one wave of my hand. Multiply that by twenty and it'd be the inevitable outcome if any warlocks pissed off those outcasts. No… resolving Harvey's delusions of conquering the guild would require a delicate touch.

Considering both my hands unpredictably went up in flames, 'delicate' was not an accurate word to describe my own touch. Seven hells. The idea of keeping the rogues' existence secret when one of them might be the killer made me uneasy, but with no proof, I'd just be creating unnecessary conflict. I'd check back with Lydia and demand to know why she'd neglected to tell me just how many there were, and that they hadn't been the same outcasts as the ones I'd already killed.

Fiona stood on tip-toe, peering over the houses. "There's a fire over that way. Wait—isn't that where Nikolas's house is?"

"Shit." She was right.

Either another demon had attacked, or Zadok had been responsible. Given the sort of day it was, I'd bet on the latter.

I ran all the way to Nikolas's house, and halted in front of the doors. Thick clouds of black smoke came from upstairs. I didn't see any flames, but I approached the door warily. Rather than fire, the smell was distinctly brimstone, and the smoke looked suspiciously shadow-like. I nudged the door open, and shadows filled the hallway. Oh boy.

"Zadok, cut it out!" I yelled, running through the living room and upstairs.

His door was still locked. I kicked it in, and found him half-standing against the wall with shadows spilling out from every inch of him. His eyes were closed, and he muttered something in the demon tongue under his breath.

"Hey. Zadok. Stop flooding the house with magic."

His eyes snapped open. They were bloodshot and jet black. "You would have left me for dead here?" he rasped, speaking in Malthric, the demon tongue.

"What in the world are you talking about?" I said. "You're not supposed to be able send your magic beyond the boundaries of the room. Did you sense those demons show up?"

He blinked, as though only just becoming aware of who he was facing. "Devi?"

"That's me. Where were you?"

He blinked again. Golden eyes. *What was that?* "I sensed them coming," he said, in English.

"The demons?" I said. "I already took care of them. Can you remove your shadowy magic from the house so nobody walks into it by accident?"

"It's a defence mechanism," he rasped. "Where is my dear brother?"

"Right here." Nikolas walked into the room, at a slight angle to fit his wings through the door. He was in full demigod mode, eyes burnished gold, and while Zadok looked diminished beside him, he didn't look totally defeated either. "Turn your magic off."

"I'm afraid I can't do that. Not until the demons stop trying to kill me."

"Nobody's trying to kill you, idiot," I said. "They went after the humans, but we already took them to pieces."

He laughed.

"What?" I said. "What's so funny."

"It was me they attacked," he said. "Your friend defended me. And to think you were so adamant she wouldn't choose to help me."

What? Fiona did? Crap, I did *not* need this—though I was relieved as hell that Nikolas had come back in one piece.

"Zadok," Nikolas snapped. "Turn the magic off before Javos comes here and finishes Casthus's job. You know perfectly well that I'm keeping you here against the laws of our kind, and unlike Babylon, there are no exceptions. There'll be blood."

"Yes, there will be," said Zadok. But the shadows had begun to pull back from the floor, returning to their owner. His body glowed, outlined in luminous shadow not unlike Nikolas's dark lightning. So similar and yet so different.

I turned my back on him. "Niko, I need to talk to you alone."

Zadok's soft laughter followed me downstairs. Nikolas's wings faded as the shadows disappeared from the landing.

"He's starting to creep me out. More than usual, I mean." I had no doubt Fiona had acted in self-defence. She was too wary of demons to let him get under her skin that easily. Now I needed to keep him from getting under *my* skin.

"Did those demons come from Babylon?" I asked Nikolas.

"Some of them might have, but it's more likely to be Pandemonium. I worried this might happen."

We reached the living room, where Fiona sat on the sofa, examining the mark on her hand.

"You didn't touch the venom, did you?" I asked her.

"Nope."

"Good. The first lesson with those demons is avoiding that bloody stinger. I had to supervise a pack of celestial novices facing those demons in training and the level of crap they put me through was unbelievable."

She pulled a face. "They're nasty little bastards. But for all

I know, I picked up immunity as well as my other weird demon powers."

"Better off not finding out the hard way."

Nikolas studied the demon mark on her arm. "That's new."

She nodded, biting her lip. "I know. Do you know whose mark it is?"

I gave him a questioning look. "It's not Themedes's, or…?"

"Possibly," he said. "If it is, she's her own person, unclaimed. He's dead, and nobody survived to follow in his footsteps. When it comes to arch-demons' marks, however, I can't pretend to have extensive knowledge of their effects on humans."

"Except for me." I heaved out a sigh. "Is Zadok going to behave? I need to tell Javos the latest before he hurts Lydia. You've missed out on a bunch more drama. Fiona… you might want to stay here. But really, watch out for Zadok. He knows about your mark."

"I'm wise to his tricks," she said. "Not to worry. He knows I can set him on fire if I like. He's seen it."

I updated Nikolas on the latest while we reset the spells around Zadok's prison, and then walked back to rescue my poor car from where I'd had to abandon it.

"In conclusion," I said, climbing into the driver's seat to take us to warlock HQ, "we're screwed. If I leave those people be, they'll start a war with the guild. If I tell anyone else, it'll have the same outcome. What's a reasonable solution to dealing with absolute lunatics?"

"Use your demon mark," Nikolas answered. "You can take them. I'll help."

I shook my head. "I can take one or two of them at a time, but not all at once. Not to mention, I know them, and I can't figure out how. It's going to keep bugging me. I'm sure I'm missing something."

"They seem to know enough about you," he said. "If they want you as their leader."

"They're seriously loopy." I started the engine. "We should check in with Javos. I don't know if Lydia was working with those outcasts or not, but she's the one who gave me the address. I think they might have some kind of hold over her. But Javos is the only warlock around who wouldn't burn to a crisp by going near them. Yes, that includes you, Nikolas."

He tilted his head. "They can try. There's little I can't regenerate from, and I'm certain one of them must be the killer."

I gripped the steering wheel tightly. "You're probably not wrong, but they're working behind the scenes with warlock traders. This has been set up for longer than all this nether realm crap's been going on."

"Really?" He frowned. "Javos knows all the trade in the city. What exactly were they buying?"

"Props. Warlock-style spells. Look, I know I'm gonna have to report them. I'm just trying to minimise the collateral damage. They're bonkers. Cultist madmen who want *me* to lead them to glory. They think I'm superior to the guild and will lead them to heaven, and somehow they're totally fine with working with the warlocks, too. Doesn't mean they aren't lying through their teeth, but..."

"No," he said. "We definitely need to handle this case carefully. It has the potential to escalate."

I rounded the corner and found a parking spot outside warlock HQ. "Firstly, I need to make sure Javos hasn't killed the one person who *didn't* murder any warlocks. Also, I should have asked—how's Babylon? If he's gone—are the fallen still in the dungeon?"

"Last I checked—yes. I made sure he didn't hurt anyone. He left the warlocks behind."

"But not his servants." Dammit. If we'd had an actual

concrete plan, we could step in to smuggle them out—but the arch-demon might well retaliate. And Earth would pay the price. "I can't see how this could have gone differently. Since Themedes died, someone would have had to step in to take power no matter what. And they'd have ticked off the other demons by doing so. I guess it's just unfortunate that Earth got as involved as it did."

There was a moment's pause. I turned to see him examining me with his eyes slightly wider. "What? Isn't it true?"

"No, you're right," Nikolas said. "I shouldn't… I apologise for doubting your knowledge of the netherworld. You're intelligent enough to understand hell's workings even though those in charge insist on keeping that information from you."

"And you thought I was stupid."

"No." He touched my hand, the impact sizzling through my demon mark. "You're reckless and exasperating, but neither of those traits exclude intelligence."

"I'm so flattered."

"I'm trying to apologise for not giving you the credit you were due when we met."

I grinned and shrugged. "You thought I was a brain-washed follower? I was. The guild was all I had. Same for Lydia. What's happening with those rogues is a direct result of that brainwashing, which is why the guild should be the ones to deal with the Grade Fours. They know their own game. Or do you disagree and think I should tell Javos?" I jerked my head in the direction of the devil horns on the gate. "Last chance to object."

He shook his head. "I'm treading a thin line. Are you certain they weren't the killers?"

"Nope, but they're a wild card. I know Javos is immune to them, but nobody else is if they decide to attack, or he sends in an army because he thinks they're dangerous. I have no idea *what* the solution is, to be honest. I'm going to talk to Lydia first, since she definitely has first-hand knowledge of how their group formed."

"Good idea. We should certainly tread carefully. Javos's immunity is a very unusual power, and not one that many other warlocks possess. The celestials could wipe out an army, but the effects across the realms would be catastrophic."

I shivered. I barely had my own celestial mark restrained, and even now, I felt its power humming under the skin of my left wrist. I was always one step away from losing control and seriously hurting someone. And aside from Fiona, all my closest friends were warlocks now. I was glad Nikolas understood, but hell, maybe even the celestials couldn't take down the outcasts. They were outnumbered. *Who* in all the nether realms had given a bunch of deranged people like them a shortcut to the top level of celestial power? Had they all gone rogue at once? Whatever the reason, something was seriously screwed up on heaven's side as well as hell's.

12

I found Javos in the kitchen of the warlocks' headquarters, pulling the skin off a dead venos demon. I gagged on the smell. "What the hell are you doing?"

"It's a shame to waste fresh meat."

"You're sick in the head." I covered my mouth and nose and backed out into the corridor. "Please tell me the prisoner's still alive."

"For now."

I gave him a stern look. "Watch it. She's not the one who did it. Even if she's still a celestial vamp, she doesn't have the firepower."

Javos tailed me to the prison room, like he expected me to sneak her out of there. Which I would have done if I was a hundred percent assured of her innocence, and I wasn't. She had some serious explaining to do.

Lydia sat in the same position as before, and gave Javos a wary look. While he wasn't doing anything explicitly intimidating, he looked terrifying without even trying, and I didn't blame Lydia for sitting as far away as possible from his blaring aura and menacing stare.

"You're scaring her," I told Javos. "If you want her to tell you anything at all, let me speak to her alone."

"If she's a criminal, I intend to treat her as such. Participating in the murder of my fellow warlocks is not an act I will brush aside."

"She didn't do it," I said firmly. "She's not Grade Four and was infected with demon venom until recently."

"She's hiding something."

No kidding. I was less than convinced the Grade Fours were a secret worth keeping, but if anyone needed to know and deal with them, the guild did. The inspector's head would explode if he found out that a whole bunch of other Grade Fours had gone rogue. If I told Javos, someone else's head would explode. Probably a lot of someones.

"Tone it down," I told Javos. "If she has anything useful to say, I'll tell you."

He grunted and slipped out of the room, as lithely as it was possible for a gigantic warlock to move.

"You have got to be kidding me," I said to Lydia, once I was sure we were alone. "Grade Four celestial vigilantes? Are you seriously working with them?"

"No, of course I'm not working with them. They're terrifying fanatics."

"I knew that charm was all an act," I muttered. "They tried to recruit me. Know anything about that?"

"That's why I sent you to them. I thought they'd tell you the truth."

"How did you wind up tangled with them in the first place?"

She sat up straighter, running a hand through her matted hair. "They kidnapped me after the battle."

"Seriously?"

She nodded. "Like I said, fanatics. They made these odd claims about you being their potential saviour... that you were a celestial demon with your own soul, owned by both heaven and hell at the same time. Because the angel who marked you fell from grace."

A chill raced down my back. It wasn't as though I'd spread the information wide before the battle had given me no choice. I was pretty sure none of the celestials save for Clover had known at all, certainly not before the celestials had put the arrest warrant out for me. Which meant either the group had had an insider amongst the demons—entirely possible—or they'd formed recently.

Someone had started the band of outcasts while the guild had still been functioning. That much was clear. And the rest? I hadn't a clue *how* they could possibly have found out something I hadn't known for sure until I'd *met* the archdemon who'd marked me.

"Why not tell me before I went to them?" I asked.

"I didn't want them to suspect we might be working against them. It's lucky they seem to want you to help them, whatever the reason."

"They're all bonkers in a weirdly rational way. They sound like their own book of propaganda. The majority of the celestials all but fell for it once already. Guess that's how they recruited so many." I clamped my mouth shut as her expression crumpled.

"The guild was all I had," Lydia whispered. "I don't think they're evil. Not all of them, anyway."

"I'm going to tell them," I said. "I have to report this to someone, and it's either the guild or that warlock you just spoke to."

"Ah." She paled. "They don't know…"

"I can't let this slide. If they attack, the only people who could reasonably take them down are those two and me, and you really don't want to know what other crap I'm dealing with at the moment."

Her lip trembled. "Then tell them. But the inspector—"

"He has zero clout. Look, I'll level with you. If you hide the truth, you're not getting out of here anytime soon. Javos thinks you're guilty, and it's plain to see one of those celestial rogues committed the murders. I'm going to try to find out who, but for crying out loud, use your common sense. It's not worth keeping secrets from Javos. I'll tell the guild, anyway."

They'd better actually act this time. Not that I thought the celestials would be of any use whatsoever when it came to arresting their wayward brethren.

Once I was out of the room, I checked Javos wasn't lurking nearby and called Clover, summarising the situation as quickly as possible.

She swore in one of the demon tongues. "One of heaven's own has gone rogue, or worse is afoot."

"What's worse, more war? Bloody wonderful. What with the demons showing up everywhere, I'm convinced heaven has given this realm up entirely."

"Not entirely." She paused, and there was an odd noise in the background, like the sound of a motorcycle engine. "I'd advise you to go ahead and tell the guild. But it doesn't sound like the warlocks would deal with the situation in an appropriate manner. The guild might be able to entice the rogues back into the fold."

"Back," I said slowly. "I'm going out of my mind trying to figure out where they came from. They know Haven City. And I swear one of them looked familiar, but he wasn't one of the Grade Fours from last time. It's been too long since I spent any substantial amount of time in the guild..." I trailed off.

I knew where I'd seen him before. Harvey had been assigned to one of the missions I'd taken with Rory as a Grade Three. Just a week before he'd died.

Did he ascend to Grade Four in that time? "Er, Clover, do you know someone named Harvey? Grade Three?"

"You know I stopped learning everyone's names after I retired."

"Look, you're an angel. And besides, weren't you supervising the Grade Four ceremonies two years ago?"

"Occasionally. What about this Harvey person?"

I took in a deep breath. "He's Grade Four. But the last time I knew him, two years ago, he wasn't. Did he ascend here in Haven City in the last two years?"

"No," she said. "There haven't been any ascensions in a while—certainly not since the stunt you pulled in Purgatory."

I went still. "Oh shit."

"What is it?"

"They… I think they stole my idea."

They weren't originally Grade Fours. Not at first. And they'd never ascended under the guild's orders. Somehow they'd gone behind their backs and upgraded themselves, like I had, and succeeded.

This wasn't good. At all.

She hissed out a breath. "Are you certain?"

"Why the hell are you asking me? Can't you get into Purgatory? What even are the rules on angels?" I hadn't meant to yell at her, but that explained why they'd looked so familiar. Grade Threes rarely settled in one place, but I'd met at least some of them on missions at one time or another. And Grade Three was one step below the highest rank. If you were chosen.

Unless you were audacious enough to break the rules.

If I was right, they were gods in their own right without the discipline to back it up, and outnumbered the number of their genuine counterparts left in the region.

Never mind hell. Heaven had a real problem on its hands.

"No, I can't get into the heavenly realms at all," she said.

"As for Purgatory, it's different for every initiate. And it's a very serious accusation, too."

I gripped my phone tightly. "What, you don't believe me?"

"I believe you. I don't think the guild would, however, unless they sent their people in person, and there aren't even any Grade Threes in the city who aren't retired or injured."

I swore. "This is ridiculous. I can't watch Purgatory on top of two demon wastelands and the bloody warlocks."

"The angels living in Purgatory are hand-picked representatives of heaven's own, put there as a test to gain a chance of re-entering heaven."

"How *do* you know that?" I shouldn't need to ask. Earth had no angels of its own, except the one I was speaking to. "So one of them went rogue? Or does heaven actually want those Grade Fours running around trying to take over the guild with no leadership experience and a habit of kidnapping and coercion?"

"What are you yelling about?" Javos elbowed the door open.

"Nothing," I growled. "I'm going to talk to the celestials."

"I hope that means you're considering telling me where you've been," Javos said. "Without me having to do anything unpleasant to my prisoner."

"Javos," I said, through clenched teeth. "Leave her alone. This is bigger than all of us."

I did not have the mental space to deal with any more unwelcome revelations. And I'd accidentally hung up on Clover. Not that she'd been particularly reassuring this time.

I marched past Javos to where Nikolas stood near the lab, in conversation with Rachel.

"Nikolas," I said. "Can you tell me anything that's going on in the netherworld which might impact a visit to Purgatory?"

"No," he said. "You're going there now?"

"Yes. I think I'll have to." I waited until we were outside to explain what I'd concluded. "Unless heaven's drastically changed the rules, someone on Purgatory has betrayed them. Creating a whole army of rogues to take down the celestial guild seems to be the sort of thing that'd get you exiled to hell."

Not that I knew the behind-the-scenes rules which dictated who got to stay in heaven or not. But someone had kept the celestial guild running for years on faith alone. Had that fallen angel I'd defeated been responsible for the new wave of rogue Grade Fours—or was someone else working against heaven and hell alike?

13

"Will Zadok know what we're doing?" I asked Nikolas, when we were back in the living room of his house, ready to open a door into the between world.

"Possibly," he said. "I'll keep an eye on him. Are you sure you want to do this?"

Nikolas himself hadn't been there last time I'd taken a potentially fatal journey into Purgatory. He'd been held captive in another dimension by a demon determined to keep him out of the fight. If I left now, anything might happen in my absence. I'd left a message on the guild's answering machine on the drive back, for all the good it'd do. If they refused to see the truth, I'd find out what was really going on, one way or another.

"I'm ready," I said, and used my celestial light to burn a pentagram into the floor. Then I spoke the heavenly words, and stepped into the light.

As the whiteness died down, barren empty ground greeted me. Nothing was real here, not even the wasteland beneath my feet and the blank red-tinged sky. Purgatory was a between-realm, a place of nothingness between heaven and hell. The place where the best celestials were put through trials to see if they were good enough to ascend to heaven's battlefield.

I looked around. No angels, fallen or otherwise. I could see through disguises now, but the wasteland seemed as empty as any demon realm. Blank, burned sky. Lifeless ground, devoid of any plant or animal life.

"Hey!" I called. "Is anyone out there?"

I took a few steps forwards across the rough stone ground, reluctant to wander further and lose sight of the pentagram. I might be able to use demonglass to get around, but I'd never tried to do it from here before, and however much this realm might look like the netherworld, it wasn't. For all I knew, demonglass didn't work the same way as it did on Earth and in the hellish dimensions.

I squinted at the wasteland ahead, frowning. The flickering outline of a person appeared, someone shrouded in too much darkness to make out their features. I called out again, and my voice echoed back. The stranger had heard. They were human-shaped, without the wings of an angel—fallen or otherwise.

This was Purgatory. It stood to reason that some humans might end up here after death, and yet...

"Hey!" I called out again. "Who are you? Is there an angel I can speak to?"

The person walked towards me. Fast. Definitely human. Curly dark hair, lightly tanned skin...

I stopped dead.

Her face was mine.

I stared at her. Reached out a hand as though I could cross the metres between us to touch her face and see if she was real.

She raised her right hand, celestial mark blazing. She was

my reflection: celestial mark on her right hand, demon mark on the left.

Revulsion clawed up my throat. The celestial mark could only exist on one side. Nobody knew how it worked. It just *was.* I struggled to quash my revulsion, which made no rational sense. Maybe the guild had left a deeper impact on me than I'd thought.

She was the inverse of me—yet she was also as solid as I was.

"What *are* you?" I whispered.

"I'm the other side of your soul, Devi," she said, in my voice.

Dread gripped me. "You're *what?*"

"I am the part of you trapped in limbo. This is the fate that awaits you after death."

Okay... My magic bound me somewhere between heaven and hell—so Purgatory was the logical place for me to go after death. Better than hell, obviously, but I was far from at death's door. "I'm not dead yet. My soul is my own. Nice demon disguise, but I'm not falling for any of your crap, whatever you are."

But my magic should be able to see through disguises...

"Maybe it's you who isn't real in this realm."

I glared at her. "Yeah, sure I'm not. Whatever you are, I'm here to speak to a representative of heaven."

She studied me, a smile flickering on her face. "You're here because your soul is drawn to your other side."

"Cut the crap," I snapped. "Are you the one turning Grade Three celestials into Fours without the guild's say-so?" No... even as a Grade Four, I didn't have the power to upgrade someone else's magic. Only the angels themselves could do that.

"I can burn the demon right out of you, Devi. Your soul will be on the side of heaven once more..."

"That's not happening."

"I never said you had a choice."

The thing that looked like me walked closer, and celestial light flared from her right hand, forming a sword... shimmering white, a mirror of my own.

"I am a new creation of heaven, Devi. And you *will* be ours."

Her blade flashed down in a blur, and light blazed, searing its way up my arm, through my very soul.

Shadowy power poured out of my own right hand, and I slammed it into her. The arch-demon's power flared from my palm and spread across the Earth, the antithesis of heaven's light. The thing that looked like me stepped back, her expression calm in a way I was sure mine had never been, not in recent years, anyway.

Then she was gone.

I dropped to my knees, my body trembling. Celestial light blazed up my right arm—the wrong arm. I crawled in the direction of the pentagram, my vision blurring. The light she'd hit me with was still inside me. An alien substance, burning at the demon half of me.

No. If I pass out here, I'm dead no matter how much demon magic I have in me.

My right fist clenched on the demonglass in my pocket. I let it pull me in, images of spired towers and temples shimmering before my eyes. *Earth. I need to get to Earth. Now.*

Celestial light flared inside me, cold and merciless. A different light burned behind my eyes... the light of death.

The promise that I'd come here or go somewhere worse afterwards.

The demonglass pulled me in, and I fell into a heap on Nikolas's floor, screaming as the pain intensified. I hadn't left the relentless celestial power behind, but it'd come with me, determined to finish its job.

"Help!" I shouted. "Someone—get it out."

"Devi!" Nikolas ran to me, his expression the closest to panicking I'd ever seen him. "What is it?"

I raised my head and gasped. "Heaven has some new… thing. It tried to burn the demon part of my soul right out of me. It's… like poison."

My body glowed with light. I shouted a warning, knowing what that light would do to a demon, but Nikolas disappeared into shadows, evading it. He appeared again, closer, and grabbed my right hand.

I drew his magic into me like a lifeline. He gasped, eyes widening at the sudden drain. His power flooded me, dark lightning pushing against the celestial flame. I drank it in, greedily, desperately. The colour drained from his face and he dropped to his knees beside me.

He'd given everything to me. And I was killing him.

The door exploded from its hinges and a second winged figure walked in, close enough to the light that surely he should have burned.

"He will die," said Zadok. "Or you will. Whoever breaks first."

My demon mark latched onto his magic without conscious thought, drawing his power in. The celestial flame faded, but it was still there, searing my soul. *Yes. Kill him instead.*

He laughed. "Your mind's made up, then."

I shook my head, desperately trying to break the connection. The mark wouldn't be satiated. It'd take everything.

"Devi, dearest, when will you accept that you need me? I saved your life once before… let me save it again."

Zadok's magic pumped into my arm, and my body trembled with it.

"You're not supposed to have any power left," I croaked at him. "Stop…"

The burning sensation in my veins faded out as his shadowy magic pulsed through my demon mark, into my soul.

Despite the tremors, my body was too limp to get to my feet when he stalked past me, towards the hall.

No. He can't get out on Earth...

The door slammed. Zadok was gone.

There was a long pause. Then Fiona ran into the room. "I'm so sorry," she whispered. "He trapped me. Locked me in my room... Devi. Are you okay? Please... speak to me."

"He pretended... to be weak..." My vision was fading. "Nikolas. Please. Is he alive?"

I breathed out when I heard her say yes, and blackness rushed in.

———

Light streamed across my vision. Sunlight. I rolled over and buried my head in Nikolas's chest. He murmured my name and drew an arm around me. Warm and sleepy, I wrapped myself in him. I was so tired. Like I'd crashed after one hell of a day... wait, why were we both fully clothed?

Oh hell.

I jerked upright and grabbed Nikolas's arm. He was breathing, his heartbeat was steady, and though he looked a little paler than usual, he was alive.

My eyes welled with tears and I collapsed onto the bed, shuddering. That alien power inside me... pain beyond reason... had nearly caused me to do something irreversible.

Until Zadok stopped me.

My body stiffened when Nikolas moved, his eyes opening a fraction. "Devi? What...?"

"Don't move," I said quickly.

He didn't look as bad as Zadok had when his power had

been gone, but he hadn't walked headlong into his own weakness either. Instead *I'd* nearly killed him, thanks to whoever that assassin had been.

He blinked sleepily. "Are you okay?"

"Am I… I nearly killed you." My voice cracked. "Tell me you remember. I didn't cause you brain damage, did I?"

He rolled onto his back, his body shaking with laughter.

"Nikolas Castor, what's so bloody funny?"

"You might as well be concerned about throwing a rock at an arch-demon."

"I'm really glad your ego is in one piece, then."

"Devi, I'm fine," he said, grabbing my wrist and pulling me into him. I yanked my arm away indignantly, but he was warm and smelled of brimstone and heat. It was such a relief to see him alert that I couldn't stay angry with him. I shuffled closer and let his warm arms blanket me from behind.

"Celestial fire is poison to you," I mumbled into the pillow. "Hell, it's poison to *me* as well, apparently. And it nearly killed both of us."

"I apologise for making light of the situation." He kissed me on the side of my jaw, his strong arms as steady as ever. "I don't blame you. At all."

"Zadok is free. On *Earth*." I groaned. "Or on Babylon."

"Babylon, most likely." He released me and got to his feet. "I don't blame you, Devi, but this is possibly the worst crisis the warlocks have ever been in since I moved to this city. I'm going to have to be extremely careful when I explain this to Javos."

"We could just not tell him. Otherwise, we might not need Babylon to unleash the apocalypse." My words were half-hearted. After all, I'd possibly unleashed worse on my own power.

I climbed out of bed, aching like I'd run a marathon. Apparently nearly dying expended more energy than I thought. "Ugh. I feel like crap." I deserved it. Nikolas might not blame me, but it was hard to imagine screwing up any worse. "Are you sure you're—"

"Yes." He opened the wardrobe, reminding me that I still wore my rumpled clothes from yesterday, and they were covered in Purgatory's dirt.

I opened the drawer I kept my clothes in. "You didn't let me finish my sentence."

"I need to recharge my power, but that's an easy fix."

"Except if it involves Babylon." Clothes in hand, I walked into the en-suite bathroom. "Do you think Zadok's there? For definite? Even after last time?"

He'd been hiding his power. How much else had he done while pretending to be a helpless prisoner?

"I do," Nikolas said. "You know… I always thought he'd wreak total destruction on Earth, but he's a lot more subtle than I gave him credit for."

You're telling me.

Once we'd both showered and dressed, we found Rachel in the kitchen.

"Hi," she said. "You probably don't remember last night, but you freaked out Fiona. I found the two of you totally passed out in the living room."

"So how'd we end up in bed?" I asked.

"I shapeshifted into Javos's form to carry you. Speaking of Javos, he's been hassling me all night. I told him you were dealing with Babylon."

"Huh." I grabbed a plate and piled it high with toast, which was all Rachel could cook. "I'd count Zadok not being here as good news," I said. "But it probably means he's off stirring up trouble."

Despite Nikolas's assertion that he was likely in Babylon, it didn't seem characteristic of Zadok to walk back to the place he'd nearly died, to the home of his enemy, without a plan. But anything that took just one enemy off my list was an advantage. I'd abandoned Lydia to the wolves, and I never did speak to the guild yesterday about their wayward outcasts.

Speaking of whom? I *knew* they were up to no good. As for Clover, for the first time, she'd been unable to give me helpful advice. It floored me. She *knew* heaven. She'd been there. What would she think if I told her about the creature that had attacked me? It gave me a headache even thinking about it.

"Right," I said, putting my plate aside. "My first order of business for the day is to find a demon with the ability to clone itself so I can go and stop Zadok, Javos, the rogue celestials and the arch-demons from breaking things all at the same time. Oh, and tell the guild. Not that they have the resources to stop an army of their own. On top of that, my evil doppelganger is wandering around Purgatory."

"Evil doppelganger?" asked Rachel, grabbing a piece of leftover toast.

"She claimed to be a new creation of heaven. She looked like my walking reflection. These—" I held up my hands to show the marks—"were reversed. Seriously creepy. Then she blasted celestial magic into me and claimed to be able to burn the demon right out of me. I managed to get out, but I was dying. I needed demonic power."

And now I have some. I'd taken in an indeterminate amount of Zadok's power. He could use the shadows to hide himself —and create clones. Hmm. Might come in handy.

"I would guess that it's heaven's way of reacting against the arch-demons," said Nikolas. "But that creature shouldn't have been able to counter your demon mark. Your celestial and demonic powers are equal. Only a true angel might be able to undo them."

Or an arch-demon. Or... a Divinity. She'd been none of

those things. "I have no idea what she was, but I'm pretty sure she's not the only rogue in Purgatory. The guild needs to be warned. They must have the resources to defend against their own. It's not like they've never jailed a celestial before." Rare, but it happened. "I need to speak to them in person, but there's also Lydia to consider. That creature that looks like me—maybe it's the one committing murder. If it's not the celestials, it's the next logical choice. And now Zadok's on the loose. Does Javos know none of this?"

"No," he said, biting into a piece of toast, "but he's aware that there might be another incident like the venos demons and is also taking steps."

"There's a world of difference between a few scorpions and the apocalypse. What'd happen if I opened a pentagram leading to Babylon on top of those celestials?"

"Nothing good," he said, dismissively brushing crumbs of the front of his shirt. "They'd attack my own army of warlocks, my father would smite them, and then he'd turn on Earth's celestials."

"Damn." So much for that idea. "What does that leave us with?"

"Babylon," he said. "Zadok will be there, most likely, and if I find him, I intend to know what he did to replenish his power. It shouldn't have been possible for him."

"He gave me some." I ran my fingers over my demon mark. It came as a relief when it responded with no pain, not like when the fires of heaven had burned inside me. "Shadow power."

"Devi," Nikolas said warningly, but I'd already slipped into shadows.

I waved my hands around. "Neat trick. Can I sense him like this? Wait, can't *you* sense him?" I let the shadows disappear and returned to my seat at the table. Rachel gave a round of applause.

"Not here," he said. "There are too many warlocks living close together in the city. As for Babylon… normally I would be able to easily detect him, but not with the arch-demon close by. His aura masks everyone else's."

"And he and Abyss had a nice discussion. Maybe he wants to get into it with Lythocrax next."

His mouth thinned. "I don't know why he's staying. If he expects something from Earth… but he's expressed no interest in the bridge. It might be that he plans to act against Abyss after all."

Or he's like the others. Not acting on his own orders. "Maybe. One problem at a time. The rogue celestials… or the murders. Which first? Javos hasn't hurt Lydia?"

The guild certainly seemed to be taking their sweet time coming out in defence of one of their own members. I almost wanted to let them fall, but the majority of people there were innocent. They didn't deserve to be taken over by murderous cultists. Frustration burned deep inside me. Where in hell had the angels gone?

The fallen.

Of all people who might know where their predecessors were—the fallen might. They were the ones who'd clued me in about the ritual to upgrade to Grade Four in the first place.

Problem: Casthus had them in his castle, and thanks to my ill-advised trip to Purgatory, I'd possibly missed my shot at rescuing them.

"I'll handle Javos," said Rachel. "Nobody else was murdered, so he can hold off on attacking the celestials for now. As for the rogues… sorry, no clue."

The rogues could collectively destroy the city's entire warlock population if so inclined. Not to mention the guild.

I have to stop them. I blew out a breath. "Right. The fallen it is."

"What?" said Nikolas. "Who said anything about the fallen?"

"I just did. They might know who's messing up in heaven."

"Or you might poke the arch-demon," Rachel added.

"Did Casthus ever actually return from Pandemonium?" I asked. "Wouldn't we have felt it if he did?"

Nikolas frowned. "Perhaps. If not... he might return at any moment. It's risky."

"Zadok might be there," I said. "If we can confirm he's not on Earth, Javos need never know he was here, and that's two of our problems solved."

"I doubt you'll get that lucky," said Rachel.

"You're supposed to cheer for me."

"That's Fiona's job. I'm the voice of reason."

I snorted. "Sure you are. Thanks for getting Javos off my back. I'm going to need all the luck I can get."

Nikolas shook his head. "I'm weakened. I can't get us both out of there if it turns out the arch-demon *did* come back."

"Lucky I stole someone's power." A brief rush of guilt rose. "But seriously—the fallen *were* the children of the Divinities. They knew how the ritual worked for making someone a Grade Four. They'll talk." At least, I hoped they would.

"I hope they do," said Nikolas. "Otherwise, heaven is in for a reckoning."

Not just heaven. Whatever the Devi creature I'd faced was, I was certain it was killing the warlocks... and that nobody but me carried both demonic and angelic power to stop her.

14

Before we left, I called Fiona over, to reassure her I was okay, while Nikolas checked into Babylon to make sure our evil shadowy overlord hadn't made an unexpected reappearance. Rachel, meanwhile, went to check Javos hadn't done anything rash, and to send Fiona my way if she was at the warlocks' place. I needed to tell the celestial guild about the rogues in person, ideally, but Babylon couldn't wait. Nor could I think of a tactful way to tell them their own members were planning to single-hand-edly take over the war with heaven. But if the enemy had given them the upgrades, they weren't on the guild's side either. Someone had to tell them. And I'd drawn the short straw yet again.

"Hey there," I said, when someone picked up the phone. "Can you put me through to the person at the guild with the highest celestial ranking?"

"That would be me," Inspector Deacon answered.

"They've got you answering phones now? Don't hang up," I added hastily. "I have something important to tell you."

"Contrary to what you apparently believe, I have important work to be doing."

"Theoretically, Sir, what would you do if I went rogue?"

There was a pause on the other end of the line. "Is this a confession?"

"No, it bloody well isn't. I'd like to know if you have a contingency plan if I decide to run amok with my celestial power and single-handedly declare war on hell."

"Considering your role is *supposed* to be to fight on the side of heaven, despite your dealings, the guild would leave you to it."

I wished I could punch him through the phone. "And if I went rogue and started attacking warlocks?"

"Attacking them rather than fornicating with them? I don't need to hear your relationship drama."

"Pull your head out of your arse," I told him. "I'm not talking about me. I'm talking about other celestials, and if you're going to be obtuse, then imagine there are celestials with my level of power who might want to usurp the guild's highest members. What would you do if they tried?"

"The only highly ranked members aside from yourself answer to heaven, and us."

"Yeah, nope," I said. "That hasn't been true for a while. Did you ever keep tabs on Harvey… no idea what his surname is? Grade Three, used to work here a few years ago?"

"I believe there's a celestial with that name listed as dead. Your point?"

"He's not dead. He was reborn as a Grade Four. I felt their power. The angels upgraded him, and quite a few others, too."

"What?" snapped the inspector. "You're lying."

"I'm not. Lydia is locked up for their crimes, but it's likely they're working with the killer."

If he didn't believe his own people were rogues, he wouldn't believe there was a creepy Devi-doppelganger going around murdering warlocks, either. And realistically, there wasn't a whole lot the warlocks themselves could do against her, even Javos. They didn't frequent Purgatory. The top-ranking celestials did. And *they* were immune.

More to the point, they knew I was a wild card. I'd have thought they'd have a plan in place to capture me if it came down to it—even if they'd refuse to tell me the details, for obvious reasons.

"Killer?" he said.

I groaned. "The *warlocks'* killer. They're blaming the guild, and you by extension, but there are a bunch of rogues out there and I'm not about to send the warlocks after them. Since I know you've wanted to get your hands on *me* for a while, I thought I'd let you do the honours."

"You're a liar," he said. "What reason would I have to believe that anyone not tempted by hell would betray us?"

"Oh, they're working with hell, all right," I said. "I didn't see any demon marks, but that doesn't mean their orders aren't coming from that direction."

I suspected not, but if I told him heaven was likely giving them orders, he'd clam up. If the guild took out the celestial rogues without finding out they were answering to their own so-called allies, then I'd have one less problem to worry about.

"Bring me proof," he growled.

"What, bring them directly to you?" I asked. "I can't do that. I told you—they want to take over the guild. If I bring them into your headquarters, I'm potentially setting a demon loose. They're unpredictable and clearly have a plan. All I ask is that you take the threat seriously. I can even facilitate a meeting, but I wanted to gauge whether you actually have the necessary firepower to take out a dozen or so rogue celestials."

"Absurd," he said. "Why would I listen to you? Your antics nearly got me killed. You *did* get the others killed."

"Feel free to toss around blame later," I said. "Fine. You know nobody can reach Grade Four without visiting Purgatory. That's where their upgrades used to take place. So: have you been there recently? Seen anything odd?"

His tone was sharp. "That information is confidential. You never should have been allowed there in the first place."

"I'm trying to save your damn necks again," I snapped. "I've been there recently. If you have too, then you'll know exactly what I'm talking about."

"What you need to understand, Devi," he growled, "is that none of the top echelons of this guild have been able to get into Purgatory since your little stunt."

My heart sank. "What? I didn't bring anyone with me. They might even have turned before I did."

But... *I'd* been allowed in.

And that creature who looked like me had been to Earth... more than once. Recently. So why would the other celestials no longer be able to get in? Damn. I didn't have the power to bring that monster down on my own, not until I knew *what* it was.

A hand closed around my throat, lifting me off the ground. My phone slipped from my grip as my vision darkened at the edges.

Javos.

Shit a brick. I hadn't seen him sneak up on me.

With a horrible crunch, his foot came down on my phone, smashing it into fragments. He wasn't using telekinesis. He was really, really pissed off.

"Rogues?" he said. "You caught the killer but neglected to tell me?"

"Put… me… down," I gasped. Shadows exploded from my right hand, wrapping around him, dragging both of us into the shadowy between-world of my own creation.

He dropped me. I landed on my feet, glad Rachel's boots held off the impact. Wheezing, sucking air into my lungs, I pressed my fingers to my bruised neck. "You're going to regret that."

"Remove us from this place immediately," he said. Oh. The shadows. He'd likely know I stole the magic from Zadok, but I'd go scrounging for a fuck to give when I got my breath back.

"Actually," I gasped out. "I've no idea how."

Classical music blared through the air, and the shadows receded from Nikolas's front garden.

Rachel ran up to us, wielding a radio. "I'm sorry!" she gasped. From her wild appearance, she'd followed him all the way here on foot. "Devi—" She whirled on Javos. "You *bastard.*"

His eyes burned, his aura raging. "She's been holding information on the killer."

I coughed, my throat dry. "I didn't know who it was until she nearly killed me last night. And her other target is the guild, so I decided to give them advance warning before I sent you on a rampage."

"She?" he echoed. "These rogues of yours are the killers, are they?"

"Not to my knowledge. Lydia would have told you about them if you hadn't terrorised her. I've been too busy putting out fires to deal with your temper tantrums." I rubbed my neck again. "You know, I might pay to watch what Nikolas does to you for this. But maybe I'll use my own power instead." My hand blazed with shadows, hungry to devour everything in their path.

Javos stepped backwards, his expression the closest to

ashamed I'd ever seen him. "I forgot myself… forgot you're human."

"Really?" I said. "Too bad. I'm out, and you can stay away from Fiona as well. Also, I have it on good knowledge that Nikolas has been nominated as your successor at least a dozen times, so he gets my vote for your replacement when we scrape what's left of you off the floor."

"That's a delightful sentiment, Devi," he said. "But your dear friend Lydia escaped. Leaving this." He held up a piece of glass, which gleamed faintly gold. Demonglass.

"They're… using my glass. She is." Horror coursed through me, momentarily distracting me from my rage. "The killer. I literally found out who the killer is about twelve hours ago, and Nikolas and I nearly died thanks to what she did to me."

"She?"

"I don't know what she is. A celestial demon. Doppelganger… she looked exactly like me, but like my reflection."

In demonglass.

My ability was tied to demonglass in some way. Demonglass absorbed magic, and so did I. But what did that make her?

"Your reflection?" Javos said. "What manner of demon is she?"

"She's not a demon," I said. "There's a rogue working for heaven sending her after warlocks, I guess, but I don't know how to kill her. She's no regular demon, nor like anything else I've faced. If you want to go into Purgatory, it's up to you. Hell, I'll even throw you a farewell party, if it's all the same to me."

"Why did you go there?" he growled. "You started this, didn't you?"

"No. I went there to look for the angels. I found her instead. She's killing your people to start a war."

His aura blazed white-hot. "And these rogues of yours? Where are they?"

"I told you, they're not the killers. And if they are, your warlocks can't beat them." Not to mention Javos himself was wildly unpredictable, and if not for the regenerative power I'd picked up from the two demigods, he'd have put me in the hospital for a week with the way he'd half strangled me. Not to mention he'd broken my phone. I hadn't lied. I *would* vote in Nikolas as a replacement. Actually, I'd vote for the were-warlock with the deadly paintbrush over him, but that was beside the point.

"Tell me where they are," he ordered.

"To be honest, Javos, you've done absolutely nothing to deserve that information. It's on the guild, not you."

"Then we're at war with heaven," he said. "I will inform the warlocks—"

"Don't be rash. The killer is deliberately trying to provoke a war. Besides, the Divinities like to play games with mortals. They're probably setting us up to entertain them, and we're walking into their trap. I'll kill that creature. She won't get the jump on me again."

Javos's blazing eyes narrowed. "You seem certain enough to stake others' lives on your guesswork considering you nearly died, Devi."

Ouch. Guess I deserved that one. "If you want to go and face down that creature yourself, you're more than welcome to. Pretty certain it's after you anyway, considering it's trying to provoke the warlocks into a war."

And you're rising to the bait.

The Divinities wanted a war. And they'd try to provoke every conscious being in both heaven and hell in order to get it.

He took another step towards me. "Tell me, Devi. I don't want to hurt you again."

"Look, Javos, I'll level with you. I am under a crap-ton of stress. You also just violated what was left of my trust in your ability to do your job, so forget it. If you want into Purgatory, I'll let you fight the killer. If not, then she'll keep killing your warlocks. Your choice."

"I choose to hunt your rogues." He turned heel, and stomped off.

Rachel didn't follow him. "Seven hells."

"Tell me about it." My neck smarted with pain. I still had regenerative magic, so I directed some of it at the wounds to heal the damage, while Rachel watched.

"Is Nikolas still on Babylon?" she asked. "He's going to kill Javos."

I groaned. "Yes. I know. I guess I'm officially unemployed."

"So am I," she said. "That was out of line."

"Damn right he was, but he's the least of it all. I'm not... not powerful enough to beat her. The killer." It stung to admit it, but it was true.

Her mouth turned down at the corners. "Are you sure? It can't be an angel."

I blew out a breath. "She called herself a new creation of heaven. I have enough demon in me for her magic to be fatal. I have no idea whether she's killing the warlocks or not, but she might well be linked to the rogues, considering they got themselves upgraded right there in Purgatory."

"Enough demon in you," she repeated. "The other celestials' power didn't do that. I've never seen magic like that before. When you came back... it was like your body was breaking apart. If Niko hadn't given you most of his regenerative magic, you would have."

I winced. "Breaking..." Like glass. "Demonglass," I said. "She... whatever she was, she didn't actually use my demonic power. She's probably a shapeshifter creature, like a demon.

Demons come in all forms, and for all I know, angels do, too."

A new creation of heaven. Like the fallen? The children of the Divinities? I'd been so sure they must know something, but now doubts crept in. Heaven had changed the playing field.

I ran a hand through my hair. "The arch-demon isn't on Babylon. I don't know what Nikolas is doing that's taking so long, but if he sees this mark, he'll go to war with Javos, and we don't have time. I'm heading over there."

"You sure?"

Doubts or not, I needed to speak to the fallen. "I'm bloody sick of always being the person who has no clue what's going on."

Not that anyone else knew, either. Aside from the highest denizens of heaven and hell. Since heaven was off the table: hell it was.

"I'll be your backup," Rachel said. "But *only* if Casthus isn't there. If so, we get out. Deal?"

"Sure. I have the demonglass right here. I'll just throw together another blister trap or two."

After all, it didn't look like I'd be returning to the warlocks' place any time soon.

I re-entered the house with Rachel and made my way to the lab in the living room.

"Fiona was behind me," she said. "I hope she didn't run into Javos on the way back."

"*I* hope she's far enough along in her training that she can control the fire without any more lessons from him."

"Me too," Rachel said.

Five minutes later, Fiona rang the doorbell. Rachel let her in, and she came and watched me put the final touches on the anti-warlock trap.

"What're you brewing this time?" she asked.

"Blister trap." I slipped the spell around my neck. "Maybe I'll use this one on Javos."

"Javos was in a real temper," she said.

"Yeah, he was." I checked my weapons were in place. "I know Nikolas isn't back yet, but we're running on a time limit here. Rachel and I are going ahead to Babylon. We'll meet him there. Maybe he's dealing with the other warlocks."

Fiona nodded in understanding. "Sure. I'll keep watch in case any more of those scorpion things come back."

"Thanks," I said. "By the way… I kind of quit working for Javos. So did Rachel. I'll tell you the rest when we're back."

Her eyes widened. "Seriously?"

"Yep. Be careful, and if Javos comes here, don't let him in. That okay?"

"I'm ready." Her face was set, her demon mark uncovered. A new mark. I needed to look into the matter when I had a spare moment, to make sure the mark wasn't harmful. I sincerely hoped it wouldn't cause her as much grief as mine had caused me.

And if the fallen didn't have the answers? I had to go back to the demon who'd marked me in the first place. For all I knew, he was behind this. Lythocrax. As the arch-demon who'd most recently been in heaven, *he* must know if there was a new conspiracy to bring down the celestials or start a war. Maybe both. Heaven's warriors were mere pawns. So were hell's.

Then I'll bring them both down.

15

Rachel and I crossed over to Babylon, landing in an unfamiliar corridor surprisingly free of debris. The demonglass pillars had been in shattered ruins the last time I'd been here, but apparently, the arch-demon had redecorated. The tall, wide windows had gone, masking everything in gloom. My extra-sensitive Grade Four magic would pick up on any demons or warlocks present, so the darkness didn't bother me that much. Maybe it was because I'd already fulfilled today's danger quota, maybe it was that I'd damn near died yesterday, but I kind of wanted to laugh at Casthus's blatant attempt to play up to the image of himself as a terrifying shadow demon. Okay, he *was* terrifying, but so were ninety-nine percent of the people—or not-people—I ran into these days. And hey, the apocalypse was coming. I needed all the entertainment I could get. The poor warlocks in this castle probably did, too.

"Whoa," said Rachel, from beside the arrow-slit window, which had replaced the wider windows overlooking the area below the castle. "That's new."

I moved to her side, squinting through at the castle

grounds. Whoa indeed. The tower—Zadok's tower—had *gone.*

"Talk about burning bridges," I said. "Or knocking them down."

He'd even destroyed Zadok's home? Harsh. It seemed a tad excessive, not to mention… where had the demonglass disappeared to? Aside from the pillars, the whole tower had been made out of the stuff.

Weird. Really weird. Casthus might have broken the damn thing into pieces, but those pieces must be somewhere. I doubted he'd destroy a valuable magical source.

Rachel and I kept walking. The castle smelled stale, with the occasional whiff of something rotting and foul. Not unusual for an arch-demon's abode, but dread stalked my steps, like he lurked in the shadows waiting to pounce.

"This place is too quiet," Rachael whispered.

I nodded in agreement. "He went into Pandemonium, and we'd know if he came back. Let's get to the fallen."

Not that I'd yet figured out how to get them out of here—or where to hide them when I did.

I tiptoed down the corridor, cloaking myself and Rachel in shadows. If Zadok was here, he'd doubtless be able to find me, but the extra security calmed my nerves.

The dungeon had been opened after I'd freed the fallen, but of course Casthus had rebuilt the castle. I stopped at dead ends more than once where he'd moved things around. Rachel looked equally lost, and she generally had a better sense of direction than I did—as I inferred, due to her having grown up in a warren of confusing tunnels. Finally, we reached the spot where I thought the dungeon should be, only to find the doors sealed.

"Crap. Please tell me he didn't kill them."

"They can't die," said Rachel. "From what Niko said, it sounds like he already tried. Unless he took them with him."

My heart lurched. "Damn. Okay… let's speak to the other warlocks. We've left enough traces for a certain shadow demigod to guess we were here, assuming he came back."

Rachel gave a doubtful head-shake, but followed me towards the entrance hall.

Unlike the rest of the castle, the entrance hall lay where it'd always been, and looked much the same—large, wide and gloomy. And not empty, though the warlocks didn't mingle as usual. They were gathered around the edges of the room in regimented lines… and in the centre, two people grappled with one another. Both were hairless, their hands clawed.

Fallen.

"Hey!" I shouted. "Stop that. Now."

The warlocks turned on me. Formerly indifferent faces showed outward hostility. One warlock pointed a hand at the fallen. "Kill the traitors."

The two fallen stopped grappling and turned to face us. Their features showed no signs of recognition as they moved forwards—faster than I'd ever seen them move before. Their bodies were streaked with blood—and symbols. Marks.

The fallen lunged at Rachel and me, claws swiping.

I leaped forwards in front of Rachel, activating my celestial hand and summoning my blade. Blood spurted from their chests and I jerked backwards in surprise, letting go of the blade. It shouldn't have damaged them. The blade hovered in the air, both fallen impaled… and black blood dripped to the stone floor.

Like demon blood.

"What the hell did you do to them?" I demanded of the nearest warlock—Vulric, the former supervisor of this place in Nikolas's absence.

"Not us," he said. "Him."

Casthus. "You're watching them fight one another for sport."

"Those who resisted are mounted on pikes outside," he snarled. "You left us to him, and you will pay."

"Er, no." My celestial blade glowed as though to underline my point. "Firstly, I'm not your boss. That would be Nikolas, and he wouldn't want you killing the fallen, either."

He wasn't here. So where in the seven hells was he?

"Secondly," I added, "your own superstition tells you that killing the fallen is a bad idea, so you're damning yourselves by your own logic."

The warlock's forked tail lashed. "They are no longer of heaven. But they can be changed."

"What, tortured for your own entertainment?" I said. "Tell me why I shouldn't blast the lot of you to pieces. You know I can. I led you to war. I protected your world. And you do this."

The warlock turned his back on me and walked to the door, kicking it open. "Look upon his handiwork, human."

The area in front of the castle had transformed. Outside, a collection of bloody heads had been mounted on a row of pikes. So those were the dissidents, then. And that made the people inside the castle complicit in the murder of innocents. Crap on a stick. Nikolas *probably* wouldn't want me to blast them all with celestial power, but damn, was it tempting.

"What the hell is that in aid of?" I asked, jerking my head at the fallen's limp bodies. "Punishment just for their existence?"

"No," said the demon. "Preparation."

"For you?"

"For them."

At his word, several fallen shuffled into view outside the castle. They stood tall, moved faster than before, and their arms were marked with arcane symbols. Hell's symbols. Their auras were shadowy-black on top of their usual rotting yellow colour.

I nearly vomited at the warlock's feet.

Casthus… he'd decided to make them into an army. They were immortal, so they made easy cannon fodder. I could think of no other explanation. I swallowed hard, and dragged my gaze away.

Rachel yelled aloud. I whirled around, re-summoning my blade. With a hissing noise, Rachel sprang away from the dead fallen—who suddenly weren't so dead at all. The two fallen who'd been impaled on my sword rose to their feet, no longer bleeding, no marks remaining from the celestial power I'd hit them with.

"There," said the warlock. "They suffered no damage."

"Pity I can't say the same for you."

I slammed my fist into his cheek. Through sheer luck, I managed to hold back on my celestial power, though my sword blazed in my other hand. The other warlocks crowded me, but none seemed keen to get near the blade.

"Are you really so easily swayed?" I asked. "I'm here to rescue the fallen. Not kill them. I wasn't even going to kill you, actually, but you're making it pretty tempting."

"You can't take them," he said. "Their souls belong to Casthus now. He marked them."

Oh no. Might it be true? They were the children of the Divinities, but considering they'd been abandoned, our delightful overlords plainly didn't care for them at all. Was it even possible to undo the mark of an arch-demon, especially from someone like him?

"They're not his," I said. "He has no right to claim them."

"Feel free to tell him that yourself."

"Devi," said Rachel urgently from my side. "He—"

Shadows fell. The warlocks cringed back as the monstrous shape of the arch-demon appeared overhead, wings blotting out the huge luminous moon.

Dammit.

I grabbed Rachel's hand, deactivated my blade, and plunged my hand into my pocket to grasp the demonglass. Ignoring the warlocks' shouts, I pulled us back to Nikolas's house.

"That was too close," Rachel gasped. "That was him?"

I took a step backwards, breathing heavily. "Yeah, it was. But where's Nikolas? I thought he was there. On Babylon."

Had the arch-demons taken him again? I hadn't wanted to run like a coward, but I knew a losing battle when I saw one, and risking Rachel's life hadn't been on my plan. The other warlocks sure as hell wouldn't help either of us.

Shadows exploded through the room. I jumped to my feet, light blazing from my hand—and immediately dropped my hand when Nikolas stepped from the shadows. "Where *were* you?"

"Don't tell me you were on Babylon," he said.

"All right, I won't."

"Devi."

I folded my arms, my hands still shaking. "He's turning the fallen into a dark army. Did you know?"

My insides went cold. *He* didn't *know—did he.*

"No, of course I didn't," he said. "Otherwise I wouldn't have supported your attempts to rescue them. It's out of the question now."

"So what were you doing?"

"Inspecting the damage," he said. "And looking for allies. My own warlocks refuse to listen to reason. I'm sorry, Devi, but the fallen are lost."

My heart plummeted. "No."

But my celestial light couldn't heal the damage. It only destroyed what it saw as evil... which now included the fallen.

"They can't be saved," he said. "And it would have been all

but impossible to bring them here in any case. They might attack humans. Even without those marks."

I dropped my arms to my sides. "I'm at my wits' end. I didn't even see Zadok there, so *what* he's doing is anyone's guess. But Rachel and I left before Casthus spotted us. And I have no bloody clue what he and Abyss were talking about, but if they want to punch anyone, they can do us all a favour and deal with that bloody evil clone of mine. If heaven wants a war, they should have sent her against them, not against a bunch of innocent warlocks on Earth."

Nikolas crossed the room to me. "I don't know what their strategy is. They're playing the long game. That's what the demons do, anyway."

"And you?" I asked. "Have you given up?"

"No."

I tilted my head at him. "You just said the fallen can't be saved."

"I'm not the one who can save them," he said. "But Devi —*you* might be able to."

"Yeah right." I laughed, without humour. "My soul is split. Apparently I'm bound for Purgatory when I die, but I'm still holding out hope that that's a long way off. Anyway, the only other plan I had was to talk to Lythocrax. I mean, he knows demon marks. He might know what that clone is, too. But he kind of hates my guts. On the other hand, he was on Abyss's side, so presumably not Casthus's."

"I never got the impression the feeling was mutual. She needed him: not the other way around."

Damn. He was right. "Okay, but they worked together. If Purgatory isn't an option, that place is. I know his name. Unlike the other arch-demons, I can get him to listen to me." I hoped.

More than my own life was at stake. Saving the fallen was vital. I wouldn't leave them to die.

"If you're sure," he said. "Abyss also has a long history of stealing Casthus's servants for her own amusement. The fallen might be a target."

"What, she might *steal* the fallen?"

"I may have planted some hints to that effect."

"So you *are* playing the demons' games."

"I know how those two work," he said. "I think he's planning to trade them to her in exchange for territory on Pandemonium."

"Demon territory squabbles, and betting lives on it. How very… netherworld."

Rachel gave a short laugh. "She's not wrong."

From what I'd heard in my studies, arch-demons' petty arguments and constant bickering were par for the course. Even the celestials' doctrines said so, though they never went into specifics. And the guild had never mentioned the fallen existed. Probably didn't know.

Oh, who am I kidding? Someone knew—someone who had no intention of telling the rest of the celestials what in hell was going on.

"The eventual goal, I believe, is Pandemonium," Nikolas said. "But he won't steal it outright. He'll play the game first."

I frowned. "How long do the fallen have?"

"Honestly? Not long enough."

"Then I'll speak to Lythocrax next," I said. "He might hate me, but he can't hurt me, and he also can't disobey my orders if I call him by his true name. And he's the most recent arch-demon to fall."

If anyone might know what the gods wanted with me, it was him. Last time, the Divinities had wanted to see me open the bridge and invite Armageddon in myself. Who knew what they wanted with me this time, other than my death?

There were far too many people counting on me to defend them.

16

<hr>

I felt no fear this time when I set up the pentagram to take me into the realm where I'd been reborn for the second time. The place that had taken so much from me, yet given me the powers I needed to save this realm from darkness.

Unlike the shadow dimensions, the world Lythocrax had claimed was a wasteland devoid of beauty… and pretty much anything else. Almost like Purgatory. If Lythocrax was a new arch-demon, was his world a new demon realm? Possibly. But unless it'd sprung up from nowhere, it must have been a heavenly or earthly realm beforehand.

I stepped into the pentagram, and crossed over.

Immediately, my demon mark ignited in warning. Shadowy power rose to the surface first, countering the instinctive fear conjured up by the approach of an arch-demon. Even one who couldn't harm me.

"YOU WILL NOT USE HIS POWER HERE."

Fire flooded the otherwise barren earth. Orange light gilded the horizon, and with it came a roar that shook the world.

I stood my ground as the roaring died down and the scent of brimstone rushed in. "I wasn't going to use it until you decided to drag it out of me," I said, as though the noise wasn't absolutely terrifying. Not to mention the arch-demon, who had ashy wings and a huge form cloaked in lava-covered skin, an embodiment of terror that nobody could equal. I'd faced literal death too recently to brush off the primal rush of terror at his appearance—but for all his pomp and ceremony, I held his true name.

"Altheare," I said. "Haven't we talked before about not messing up my demon mark without my permission?"

He hissed at my use of his true name. To everyone else, he went by 'Lythocrax'—fallen angel, former Divinity, and the newest arch-demon who'd nearly destroyed the realms when he'd decided to enlist the help of Abyss with the promise of helping her gain a body that was immune to the sunlight. I didn't need to know his weakness. If I used his true name, he couldn't hurt me.

"Casthus is back," I told him. "One world away from Earth, to be precise. Just in case you didn't know. I need information."

"I care nothing for the shadow dimensions."

"You did when you were manipulating Abyss on the Divinities' orders," I said. "And for the record, it doesn't take a genius to see something is screwed up in heaven. One would think they wanted hell to win."

Except the false Devi and the rogue celestials still wielded heaven's light as their power. If anything, that made it worse. As for the fallen, the Divinities had already proven they didn't care a bit.

He watched me with fathomless eyes, his aura flickering like a flame. "The ones who rule, in heaven and hell, are inscrutable."

"You *are* one of the rulers," I said. "Of a dismal wasteland, but it's yours. You fell yourself. You must have done something to deserve it."

I looked up at his huge demon form. If not for the demonic aura, he'd appear almost angelic… a stark contrast to the shadowy monstrosity of Casthus. And still different from the almost human-like form of Abyss.

"The old ways are dying," he said. "The Divinities know it, and they fear it. They are not what they were."

"So say we all," I said. "You're still stuck here, alone? Why? Because you're the runt of the litter, being a new arch-demon, and you're scared of the others?"

"I fear nothing," he growled.

Sure you don't. Arch-demons could feel fear. They were undeniably mighty, but they still had weaknesses.

"Look, weren't you supposed to put me against Abyss? That was your goal?"

"Not my goal. Theirs. They pushed me out of heaven for their own gain."

Finally. A proper answer. Maybe he lied… or maybe he was helpless against heaven as I was.

"Then I need your assistance," I told him. "Tell me about the war in heaven. Tell me what their plans are."

"Do you think they told me?"

"You were one of them." So much for useful information. "You have more knowledge of what's going on than anyone else I've met save for the other arch-demons, and I've had bloody enough of tiptoeing around. Fallen armies, world-hopping venos demons, temper tantrums—you're all a bunch of petulant toddlers."

"Fallen armies?" he echoed. "The armies of heaven have yet to descend."

"Not heaven. Well, they *were*. The fallen. Children of the Divinities. The ones they—*you*—threw out of heaven when Babylon fell, or whatever went on there."

He roared. The ground trembled, and I braced my feet on the stone to stop myself from being blown over.

"Seriously?" I yelled at him. "You're proving my point about childish temper tantrums."

"Those fallen," he said, "were mine."

Crap. "What do you—?"

Lines spread across the ground. The air burned, and fiery rocks rained down.

"Turn off the bloody meteor shower!" I bellowed. "I was planning to save the fallen myself, actually, but I thought I'd check in with you, first. What do you know about them?"

Fiery rocks struck the ground on either side of me, close enough for me to feel their heat. Shadows rushed from my hands, forming a barrier between us. The mass of shadows grew as I poured more power into them, and blasted him in the chest with demonic lightning.

"YOU DARE?" Power thrummed in Lythocrax's gaze, and he raised a hand.

"Don't *you* dare strike me, Altheare. Heaven is trying to manipulate you. *Who* are the fallen to you? Are *you* one of the Divinities who abandoned them on Babylon?"

"Not abandoned," he growled. "Stolen. By hell."

I let the shadows die a little so I could look into his fiery gaze as though it would give away whether or not he was lying. "You mean, they fell. They told me themselves that you ditched them there."

"You know absolutely nothing, mortal." His tone was quieter, and mercifully, it'd stopped raining fiery rocks. I bloody well hoped there wasn't anyone else living here who'd been engulfed in meteoric fire.

"Enlighten me. The fallen were from this realm, right?"

"Correct. They were mine. But when they went to war with the shadows, they lost."

"And the fallen fell... wait a moment. You only fell

recently. The fallen have been there for years." Since before Nikolas was born, at any rate.

"Who told you they fell when I did?"

"They did," I said. "Are you messing with me? The fallen distinctly said, *we fell when they did, and they hardly cared.* So unless you're blatantly lying—"

"They were my army. The enemy must have told them I fell. They lost their divine powers when the realm of shadow cut them off from heaven, and the other Divinities cared nothing."

"Do you swear you're telling the truth, Altheare."

"I swear."

Hmm. There was no way to guarantee truth, especially from a being cast out of heaven and who seemed to *want* to be here. He'd fallen, damning both of us, to drive me against Abyss at his command. When I'd escaped his command, he'd used Inspector Angler's demon mark for the same reason. And he'd made no overt effort to go and reclaim the fallen even when he'd had the chance to.

He's lying. Not that it came as a surprise, with him being an arch-demon, but come on.

"I don't think you're telling the truth," I said to him. "The fallen are immortal, and can't die. They've been suffering for years, and you're seriously saying you had no clue they were still alive?"

"They were punished for all their crimes. Arch-demons and Divinities both."

"Yeah, don't go pinning the blame for this on anyone else. Casthus owns them now. He marked them. Know how to reverse that?"

The ground gave another tremor. "We cannot normally mark anyone unless they were already tied to us, but the fallen are close enough to demons that they can be controlled in the same way. It's typical of the dark one that he would choose to do so."

"And—can I free them? That's what I came here to find out. Is there a way to break a demon mark?"

"Remove them from their own dimension. He won't have laid his personal mark on them. He wouldn't waste that on the dead."

"Are you sure?"

"Yes. Bring them here, and they will be mine again."

"You're asking me to put an awful lot of faith in you. How do I know you don't plan to turn them into an army, too?"

"I never said I wouldn't. But they are mine."

At least he was honest about his intentions, even if he'd probably lied about the rest of it. Like it or not, the best place for the fallen was another demon realm—there was no hope for their re-ascending to heaven, and they would never be able to adapt as humans, not on Earth, at least. But who was I to make that choice for them? As long as the shadow demon's mark remained in place, though—they had no free will to make any decisions.

"Is my claiming the fallen worse than what he's doing?" he enquired.

Damn him. "Maybe. You arch-demons are all the same in my eyes. You might have fallen recently, but you're still damned, and if you're in contact with heaven, that makes you *less* trustworthy than the shadow demon."

"A valid concern," he said. "What if I were to tell you that if those fallen go dark, they can obliterate the celestials and everyone you love?"

An icy pit grew in my chest. "I'd say I need proof."

"And what if I were to tell you that I alone can save them?"

"No arch-demon can save anyone."

"I saved you."

"That's not the same," I said. "Your ability to raise someone from death, however you did it, doesn't make that person a celestial any longer. You can't deny that."

"No," he said, "but the shadow demon's magic runs deep. If he gets the fallen to serve him, they will live forever, and they will wish for death every second of the way."

Despite the lingering heat, chills raced up my arms. "You're still using people's lives as bargaining chips, even if they are your children. I don't trust you one bit."

But what choice did I have? No other realm had a place for the fallen. They *were* vulnerable to influence. And Lythocrax was their father… possibly.

"Your distrust is valid, Devi."

"You tried to kill me yourself. How do I know you won't kill the fallen or turn them against me?"

"I will promise you something else in return, Devi," he said. "A true name."

My heart skipped a beat. "I thought you were born with them."

"There's one exception," he said. "The true name of an arch-demon is not the same as the name they had when they were divine."

"Interesting," I said. "The answer's still no."

"Then the fallen will die," he said. "If you wish for some time to think about your decision, however, I will grant you that."

How generous of you. "Fine. I'll consider it. Also, I had another question. There's a being out there, a creation of heaven's, who looks exactly like my reflection. She seems to have some new celestial power, and she nearly killed me. Know anything about that?"

"I'm not privy to heaven's manoeuvres."

"Like they didn't send you here." I gave him a glare. "Nice try, Altheare."

He growled, and the Earth trembled. I'd had bloody enough of arch-demon theatrics for one day. Without breaking his gaze, I gripped the demonglass in my pocket, transporting myself home.

"Well, that was enlightening." I kicked ashes out of the pentagram.

"What is it?" asked Nikolas.

I explained. "I know he's a liar," I said. "But they're being turned into an army. If they go back to the Divinities—it's where they belong. I can't pretend to know what he's scheming, but if I speak to them and find out if it's true that they belonged to him…"

Nikolas's mouth tightened. "Not with Casthus there."

"He's turning them into an army *now*. Rachel and I got into the castle once already."

"When he wasn't there."

My fist clenched on the demonglass. "If we get them here, just for a minute, his hold on them will lift and I'll be able to ask them if it's true. We don't have a lot of other options. Also, Lythocrax promised to give me a true name. Like a demon. I can stop people from controlling or summoning me using my given name."

"Devi, nobody has tried to do that to you. And is it worth taking his word for it?"

"Well, no. I need to confirm with the fallen. I have no idea what he's scheming, but we need to get the fallen out of that realm regardless. It's that or ask Clover, and she wasn't much help last time."

I checked in my pocket for my phone. And then I remembered Javos had smashed it. Also, I hadn't told Nikolas about our little altercation yet. Not to mention I hadn't even figured out how to handle Javos's crusade against the outcast celestials, the guild's refusal to face up to the situation, and the band of lunatic outcasts wanting my help.

I half-fell onto the sofa. "This is… this is too much. The only person I haven't spoken to in the last day is Abyss… and he already traded two of the fallen to her. Maybe she'll listen."

Maybe hell would freeze over… which would still be better than the alternative.

"I highly doubt she will, but she's also less likely to kill you." Nikolas took a seat beside me. "However, this time I'm coming with you."

I lifted my head from the cushions. "Fair enough. I'll tell Dienes to give her a warning. Also, she has assassins running around, but they're pretty amateur. Surely she must know that Casthus plans to take over her territory, but for all I know, she already has an exit strategy."

I flipped the right way up on the sofa, casually burned another pentagram into the wall, then yelled, "Get out here, Dienes."

Nikolas raised an eyebrow. "I'm starting to get the impression that you're at the end of your tether."

"Oh, I'm past that point."

Dienes popped into existence, a puzzled frown appearing on his forehead at the sight of me half sprawled on the sofa against Nikolas's shoulder. "Devi! You are—"

"Don't you start grovelling. It's not a good look. I don't suppose you were allowed into Abyss's top-secret meeting with Casthus?"

"No, Devi, I wasn't," he squeaked.

"Worth a try. I'm coming to see Abyss, and if she traps me in a demonglass maze last time, I'll strip the glass from the palace and feed it to her."

His brow furrowed in an apparent attempt to decipher the logic of that pronouncement. Then he vanished back into the pentagram.

———

I gave Dienes an hour, during which I changed into a fresh outfit that didn't smell of Lythocrax's realm, refuelled on coffee and a plate of sandwiches, and updated Fiona on the latest. Apparently she'd been with Rachel while I'd been gone, who'd helped her retrieve her possessions from Javos's place without him trying to rope her into another contract—Nikolas's sharp eyes narrowed at that word, but he didn't ask me until both of them left the room.

"Did something happen between you and Javos?" he asked, casually.

"Firstly, promise you won't overreact."

"It depends what you say." His words were calm. His aura told a different story.

"He broke my phone," I admitted. "He caught me red-handed talking about the rogue celestials, and he snapped. Now he's claiming he's going to hunt them down single-handedly."

"By snapped," he said, his words measured, "you mean he attacked you."

"Rachel was a minute too late with the radio. He's scared you'll hunt him down, so he won't be coming after me again."

"No, because I'll go after him first."

I held out an arm. "Any other time, I'd say go ahead. But seriously—we have an oncoming apocalypse to deal with. I might need to borrow your phone. I should have memo-rised Clover's number. She doesn't know what's going on, anyway. No more than we do. All I know for sure is that the demons are all dickheads and might be lying at any time."

Lythocrax being a prime example. For all I know, he was working with heaven, and the evil Devi clone by extension... *stop that. Now isn't the time.*

"Let's get this done," Nikolas said. "Then I'll sort out Javos."

"I'll buy a front row ticket, assuming the arch-demons don't smite us first. This is Devi, from the department of eternal optimism."

"I think you have a realistic view of the situation."

I shrugged. "I have to. When you lose everything, when you're scraping the bottom of the barrel… you get up again. You have to. I don't know whether it's my celestial power or just the way I am, but I'm not capable of staying down."

"It's one of the qualities I admire most about you," he said. My demon mark tingled at the heat in his stare. *Not now.* I was tempted to say screw it and have a fantastic time banging him up until the literal end of the world, but the idea of having Nikolas's company for my next argument with an arch-demon was fairly appealing, too.

"Along with my killer wit and great sense of style, obviously." I burned another pentagram into the floor. "Let's go and say hello to Abyss."

Nikolas took my hand and stepped after me, into the whirling flames.

A moment later, demonglass walls surrounded us on every side, reflecting both of us—Nikolas, tall and winged, his aura shadow-black, and me, half light and half dark, and wildly pissed off.

"Hello?" I said. "Oh, for the Divinities' sake. It's the assassins' maze again."

I clenched my right fist, and shadowy power flowed to my hand. Nikolas looked at it. "Is that what I think it is?"

"Yep. It can destroy demonglass."

I blasted the wall down, revealing Abyss's throne room. Tall ceilings, stone walls, and Abyss herself, clad in her human-like guise. Her armour reflected the shattered pieces of demonglass back at us.

"Two of you this time?" she said. "You dare to bring the son of shadows with you?"

I approached her, my footsteps crunching in the demon-glass. "I thought you didn't mind. You and Casthus certainly had a long chat. Anything you want to share with me about our shadowy overlord?"

"Certainly not with you."

"Worth a try." I shrugged. "We're here because you're an easy target. Also, in case you weren't already aware, Casthus intends to take your throne. Where are the fallen?"

"These creatures?" She gestured carelessly, and two fallen appeared at her left side, softly and silently. Their bodies were covered in marks, like the others, and they didn't meet my eyes. My stomach tightened. "They're obedient and resilient: two qualities I value."

"Casthus is playing you," said Nikolas. "He intends to take this realm as his own. He's biding his time."

"I suppose you would know." She looked down at him. Very few people could do that, but the arch-demons towered over humans and warlocks not just height-wise but by sheer force of their presence. "He is ancient and inscrutable, but he will not take what is rightfully mine."

"Technically, I'm the one who pointed you to this place just because there was a vacancy," I said. "I never said it'd be easy to keep it. He wants this realm. How do you know his servants won't turn on you?"

She gave them a dismissive gesture with one hand. "They're empty vessels, nothing more."

"They're the children of the Divinities." I folded my arms across my chest. "Do you know who those fallen belonged to, once? Your old ally."

"Lythocrax? He lies."

She sure seems certain of that. "Really? He was a Divinity. It's not so unlikely. Also, as you pointed out, most people wouldn't want them. If he's not their father, then what does he want them for?"

"For his own, the same as I do."

"I thought you and Lythocrax... were you on the same side?"

"For a time. Until he granted me access to the Divinities again."

"So he does have access to the Divinities? Now?" My blood chilled. Ninety percent of me had known he was a liar, but how deep did the deceit run? He knew that he couldn't harm me, after all. Maybe the Divinities had planned to get at me through him all along--through the one who'd marked me. It was a clever plan, and I certainly wouldn't put it past them to think they could pull it off. And they might have, if not for the fact that I suspected every demon of working against me by default.

"He never told me if he did. We terminated our arrangement after the battle."

Great. Not that I'd really wanted to leave the fallen with him anyway... but if anything was clear, it was that Lythocrax hadn't severed his ties with heaven so easily. And if that was the case, then heaven wanted me dead.

I looked at the fallen, then back into Abyss's cold gaze. "What would you trade me for them?"

Next to me, Nikolas shook his head, almost imperceptibly.

"There is nothing more I need from you, Devi."

I gave her an eye-roll. "You wound me. Look, Casthus is going to slaughter you. You won't win."

Abyss looked down at me, and her form appeared to grow taller, more formidable. "What makes you think I don't have an army of my own? Themedes didn't leave this realm undefended."

Yeah, but he was dying. Damn it all. She wouldn't budge.

And she had at least given me confirmation that Lythocrax was a liar, and his words were worth nothing. If he was on heaven's side, that meant he was likely on the side of the evil monster rampaging around Purgatory and probably upgrading those celestials, too.

Maybe he'd been the one to order her to kill me.

"Tell me the truth," I said to Abyss, my quiet voice ringing out in the wide hall. "Are you on heaven's side?"

"I am on nobody's side but my own."

One of the fallen looked up at me. His eyes shone with an odd light—and he mouthed my name.

I took half a step back, and the fallen exploded forwards, claws swiping at Abyss.

Nikolas moved at the same time, his wings coming out, and launched himself at the fallen, tackling him before his claws struck the arch-demon. I ran for the other one, a wild scheme coming to mind. Grabbing the fallen, I whispered, *sorry*. Then I reached for a charm I still kept in my pocket, despite never usually needing it, and hit the switch.

A fragrant smell filled the air as the spell went off, and the fallen crumpled, unconscious. I threw another at the fallen grappling with Nikolas. He looked up, mouthing my name— and a blade appeared, spearing me through the chest.

17

A dull, thumping pain spread through my body, as shock chilled my nerves. The blade stuck out of my chest—not a celestial one, but a sharp full-length sword. I'd seen it before. Casthus's right-hand-demon had been carrying it.

A voice whispered in my ear, "The shadow demon is most displeased with your actions, Devi."

I choked, blood filling my mouth. *Regenerative magic... now.*

Nikolas roared my name, his magic slamming into my demon mark—at the same time as the demon tackled me, his wings spread wide, and propelled both of us out of the window. We tumbled from the castle—apparently Abyss's lair was further off the ground than I'd thought—plummeting towards the cobblestone path below.

The wound in my chest sealed, and I flipped over so Rachel's boots were positioned to cushion my fall, just in time. I slammed into the cobblestones, the demon landing swiftly in front of me. His dark blade dripped blood and oozed shadows. *He's from the same realm as Casthus, I guess.*

Shadow aligned, and not like any demon I'd seen before, He was huge and muscled, his legs more like a horse's than a human's, yet he was close enough to human to carry a celestial-style blade. Long and shimmering dark, it almost resembled the demonic equivalent to my own celestial blade.

"How long were you eavesdropping for?" Dammit. Nikolas was still up in the palace with two unconscious fallen and a raging arch-demon. I needed to kick this bastard into whichever hell he'd come from, and get the fallen out of here before Abyss used them for target practise. "Were you waiting for the opportune moment to announce yourself since we arrived? Because you might have had to wait all day."

He merely glared, without saying a word.

"You need to work on that scowl. It's more of a grimace." His aura betrayed the fury simmering under the surface at my mocking him. And considering his fiery counterpart had nearly killed Zadok, I knew he must have deadly magic of his own in order to be chosen to serve the shadow arch-demon. "Also, are you here to kill Abyss, or secretly working with her? Give me a clue here."

Shadows crept from his shoulder blades, a pair of wings unfurling.

"Guess I'll cut you a bit first, then."

I advanced towards him, summoning my celestial blade again. The blade would never fail me. It *should* have alerted me to his presence, but I hadn't been nearly careful enough. I should have figured a new assassination attempt would come my way. *You'd think Abyss would be his target.*

My blade gleamed, fire rippling along to the hilt as my demon mark's power combined with the ever-present celestial light. Most demons would run, or at least possess a healthy sense of wariness. This guy didn't seem to care in the slightest.

He wasn't a demigod or an arch-demon, but he was a true demon, one step below an arch-demon. I'd never seen a demon use a sword instead of magic, but his odd shadowy weapon looked like an extension of his own arm.

Time to find out what it could do.

I whirled on him, blade spearing the air. He met me blow for blow, fending me off with more skill than I expected. Demon's weren't known for finesse, but this guy had some serious talent. I ducked, dodged and feinted, tried every underhanded trick in the book, and yet somehow, he kept evading. That shadowy blade swept high and low, whipping past my skin fast and sharp enough to draw blood. My celestial training and divine magic didn't hold a candle to centuries of experience. I switched the blade to my left hand and tuned into the demon mark on my right. Underhanded it was, then.

"I'd like to say it's been a pleasure, except it hasn't."

Shadowy power rushed to my palm and I threw it in his face.

He raised his blade, deflecting that magic right back at me. I dodged, but not fast enough. As the shadows momentarily smothered my vision, he swung in and dealt a vicious cut to my arm. Blood pulsed from the wound, and magic rose immediately to heal it. But regenerative magic couldn't replace blood loss. I needed to finish this fast.

Shadowy power flared out of my right hand again—Zadok's power. I released it all, rapidly, dragging both of us into my own world.

The demon's shadowy blade whipped up. The magic shot *back* at me and only my quick reflexes stopped Zadok's magic from blasting me in the face.

Shit. He's immune to other shadow magic?

I'd have to do this the old-fashioned way, then.

I leapt back into the fight, letting my instincts take over

—the instincts that made demon killing second nature to me. Blood spurted from small cuts on my arms and legs. It didn't seem worth expending my limited power to heal them, but the wounds slowed me down, and I couldn't seem to land a hit on him. You'd think all the muscle would slow him down, but if anything, he moved faster than I did. Like a high ranked celestial fuelled by the gods' power—or the shadows.

Blood dripped from his own wounds. I'd cut him, too, and he wasn't healing. Wait… he wasn't a demigod. He didn't have regenerative powers of his own. But he'd barely slowed down, and still moved as fast as I did on my highest speed. A Grade Four demon.

Blood spurted as his blade re-opened the cut on my forearm, and pain old and new assailed me. Crap. I wasn't healing. I'd reached the limits of the regenerative power I'd taken from Nikolas and Zadok. It'd probably had to overextend itself to heal that first wound he'd dealt to me.

The demon's shadowy blade collided with my double-sided sword. My energy was flagging, and it took everything I had to push back, to keep him from dealing a fatal blow. My left hand dropped to my side as all feeling in my shoulder disappeared.

No. I'm not going to die here at the hands of this nobody. I readied my demon mark and reached for every ounce of power remaining inside it—Nikolas was out of reach, and for all I knew, there were no other demigods here. But I couldn't die. Not now. I had to keep fighting.

I pushed beyond the power in the mark to the demons I knew must be close by—

And found something familiar.

Impossibly so.

Sensation came back to my arm. *The wounds are healing.* Someone had given me regenerative power. I sent a silent thank you to my not-so-guardian-angel and launched myself at the demon with a final burst of speed.

He raised a hand, eyes widening in shock, but my celestial blade speared him through the chest.

The demon spat out blood. "Temporary reprieve, celestial?"

"Temporary or not, it doesn't matter. You're dead. You can't regenerate, can you?"

He coughed. "I have served my purpose, lord of shadows."

I wrenched the sword upright, tearing a hole in his body. He fell onto his back, blood spilling onto the road.

The shadow-like power continued to seal the small wounds he'd opened on my body. Zadok. He was here, somewhere close, but when I looked up, I saw nothing but the weird solid structure that had replaced the palace. I hadn't seen what it looked like from the outside before, but where a gleaming palace of demonglass had once stood was a fortress of stone, blocky and to be honest, ugly. Guess she'd moved all the demonglass to the inside. To keep out the sunlight.

Never mind the sun—it was the shadows she ought to be more concerned with. What in the seven hells was Zadok doing here of all places? I scanned the road, seeing and sensing nobody. Abyss must still be in the fortress—along with Nikolas and the fallen.

Grabbing the demonglass in my pocket. I transported myself to Nikolas's side—straight into a venos demon. My celestial fire obliterated it in an instant and I landed on my feet.

I'd expected to see Abyss raining terror on Nikolas and the fallen, but she'd disappeared. I blinked around, my head swimming from the blood loss, but managed to stay on my feet.

"Nice of you to drop in," said Nikolas. The two fallen lay unconscious at his feet.

"Did Abyss run off?"

He shook blood from his hand. "Security breach, I believe."

"No kidding," I murmured, thinking of the demon I'd killed. "Casthus's people—okay, demons—are already here. We need to get those fallen out before he takes them back. I have a plan."

"I hope you do," he said, "because I'm all out."

I'd expected him to at least argue about removing the two fallen, but even if he had, I barely had strength to stand. Demons' regenerative power didn't make up for blood loss, and my hands shook with the residual adrenaline. I hoped Casthus hadn't been particularly attached to that shadow demon—but why send him here alone?

"Let's go." I gripped the demonglass, hoping that I had strength enough left to transport all four of us.

The next second, we landed in Nikolas's living room. My knees buckled. "Hang on. I'll just get this set up—"

I clumsily activated a pentagram around the unconscious fallen, while Nikolas backed towards the shelves where he kept his collection of demonic tomes. "Devi, lie down before you pass out."

"Yes, O wise one." I slumped backwards on the carpet, and would have singed my hair on the pentagram if it'd been an actual fire. "That wasn't how I pictured our rescue mission going. Does Casthus have spies in the city? Will he go through in person?"

"I doubt it. He's trying to get Abyss's measure. Otherwise he would have gone there immediately."

I lifted my head. "I hope you're right. Damn, that demon hit hard. He was a brute."

"But you killed him."

I nodded, scrambling to my knees. "Yep. Shadow demon

down, fiery demon to go, and I swear I didn't go there looking to kill off Casthus's people. Not right away, at least."

Nikolas made for the corner of the living room where I'd set up the lab. "I've been wondering if this would happen."

I blinked. "This meaning… what?"

"You're not exhausted because of blood loss, Devi," he said, tipping some kind of powder into the cauldron. "Your demon… essence, it's drained every time you get into a fight with another demon. Same as all of us. We usually recharge by travelling to our own dimension, or taking in some part of it."

I blinked. "You mean your demon cocktail… things?"

"That's one way of getting a magical recharge, yes." He shook more ingredients together. "I'm using the standard recipe because we haven't yet determined what your demon type is."

"Aside from 'weird'." I moved into a more comfortable position on the carpet, my head resting against the sofa. "We can't keep the fallen in here, either."

"I planned to take them to the guest room. Here." He handed me a glass of clear shimmering liquid. I gave it a sceptical look, then took a long drink. Choking on the oddly burning taste, I nearly spat it out. Then the heaviness weighing on my shoulders seemed to lessen slightly.

"You figured I was demon enough now for this to work on me?" I said.

"You're demon enough for me."

"I'm going to take that as a compliment, weirdo." I drank down the rest of the liquid demon power. It'd work better for me if it was customised to my particular demon type, but now I felt slightly less like death. The juice was like an energy drink made of demon fuel, and by the time I'd drank the whole thing, I felt more like me.

"I guess I'm officially on Casthus's shit list," I said, straightening upright. "And Abyss's."

Nikolas finished turning the fallen over so they weren't sprawled in a heap. "You're on your own side, like all of them. I rather think Abyss has more urgent matters to contend herself with."

"You're not wrong." I looked at the fallen. "We have to deal with them. Lythocrax said the marks won't work here, but I've never seen anything like that before. Not Casthus's mark—or is it?"

"No," he said, "but I recognise them."

He crossed to the bookshelves in the kitchen, which rested above the area containing his own ingredients supply, and returned with a heavy volume inscribed with demon runes. I'd flicked through a few of his books, but didn't find them particularly entertaining reading. It didn't help that my knowledge of netherworld writing wasn't particularly extensive, thanks to my habit of sleeping through class. I'd always thought being able to talk to the demons was more practical than reading their books—most of them weren't exactly scholarly, anyway.

My gaze skimmed over the symbols on the cover. Despite the number of demons seeming to be infinite, that wasn't true. There were only seven hells, and each demon and archdemon ultimately belonged to one of those hells. Infernal and shadow were only two of them, but they were the closest realms to Earth and the ones I was most familiar with. Even my own magic was likely some variant of the infernal type, judging by its fiery hue, though that might be a result of it being the reflection of angelic power. But I was more concerned with the shadowy marks on the fallen. Each demon house had its own mark, but that's where my knowledge ended.

Nikolas turned the book's page. "Lythocrax's mark isn't in

the book because it's a new one," he explained. "The others have been known amongst warlocks for centuries."

"Yeah, I figured. Are those marks definitely not Casthus's?"

"They aren't, but there are other marks that give one some level of control over others. Obedience, hypnosis…"

"What, the mark equivalent to your psychic ability?" I thought back to my time at the guild. "I vaguely remember there was a bunch of advanced stuff in the books the guild wouldn't let me look at when I was experimenting…" I trailed off, looking more closely at the nearest unconscious fallen. The marks were all the same, but they were all arranged oddly. I tilted my head on the side. They were circles of… several symbols. All the same. "We're looking in the wrong place. Do you have a book of summonings and rituals? Those marks—they kind of look like pentagrams."

Arcane symbols—the type I'd once dealt with on a daily basis—weren't just used to summon, but as a type of magic in their own right.

He looked where I pointed. "Whatever they are, they're not pentagrams."

Something clipped and sharp in his tone made my blood chill. "What is it?" I asked. "Something about Casthus's ownership?"

"Worse," he said grimly. "I know that symbol. It's a portal."

"Portal… oh shit." They were marked as sacrifices. Some portals required blood, and a lot of it. There was a reason bloodstones had been developed, and not initially for vamps —because opening even a regular portal required a surge of energy. I was lucky my celestial power provided that fuel. "Isn't the arch-demon's power infinite, though? He can open portals anywhere he likes, as easily as breathing. That's why he's even here."

"There's a ritual," he said slowly. "It would have a similar effect as a bridge, except it would link all seven hells at once. I suspect that's what he plans. It's not something even an arch-demon can single-handedly achieve."

My mouth went dry, and a flood of adrenaline jolted me to my feet. "Seven hells? All of them? *Why?*"

He rose from the sofa, his wings momentarily shadowing his back. "Who knows? To start a war? To compile resources? To go up against heaven?"

"They can't do things by halves, can they?" I raised my eyes to the ceiling. "Surely he doesn't need all of them, if he decided to trade them to Abyss. Wait—did *she* know?"

"I would suspect not, considering it's her palace that's likely to be the site of the portal. The other necessary ingredient is demonglass."

Of course it bloody well would be.

I swore loudly. "It's the same as last time. There really isn't an original thought in hell. Abyss is pathetic and everyone knows her weakness. She's going to cave in." I could see it now. Another bridge—but worse, and this time with an arch-demon at the helm. "So will the others—or they'll fight one another. Either way, Earth loses."

The one arch-demon who might have helped me was a manipulating dickhead, who wanted the fallen for his own purposes. Unless...

"Wait," I said. "Would taking the fallen into a different nether realm stop the bridge? Assuming Casthus can't get at them?"

Nikolas's head snapped around to face me. "Yes, it would. But it depends which dimension. Most would be hostile."

I shook my head. "I shouldn't. Lythocrax... he wants the fallen himself, but he *knew* this would happen. Does that mean heaven knows, or...?"

His mouth tightened. "I would guess that Lythocrax himself does, certainly."

I looked at my feet, at the plain carpet stained in the residue of my own experiments. "He's driven me into a corner. I can't keep the fallen here indefinitely, and if the ones on Babylon might be used to make a bridge whenever hell feels like it… I need to get them out. Can the marks be removed?"

He exhaled. "Normally, I'd say no. But you… maybe you can."

Despite the direness of the situation, something inside me unknotted at his words. At his faith in me. "Not like I have any other options."

I turned back to the unconscious fallen. I'd drawn the demonic virus out of a bunch of vampires, but my own power was ranked higher than theirs. It wasn't ranked higher than an arch-demon's. But it was worth a try. I reached out a hand to the fallen's chest and touched the nearest circle of symbols, drawing on my demon mark.

The fallen's eyes flew open, and he flung himself against the pentagram's edge, his mouth opening in a strangled scream.

"It's okay," I said hurriedly. "I was just trying to help."

Celestial power didn't remove the symbols, otherwise it already would have when I'd drawn the pentagram. My demon mark hadn't reacted either. *I guess not, then.*

Nikolas strode away and returned with another book in his hand. "This details the ritual. It doesn't go in depth, for obvious reasons."

I took a step back from the fallen. His milky gaze followed me, and the knot in my chest re-tied itself. He wasn't one of the Divinity's disgraced and desperate offspring any longer. He was the shadow demon's pawn, and if Casthus stole him back, the fallen might be the end of the world as we knew it.

"Hey," I said, softly, as the fallen looked at me. "Remember me?"

"I'm supposed to kill you… celestial."

Magic pulsed from his aura, drawing my attention to the dark haze around his body. Rotten. Corrupt. Infected by hell.

I swallowed hard and took the book from Nikolas. I kept one eye on the fallen and his unconscious companion as I skimmed over the page. I understood about half the words. The ritual didn't detail the actual amount or source of the energy required, but I had to assume the fallen were different from humans or even celestials. They were immortal. So the lives of a few dozen immortals were required… I guessed I saw why nobody had ever completed the ritual before. The real question was: why now? To unite hell against heaven? To mess with his rivals? Or to give the middle finger to the Divinities?

"Tonight," whispered the fallen. "It's tonight."

My blood ran cold. "We have to stop him. Can he do the ritual on any realm, not just Babylon? Like Pandemonium?"

"No," Nikolas said. "Not without side effects, anyway. Babylon is the perfect location because it's a dead zone. Setting up a ritual there would damage that world and no others. Pandemonium… it'd cause too much damage, though it wouldn't surprise me if he ultimately intended to use the bridge to claim that world, too."

"And… Earth?"

"Only a nether realm will do."

So the fallen would be safe here, if nothing else. I nodded slowly. "Do you definitely have a safe house? I know this isn't ideal at all, but we're fresh out of options."

"I should tell you your plan is reckless and ridiculous," he said. "But I agree."

"Who are you and what did you do with Nikolas?"

He tilted his head, amusement momentarily lighting his

grim features. "I did say I have temporary accommodation set aside here, under protection. Initially it was in case I needed to move Zadok, but I can house the fallen. Without Casthus close by, they should lose the impulse to attack."

I looked at the stirring fallen on the right, trying to meet his eyes. "Can you remember who I am?" I asked him.

His gaze flickered. "He has had me only a few days. I remember you freed us."

I nodded, tossing caution aside. "Do you remember which Divinity abandoned you?"

"They all did."

"Know the name 'Lythocrax'?"

He shook his head. Slowly. Wait, maybe Lythocrax had been known by a different name when he was a Divinity. Even his true name was probably a new one. Besides, the fallen had likely been abandoned decades ago, if not longer.

"All right," I said, turning back to Nikolas. "If we're going to rob an arch-demon, we need a distraction."

What in hell would distract an arch-demon? Unless Pandemonium's forces retaliated, which I doubted would happen this quickly. If I hadn't been there, that shadow demon might even have assassinated Abyss there and then.

Think, Devi. Zadok was one option, but I doubted he'd consent to being used as bait. Neither would the other warlocks, and there was no way Javos would volunteer any warlocks from *this* realm to help out. Which left... the celestials?

Hang on. "Does this sound crazy?" I asked Nikolas. "I know, it probably does. But the rogue celestials are dead set on waging war against hell with me as their leader. It seems to me that rescuing the children of the Divinities would go a long way towards achieving their goals. Not to mention distract them from taking over the guild."

"Yes, Devi, that does sound crazy," he said. "Aren't they fanatics?"

"Exactly. They'll probably thank me for it. And they're not immortals, so he won't be able to use them in his sacrifice. They think they're serving heaven. Let him think heaven is behind it. That's what they *want* to believe."

He looked at me with his head slightly tilted on one side. "That's… devious."

"Just using my demon side." I winked. "If I get them to help me… then they'll go up against hell like they want to without threatening the warlocks or the celestials on Earth. It's a win-win."

"Unless they turn on you."

"A Grade Four celestial soldier can't outrank an arch-demon," I said. "I know that much. They're expecting an answer from me soon. So I'll give them one. Better still, it'll stop Javos from finding them. For now, at least."

"They're outside the city?"

"They're on the outskirts," I said. "But I took the liberty of leaving some demonglass behind."

He was grinning now. "Of course you did."

I leaned forwards and kissed him. "Be back in a minute."

Once again, I gripped the demonglass in my pocket tightly, visualising the empty street in the run-down part of town. One flash of light later and I landed on my feet outside the celestial rogues' place.

Alarms flared up, pentagrams kicking into action as their defences registered my presence. I raised my eyebrows at the flashing lights and raging flames, knowing them to be illusions, and didn't blink when the rogue celestials swarmed out, surrounding me.

"Have you made your mind up, Devi?" asked Harvey, striding to the front of the group.

"Yes," I said. "I'll join you, on one condition. I need your help with something important. Something for heaven."

Harvey's brow wrinkled. "Heaven?"

"Have you ever heard of the fallen?"

No recognition registered on his face. "Who are these… fallen? Angels?"

"They are the children of the Divinities," I said. "They're currently held captive in hell."

A ripple went through the group. Some celestials exchanged brief glances, but most kept their attention on me.

"The shadow demon has the children of the Divinities in his grasp." I went on. "He intends to use them to unleash hell on Earth—and tear the realms into pieces."

As I'd predicted, outraged shouts exploded from the celestials.

"What is this demon?" demanded Harvey.

"The ruler of the shadow realms," I said. "He's powerful—invincible, even. But the fallen aren't. They can be saved. But I can't do it alone."

They gradually fell silent. Watching me. My nerves spiked. They were, for all their weird powers and blind devotion to their cause, still human. Pawns of heaven, like me. Odds were, I'd be leading them to a brutal and bloody death.

"I want you to think very carefully about your choice," I said. "The fallen are the children of the Divinities. If they die, terrible things will happen. But I'm asking you to risk your own lives if you help me. I'm not going to deny that. You might die horribly. The shadow demon is capable of killing even another arch-demon. He's ruthless and evil, and tonight, he plans to kill every one of the fallen. When they die, all seven hells will unite and make a move against Earth."

I expected questions to fly at me from all directions. Instead, all I got was stunned silence.

"I can show you proof, if you like," I told them. "I

managed to save two of the fallen already, but their souls are bound to the shadow demon. The others will face the same fate, unless I stop them first."

Harvey glanced at his companions, then at me. "We will see this proof, Devi."

I thought so. I gripped the demonglass in my pocket again. "You know my ability, right? I can travel through demon-glass. I'm not sure how many people I can take with me at once, but only one of you will need to see the proof."

Rumbling mutters went through the group. It was almost a relief to see them not blindly jumping on board with my plan, because they'd need a dash of common sense if they came with me to Babylon.

"I will go with her," Harvey told the others.

More mutters followed, along with nods of acquiescence. Harvey stepped forwards to exchange a few whispered words with a couple of the others, then moved back to my side and gave me an expectant look.

"Back in a moment." I grabbed his arm and transported us both onto the landing of Nikolas's house. I'd taken the liberty of throwing demonglass around so I wouldn't transport us into my lab, or anywhere which might give away our actual location. A dark landing with plain wallpaper might belong to anyone, and I thanked the gods for Nikolas's reluctance to actually decorate the place. The fallen's room lay open, drawing Harvey's attention immediately. The two of them were unconscious on pillows we'd laid out on the floor, and Rachel had clothed them to hide the demon marks. But even then, their auras were unmistakeable. Sure enough, a gagging noise came from beside me.

Harvey stared in horror at the fallen. "What—*are* they?"

"See what hell did?" I said to him. "They were the children of the Divinities. Still are. Their lives are at risk from hell, and if we don't save them, they'll all end up the same."

"The… divine." He grabbed my arm convulsively. "I'll do it. Devi."

I nodded, hoping he wouldn't vomit on me. "Then let's go back before your people accuse me of kidnapping you."

"They would never," he insisted. "We believe in our cause, Devi."

They sounded more like they'd been reading fanfic about me on the DivinityWatch forums, but I needed all the allies I could get at this point. The celestials wouldn't hurt the fallen—if anything, they seemed to worship them. Plus they'd be distracted from the guild for a bit. Of course, if the guild suddenly decided to start taking some damned responsibility, then we might have a situation, but if luck held, we'd be back before they even knew.

In a flash, Harvey and I reappeared beside the other rogue celestials.

"She speaks the truth," he said to them, still looking a little pale. "The fallen—hell has taken them. We will not let them take more."

I turned to the others. "Are you absolutely certain you want to go ahead with my plan to rescue the fallen?"

Silent nods.

"If the gods will it," said Harvey. "We will come."

I could work with that.

"So," I said to them, "they're held captive in a castle. Here's what we're going to do…"

18

W e crept out as night was falling. Some of the
warlocks, Nikolas said, were open to working
against the arch-demon behind his back to
keep one another alive and stop him from killing any others.
None had seen Zadok, and a prickle of unease rose within
me when I remembered sensing his presence on Pandemonium—but like the guild, I couldn't afford to think too hard
about him now. I had my plan, and it couldn't fail.

Of course, Rachel said I was bonkers and Fiona wasn't far
behind. Fiona stayed at Nikolas's house to assist with accom-
modating the fallen. Rachel offered to drive, but I put my
foot down and ordered her to keep her demon form thoroughly under wraps during our mission, at least in front of
the celestials. Their hideout was too far for them to walk to
the castle if we crossed over into Babylon there, so I used the
bus I'd once driven a bunch of vampires into hiding with,
and ferried the group of celestials to a place where I'd hidden
some demonglass out of sight of prying eyes.

Then I took the rogues through the demonglass in
groups, supervised by Rachel and Nikolas. The latter stayed

long enough to check they actually had entered Babylon, and had split into groups scattered at strategic distances from the castle. The actual site of the ritual was left in doubt, but I'd bet that missing demonglass was at the centre. After all, it absorbed magic, and he hadn't just destroyed Zadok's tower out of vindictiveness. He needed it for his own purposes.

Using my ability to find the demonglass would land me right at Casthus's mercy, so I'd need to be sneakier to get ahead of him before he started the ritual. Once the celestials were distributed throughout the castle's surroundings, I transported myself back to the upper corridor with the pillars.

So far, so good. The castle was quiet, but a faint aura of dread pulsed through the place, drawing my celestial mark to attention. I hoped Casthus couldn't sense me in the same way, but if he could, the other celestials' presence would doubtless distract him. I ran to the window and peered outside. My mark ought to zero in on the demonglass, but realistically, it wouldn't be inside the castle. He wouldn't want to open the path in the middle of his own home. He'd have put it outside somewhere.

Sure enough, I looked out the window and spotted a faint glimmering on the ground below. It looked too dim to be demonglass, but nothing else shone like that. I squinted closer. *Oh Divinities. That's not good.*

Shadowy magic pulsed through the demonglass, and a line of fallen stood before it as though waiting for orders. There was no sign of Casthus, but his presence lay heavily over them. Maybe he was keeping a safe distance... or maybe he'd sensed the intruders.

It's now or never.

I used the glass to transport myself to the plains, where Nikolas waited with a group of celestials. Some were visibly shivering. This realm was much colder than they'd be used to, considering it was July back home.

"Do it," I told him. "Signals. Now."

Harvey raised his hand, which blazed with celestial light. In one bound, Nikolas took to the sky, wings spread wide. He seemed confident he could keep himself hidden, so I had to trust him.

I transported myself to the corridor directly above the fallen again. Then I opened my palm, scattering a little demonglass directly out of the window.

I'd shaved the glass down to powder so fine, it looked like mist. This part required more trial and error than I'd like, but no reaction came from below, so I assumed the arch-demon hadn't sensed or spotted me. I held my breath, scattering more demonglass, ready to leap in as soon as the signal went off.

A series of celestial lights flared up like beacons in the gloom. Even at a distance, there was no other source of light on this realm save for the moon. Blazing lights ignited the sky, and in the distance, the celestials grew closer, their lights combining to appear as though a formidable army advanced on the castle.

Shouts and roars exploded through the silence as the nearby wild demons reacted to the celestials' presence—and the arch-demon moved in the castle below. I *felt* him, his aura shifting in the direction of the noise.

Now was my shot.

I leapt through the demonglass, materialising directly behind the fallen through the powdered glass I'd scattered, and burned five pentagram points into the ground. The first three fallen disappeared into my hastily-created portal instantly. I grabbed two more, moving as fast as my celestial power would carry me. *That's half your army gone, Casthus.*

The ruckus from in front of the castle continued. I'd ordered several of the celestials to stage a fight with the warlocks, others to provoke wild demons into attacking, and yet more to create a light display to distract and dazzle anyone who went in front of the castle. Meanwhile, one at a time, the fallen disappeared to safety. Two more down. One—

A large winged shadow descended overhead. Crap.

I tackled the nearest fallen as shadows stabbed down, narrowly missing my body. We fell into a heap, and another fallen kicked me viciously from behind, his clawed foot tearing open a jagged wound on my leg. *Ow. Not good. He gave the orders to kill.*

My leg twinged as the regenerative power I'd borrowed from Nikolas kicked in. Light blazed from my hands, no longer withheld, and I drew on the shadow demon's own power. *Let's destroy that demonglass before he can use it.*

Shadows flickered through my hands, and smashed into the dark lightning that struck inches from my feet. Pieces of shattered demonglass flew into the air, and my hair stood on end with static.

"YOU CANNOT STEAL FROM ME, DEVI."

"I already did." So much for the distraction. I should have guessed he'd be smarter than that. Two fallen remained, one of them staring blankly at me with my blood dripping from his clawed hand. "You don't need the fallen. I claim them. They're mine."

My demon mark glowed. So did the demonglass at my feet.

"SO IT IS YOU." Despite his echoing voice, I still couldn't actually see him, but every nerve ending in my body told me he was close. Watching me.

"What?" I said. "What does that mean?"

The arch-demon appeared, etched against the full moon,

his eyes such pitch black pits that I could hardly look into them.

"Didn't catch a word of that." Another inch, and I'd be able to get the last fallen out—if I conjured the fastest pentagram ever.

The demon's shadows lashed at my celestial hand, and I dragged the power into me. As he raised a hand to retaliate, I unleashed every ounce of power I'd taken from him.

Right at the demonglass.

The glass shattered in an explosion of noise. The arch-demon roared in anger, the Earth shaking with the force of his rage, and I yanked my left hand free of his magic.

Lights shot from my hand, piercing the Earth around the fallen. "Checkmate," I said, the lights flaring up, and the last of the fallen vanishing into its midst. "You lose."

I held my breath as the arch-demon descended, his wings spread wide. "Then take the fallen, and let you all be damned together."

His mocking laughter rang in my ears as the lights flared around the pentagram one last time, carrying me back to Earth.

A moment later, I stood in Nikolas's very crowded living room, other fallen sprawled on the floor all around me. "Holy shit," I breathed. "That was too close."

And too easy. Sure, I'd made mincemeat of his plan, but I'd expected retaliation at the very least. Maybe it was the celestials' presence—or maybe the bridge wasn't all that important to him after all.

I should feel the thrill of victory, but the blank expressions on the fallen's faces, and their odd silence, made me uneasy. None spoke. None attacked, either. But the symbols remained the same as ever.

This isn't over.

I shoved the thought out of mind. Time to go and rescue

the rogue celestials. They'd probably had enough of fighting Babylon's monsters.

———

It was midnight by the time we all returned home, having moved the fallen to the guest room upstairs and transported the celestials back to their own hideout. I was practically swaying with exhaustion, and even our small victory couldn't raise my spirits.

"He caved too easily," I muttered to Nikolas, as we reappeared in the living room for what was hopefully the final time. "That, or I've developed some new power even I don't know about."

"Possibly." He leaned over and stroked my demon mark, and I sighed as his magic restored my strength.

"You should stop doing that," I said shakily. "You're draining your own power."

"Being with you only makes me stronger, Devi. What you did tonight—I don't think I've ever seen Casthus bow down to anyone else's word."

"You stood up to him before. It's not like I'm a revolutionary. Also, I think I accidentally became the leader of a cult of absolute lunatics. I'll have to deal with the consequences of *that* soon." I looked around the dark living room, at the lab in the corner, the stains on the floor from my experiments. Nikolas's house had become mine, and I'd moulded myself to the space so thoroughly that I hardly recalled it ever being otherwise.

"I couldn't be more proud of you."

I poked him in the chest. "You're absurd. Whatever happened to the guy who told me to leave the celestials behind and implied that I was a fool for believing a word they say?"

"I was mistaken. The demons aren't better. The celestials aren't either. This war has never been black and white, and I was naïve to believe it would never reach my own doorstep."

I blinked. Wow. Nikolas wasn't generally the type to bare his soul, and most of the time, neither was I. This vulnerability was new. It warmed my heart that he trusted me so much.

"If you were naive, then what does that make me?" I teased. "I'm going to bed before I pass out on the floor."

"I could carry you."

"If you could fly upstairs, I'd be tempted to take you up on that offer, but I think I'll walk."

My legs felt like lead weights, and when I reached his room, I collapsed onto the bed with relief. He sat down alongside me. At first his brimstone scent had been unusual to me. Now it felt familiar. Comforting.

He wrapped his arms around my back. "You don't know what you've done to me." His voice was a low, throaty growl. "Devi..."

"Huh?" I looked up at him.

"My name is Caul. My true name."

"I..." I stared at him, lost for words. "Aren't you worried I'll use it against you?"

"You already have everything I could possibly offer you."

His gaze was simmering gold. I kissed him slowly, then faster, our passion rapid and heated and necessary. He returned my kisses with equal fervour, his hands roaming over my skin, tracing familiar paths to pleasure—and eventually, rapture. I was bared to him, I wanted him, and my fire burned all the brighter for each touch.

He slid inside me, slowly enough for me to feel him fill me, inch by inch. We moved against one another, fire and darkness, celestial and demon. We knew each other inside and out, and we were one.

19

"Rise and shine," said Rachel, rapping on the bedroom door. "I've got a present for you."

I yawned, half awake. "Give me a minute."

"I'll be waiting downstairs," she said, in a singsong voice.

I blinked sleep from my eyes. That the demons hadn't attacked Earth overnight was a good enough present for me. I went looking for some clothes, while Nikolas remained lying on the bed with his eyes half open.

"I know you're awake," I told him. "And checking me out."

"Just admiring the view." He grinned lazily at me. "It's not every day that I get to wake up next to a woman who defied my arch-demon father and escaped his realm unscathed."

I grabbed my clothes. "You don't think it was too easy? That we'll look away and find he's sacrificed a bunch of nuns to the ritual instead?"

"I highly doubt it. You destroyed his demonglass, remember?"

"Demons do not give in easily." I kicked the bathroom door open. "This is my life now. I'll have to rewrite my schedule to include ruling over the fallen *and* a group of

203

rogue celestials. If anything, I think *they* gave in too easily, too, but they really believed I was acting on the orders of heaven."

The crucial question this time: which part of heaven?

I showered and dressed quickly, and made my way downstairs to find Rachel while Nikolas was in the shower.

"Surprise," said Rachel, handing me a brand new mobile phone. "Courtesy of Javos."

I took it from her. "What's this, a peace offering? Or compensation for Nikolas not strangling him?"

"Probably both," she admitted.

"Worth a try." I switched it on, finding someone had already put all my contacts into it. "Who's been snooping on my contacts? Javos?"

"Fiona," said Rachel. "You gave her the emergency numbers, remember?"

"*Oh.* Of course." Relief flooded me. I hadn't lost Clover's number after all. Whether she'd actually be able to help at all remained to be seen. *I rescued a group of fallen who aren't exactly acclimatised to living with humans* was a hell of a bombshell to drop on someone, even a former angel. Along with *I have a bunch of deranged worshippers,* I was well on my way to starting a guild of my own.

I threw some bread into the toaster. "I owe you one, Rachel."

"Think of it as a thank you for staving off the apocalypse."

"I can count on one hand the number of people who've thanked me for it, so I'm not complaining there. Where's Fiona?"

"Job hunting," said Rachel. "She went back to her own flat. Something about not being paid enough for this crap."

"She's not wrong," I said. "And now I get to spend today taking the fallen to their new home. They stayed where they were overnight, at least."

"Yep. I expect double pay for watching them," Rachel said.

"I can handle that," Nikolas said, entering the room.

"Technically, I'm their boss," I said. "I need to get those shadow marks off them. If it's possible. And what if Casthus decides to take them back?"

"He won't," he said. "If the fallen were really essential to his plans, he'd have claimed them long ago. But he also respects the rules. You bested him and took them from under his nose. He knows not to underestimate you now."

"I don't get demon logic," I muttered. "Are you sure he hasn't booby trapped those marks?"

"It's not possible," Nikolas said. "They're ritual marks. And I'd have sensed if any of his magic followed you here."

Good. Once I got the fallen out of here, I'd go through Nikolas's entire collection of demon tomes until I found out how to remove them.

"So the ritual... it doesn't specifically say 'fallen'." I retrieved my toast and set about buttering it. "He could use something else." Or some*one* else.

"Not on Babylon. You destroyed his demonglass source."

I shook my head. "He's plotting something else, I'm sure. His servant was skulking around Pandemonium. There's an awful lot of lives *there* he could use as sacrifices."

"No," he said. "The ritual specifically needs so-called pure souls. Not demons. The reason very little is known about it is because most celestials died off in the demon realms."

"There aren't enough of them left to sacrifice." I nodded. "Are you absolutely certain that he can't snatch the fallen?"

"He *could,* but he won't come here in person, and there are very few demons who can break the protections I put on the fallen's accommodation. It doesn't hurt that he lost one of his best servants yesterday."

"I'm more concerned with where his fiery friend went, to be honest. I didn't see him on Pandemonium."

Unease trickled through me. *Pandemonium isn't your responsibility. You stopped the ritual.* But Abyss remained a target, and her war strategy didn't sound like it allowed for brutally aggressive shadow demons. Unless she'd aligned with Zadok, but the two had been bitter enemies, and whatever Zadok was doing on that realm, he stood no chance against his father, either. Which left it up to me to keep the fallen out of his hands.

On top of stopping a killer. Thwarting hell wasn't enough. I needed to figure out heaven, too, and whatever monstrosity they had roaming around Purgatory. Oh, and the rogue celestials probably expected me to give them a definite answer today. They'd helped me: I owed them.

I looked at the contacts on my new phone. "How am I supposed to break it to the guild that I accidentally signed up to run a band of outcasts?"

"Good question," said Rachel. "Don't tell them."

"Because *that's* always worked out well." I turned to Nikolas. "You still haven't said it was a bad idea me promising to help them."

"No, it wasn't," he said. "I seem to remember endorsing it enthusiastically."

"You have a warped memory, Nikolas. The inspector is going to flip a lid." I took a bite of toast. I'd already *told* the inspector that there was a band of outcasts. He'd just chosen not to pursue my information. And what the hell, maybe one of them was the killer, but the way they'd accepted my orders last night made me more and more certain that if the orders came from anywhere at all, they came from heaven.

Time to face the music. I'd put off the call for long enough, helping to reset the wards on the fallen's room and retrieving the demonglass I'd scattered all over the landing when I'd brought the celestials here.

While Nikolas skimmed through yet another book on demonic rituals, I dialled the guild's number.

The phone rang, over and over. Then someone picked up. "Hey," I said. "It's Devi. Is the inspector in?"

"No—Devi." The voice sounded young. A novice. "He's missing."

My heart sank. "Missing how? Did he run off?"

"No, he... I don't know. There are rumours, and only the senior staff know the truth. Something about... about the heavens."

Oh shit. He'd *said* he couldn't get into Purgatory... that nobody could. "Can you put Mrs Barrow on the line, please? Tell her I have important information for her."

A long minute passed. Then: "Devi Lawson," said Mrs Barrow. "You'd better have a good explanation."

"Er... you're going to have to be a bit more specific. What am I supposed to have done now?"

"Purgatory," she hissed into the phone. "The inspector insisted on going there himself, after speaking with you. And he hasn't come back."

Oh no. Not that he was any real loss, but it sounded like the guild had started to pick up on the rumours all the same. And if that Devi clone came through—

"I tried to warn him," I said. "There's some kind of creature over in Purgatory claiming to be a creation of heaven, and I think it's murdering warlocks. It's like nothing I've ever seen before. I don't know why Purgatory let him in this time, but it can't be good."

Her voice buzzed with static. "Why did *you* go to Purgatory."

"To talk to the angels. They didn't want to speak. That

creature—it nearly killed me. The inspector shouldn't have gone there alone. I thought he was locked out."

"For your information, none of us have been able to follow him, so whatever tactics you're using to get into Purgatory, it would be extremely helpful if you shared them with us."

"There's nothing to share," I said. "I got in the usual way. And seriously, that thing nearly killed me and I'm Grade Four."

But it nearly killed me because I'm part demon.

And the inspector? The thing that had replaced him was gone. His soul was as squeaky clean as ever, despite his dickish personality. But then—why had whoever was running Purgatory these days let him in? To recruit him?

"The novices are panicking, and frankly, this isn't a level of disruption we're prepared to deal with—"

"So you thought you'd dump it on me? Get in line," I snapped. "I have no idea how to kill that creature. Whatever in all the seven hells the inspector is doing there, he's probably dead. And may I reiterate: there is an assassin who looks like me walking around Purgatory, a creation of heaven's, who wants us all dead."

I hung up the phone, anger blazing through my chest. My fist clenched, and it took everything I had not to hurl the new phone at the wall.

"Devi?" said Rachel. "What is it?"

"Our genius of an inspector has gone and got himself stranded on Purgatory." I slipped my phone into my pocket. "That's one rescue mission I'm not taking part in. Where's Nikolas?"

Footsteps on the stairs answered my question, and he ran into the room. "Two of the fallen have disappeared."

My heart sank. "What? They broke out? We just redid the wards, not an hour ago."

"The pentagrams weren't broken," he said.

I followed him upstairs. *What now? We'd know if someone broke in.* The wards would have reacted. Right?

The door to the fallen's guest room lay open. Though all signs of Zadok's presence had been removed, there were still faint burn marks on the walls, the residue of brimstone. The fallen sat on an assortment of cushions—it hadn't been worth procuring sleeping bags when they were supposed to be moved today anyway—and when I did a head count, there were indeed two missing.

"Someone broke in solely to take two fallen, and leave the others behind?" I stepped forwards into the room, confusion momentarily overshadowing my anger. "Er, did anyone else come into the room last night?" I asked the nearest fallen.

"Only you, Devi."

Dread flooded me. "Oh, no."

"What is it?" Nikolas asked.

I pressed a hand to my forehead. "I'm an idiot. There's a freaking clone of me walking around this realm murdering warlocks. And she's *celestial.* A creation of heaven's. She won't have tripped the wards."

His body went very still. "Are you sure? Why not confront us?"

"Someone is messing with me." I turned to the fallen. "Did you see someone who looked like me in here? Last night?"

A few nods. That settled that, then. "Great. Looks like I'm going after the inspector after all."

"Devi," Nikolas said. "Not that I'm doubting your ability, but she nearly killed you before. Is there a way she can be destroyed?"

"There must be." I swore under my breath. How did you kill heaven's own creation? If she was my equal, without the demon magic, then taking her by surprise sounded like the only option, but she'd be expecting me. More to the point, she had free run of *this* realm. But why not confront me directly, considering how she'd overpowered me before?

There must be a reason, and I could think of only one likely explanation.

"She's not acting of her own free will," I said. "She's being given orders. She's a puppet."

Of heaven? Or who?

I think I know who.

A whisper of breath on the back of my neck drew my demon mark to attention, and I felt Nikolas's magic snap into life.

"I was created in your image, Devi." Cold hands closed around my throat. "And now it's time for you to die —permanently."

I choked, feeling her celestial magic blaze a trail down my neck. I slammed my elbow backwards into her gut and spun around, striking her in the jaw with my celestial hand.

The Devi clone didn't move, blood trickling from her mouth. She bled gold. Creepy.

"You can't come here of your own free will," I said. "Someone is giving you orders."

"You should have claimed your power, Devi," said the Devi-creature. "Now it's mine."

"Bullshit." She wasn't as strong on Earth as she was on Purgatory—but this was not the place for a confrontation. Especially with the fallen right behind me.

"This house is in a pentagram, Devi. He's already here."

Lights flared up, visible even through the walls as my Grade Four senses picked up on anything close by. She'd trapped us in a portal.

Nikolas stood frozen. "Devi," he said, through gritted teeth. "This is an anti-demon portal."

She'd bound him. "Shit. I'll shut it down—"

The Devi clone slammed into me, propelling both of us

through the door to the fallen's room. Then she pressed her palm to the floor.

"Don't you dare—"

The room disappeared in a flash of raging fire, and Lythocrax's wasteland rose to surround us.

The Devi clone faced me. "So much potential, Devi. Did you ever question why you have such a deft hand with demonic sources and creations?"

"Because I'm secretly a demon, obviously."

She gave me a cold stare. "The warlock won't be able to dismantle that pentagram alone. He's trapped. None of your friends are coming to save you."

Rage filled me. She'd stolen my ideas. Stolen my *magic.* No wonder it'd looked like my magic on the victims. Her creator had engineered it that way deliberately. His magic—the same magic that had revived me from death—enabled him to create new beings entirely.

"You're his," I said. "You're Lythocrax's creation."

"Right you are." His eyes looked out from hers. They were one and the same. "You know and understand so little of your own magic, Devi."

He appeared behind her, ashy wings beating as his feet touched down on the ground.

I gave him the middle finger. "Don't you dare."

The fallen remained lying where they'd been in the guest room, before the pentagram had carried them through. The marks on their bodies flickered and warped before my eyes. They were his now, too.

Lythocrax moved towards them. "I wish you had offered the fallen to me of your own free will, Devi."

"Does it make a difference? You don't get to steal my army out from underneath me. I claimed them."

"With your true name?"

Damn him. "With Earth. They're mine. The shadow demon respected that."

"I expected more of him. I expected more of you."

"I took your name, Lythocrax. Don't think I won't use it."

"My name merely protects you from me, Devi. Not your former allies."

I glared at him. "You're talking crap, Lythocrax. If you wanted the fallen so badly, why not go into Babylon and claim them yourself?"

"Because it's forbidden for an arch-demon to cross into another's property without permission."

"You have got to be kidding me." I narrowed my eyes. "That's not all, is it? You can't cross to other demon realms, either. Someone locked you out. You're stuck here alone."

His wings beat as his feet left the Earth once more, and the ground rippled with his magic. "Your realm is directly within access to me now—through her. I can kill those you care about. The girl. Those warlocks you love so dearly."

"Empty threats, now?" Like it or not, though, he had the upper hand. His name was the only weapon I held against him. Thanks to his creature, he *did* have access to my realm… but for all his talk, he hadn't used it yet. Not directly. "You're such a demon. Why did the Divinities send you down here?"

His voice echoed through her mouth. "Who said anything about the Divinities?"

"I know you're here as a spy for heaven, Altheare," I said. "Aren't you?"

"You are correct, Devi," he said, the merest trace of a smirk on his mouth. "The fool angels knew nothing of it. Purgatory is mine. And the heavens will bow to me."

I froze. He'd killed Purgatory's angels? "You killed—"

"Of course I killed them," he said. "They gave you my name."

I could only stare at him in horror.

"There is a spark inside you," he said. "You will bow to me, or you will die."

"Fuck off, Altheare."

I felt his power flickering at the edge of my demon mark, pulled at it, but nothing happened. His was the one demon's power I couldn't take. Because part of it was already mine.

"I allowed you to live because I naively believed you would stay out of my way when you had what you wanted." He spoke through her mouth, though her body was freakishly still.

"Not if you didn't leave Earth alone. I thought you knew that. Earth is mine, and as long as I have breath in my lungs, I will die defending it."

"Then die."

The Devi clone exploded into life again. I blocked her strike, summoning my blade. It gleamed, light on one side, dark on the other. Hers blazed brighter. He'd deliberately given her more of his power than he'd given to me.

The clone's magic licked at my demon mark again.

"Don't you dare."

I flung the blade, spearing her through the chest. She staggered backwards—and the fallen swarmed her. Surrounding her.

Lythocrax watched them with eyes like knife blades. "You don't want to do that."

"I didn't give them orders, Altheare," I said. "They choose to obey me because I'm not a manipulative piece of crap. Who the hell are you really working for? Who gave you the orders to mark me? It doesn't take a genius to figure out that you didn't choose to do it yourself."

His wings beat, once, twice, and he didn't descend to the Earth to save his pawn from the fallen. "No, I certainly wouldn't have. You were tested, and you won. That's the only reason you came into your powers."

"Tested? You mean, when that portal... the first time I came here." Memories beat at the doors, of that awful day in the cave, with Rory—

It was a setup. All of it.

My body went rigid, all thought of attacking swamped beneath the cold horror of realisation. "It was you," I said quietly. "You sent us on that mission, didn't you? You left your demon here for me to kill, so... so I'd become this. Celestial and demon. That's why. Isn't it?"

"Yes, Devi, and you succeeded admirably. If only you had been as obedient as you were resourceful."

An icy sensation spread through my chest. I'd been the only survivor of that mission. "Why me? I'm pretty sure I'm not the only celestial who's ever called on the Divinities by name."

When I'd gone through that portal, I'd upgraded. I'd then upgraded again when Themedes had summoned me and my mark had properly manifested. It wasn't exactly the same as celestial grading, but close enough.

Close enough for me to know with certainty that someone working for heaven had sent Rory and me on that mission on purpose.

We'd been sent looking for demon eggs and found a portal into hell instead. But... the demon eggs had been laced with saphor demon poison. Rory had been doomed the moment he'd touched them.

Someone planted them there deliberately.

Someone working for heaven had killed my best friend.

"Who?" I said. "You can't get to Earth in person. The Divinities can't. They had a *human* plant those demon eggs there so Rory and I would stumble across them. Did they intend for both of us to die?"

"It was merely a test."

My voice sounded distant, my body locked to the spot. "It

was a fucking stupid test. Either or both of us might have picked them up."

His tone was unconcerned. "It wouldn't have mattered. Both of you bore the mark. You were the one who chose to come into my realm."

"You could have saved him. You could have, if you marked both of us."

"There could only be one champion of heaven, Devi. Your friend failed the test. One had to die so that the other could live… such are the rules of divine magic. It was nothing personal, Devi."

"You killed Rory." My voice deepened, almost inhuman. Lightning crackled over my right palm as all the power I kept hidden there burned to the surface. The arch-demon's remaining power, strong enough to shake the surface of the world.

"Tell me who it was who planted those demon eggs," I snarled. "Tell me, Altheare."

The air splintered. Screams came from the fallen as the ground cracked.

I'm not causing that.

Someone was opening a portal.

2O

The air continued to tremble as deep cracks splintered through the Earth. Demon magic or none, I was still human, still breakable. I grabbed the nearest solid object—a rock—and held on, as five lights appeared, piercing the ground. The fallen let go of the Devi clone and fled with startled cries, and between the points of the portal, a city appeared, slanted at an angle where the portal had torn into this realm.

Pandemonium.

Oh shit. Casthus must have claimed it.

A winged being flew through the air above the portal, colliding with Lythocrax at speed. The two crashed to Earth in a tangle of wings, causing the ground to tremble once again. I threw my arms over my head to protect myself from the onslaught of debris, and my back hit the Earth, rocks bruising my spine. The fallen continued to flee from the blazing portal and the chunk of city visible through the gap in the wasteland—and from the two winged beings grappling with each other, shaking the world with every punch.

I peered from between my fingers at the warring demons.

Abyss was trying to kill Lythocrax. Not Casthus. *What in the seven hells is going on?*

I turned back to the portal—and stared at Pandemonium's palace, ignoring the dirt stinging my eyes. A towering structure had replaced the palace—a single tower, spearing the sky and glowing golden as its demonglass surface reflected the setting sun. No wonder Abyss had ripped open a portal to the nearest demon realm. Someone had kicked her out of her own palace.

Abyss tore at Lythocrax with a battle cry. I'd never seen her in her fighting mode before. She was three times the size as before, with raven-black wings extending from her shoulder blades and talons like knives. Lacerations on her skin wept blood onto the Earth, but she'd dealt a few blows to Lythocrax, too. One of his ashy wings hung at a crooked angle. The fallen had hidden behind nearby rocks, but there wasn't anywhere to run out here.

"Hey!" I shouted at the arch-demons. "Stop that."

If Lythocrax killed her, that was it for Pandemonium— and by extension, Earth. If she killed *him*—no. The bastard was mine.

I summoned my blade. "Altheare," I said.

The wold went still. Abyss spat out blood. Arch-demons didn't die easily. Not unless you uncovered their weakness. Even knowing their name wasn't enough, only to insulate you against harm. Her body was broken and beaten, but she'd survive.

If she used his name.

Her head briefly tilted in my direction, registering the weapon I'd handed to her.

She looked directly at him. "Altheare."

He roared in fury, the sky shaking with the force of his rage. The portal trembled, too, the city quivering. Only the tower stood still, undamaged.

"Altheare," she said, in a ringing voice. "You forget yourself. You forget the purpose of this war. And if you continue acting as a puppet of the heavens, you will die."

"You will meet an end of your own," Lythocrax spat. His eyes were incandescent with rage and fear. He knew what she could do with that name: spread it to every demon on any realm. And he was powerless to stop her. "Kill—"

"Don't you even think about it, Altheare," I shouted at him. "You took everything away from me. You won't take Earth, too. Tell whoever is giving you orders in heaven that I'm not going to submit."

His eyes flared, his hands glowing with demonic power. "I could kill everyone in that city."

"I won't allow you try," responded Abyss.

Magic exploded from Lythocrax's hands, and a group of venos demons sprang to life, tail stingers swinging, dripping venom. He hadn't summoned them—he'd created them from the dust of this realm. I threw celestial fire at the demons—and Lythocrax took to the air.

"No!" I shouted. "Get *back* here, you murdering bastard."

Too late. He might be bleeding, but he was faster in the air than on the ground. In a single beat of those wings, he was gone. Even my celestial speed would never catch him up on the ground.

At my side, Abyss crawled to her feet, her gaze on the portal. "You have changed the tide of this war, human."

"Don't flatter yourself into thinking I wanted to help you in any way, Abyss. I want to kill him myself."

She spat out blood. "I owe you, celestial."

"No, you don't," I said coldly. "If you think I'm letting you anywhere near Earth *or* my allies, forget it. How did you break into this realm? It's never been linked with the other demon realms before."

She coughed up more blood, back in her human-like

guise again. "I knew from when I first visited him… when he tricked me into an alliance."

She's dying. He'd pushed her past her limits, and she wasn't regenerating. But it was no wonder Lythocrax had fled. If he'd fallen recently, and his demon name wasn't the name he'd worn as a Divinity, nobody would have known it. Themedes had once summoned Casthus by saying his name and accidentally summoned Nikolas instead. So clearly, a lot of arch-demons did know one another's names. Maybe even their weaknesses. Perhaps that's why they rarely succeeded in killing one another. They were at an eternal stalemate.

"Why fight him?" I asked. "I thought you were allies, once."

She dragged her gaze from the portal and regarded me haughtily despite the pain she must be in. "Why else? He planned to turn against me, and I against him. This is what we do, Devi."

"I have no idea what you're…" I trailed off, the light of the tower through the portal catching my gaze. A very familiar tower—and not at all like the shadow demon's newly redecorated castle. "Did… did *Zadok* take your tower?"

"He did." Blood trickled down her neck. "He knows my weakness."

Oh no. I'd given it to him—handed it over, thinking he already knew. And I'd underestimated the depths to which Zadok would go for revenge on Casthus. And Abyss, considering she'd been the first to drive him out of his own tower. It was almost admirable, even.

"Zadok rules Pandemonium, then?" I asked.

"Not for long." She spat out more blood. Was something wrong with her regenerative power? No—the sunlight must have slowed her down. And she made no move to find shade, because there wasn't any. Not even on her own realm. "Lythocrax will be back."

"No shit. I'm counting on it, so I can finish him off this time."

"You won't beat the betrayer, Devi Lawson."

I blinked. "Betrayer? Of whom, exactly?" *Me, for a start.* But she didn't know that. He wouldn't have told her.

"This realm was once part of heaven," croaked Abyss. "The heavens are splitting. Even after all these years, I still remember. He did it… he caused it."

I stared at her. "What? Haven't you been at war with the heavens for centuries, if not thousands of years?"

Obviously, the arch-demons had once known him in his angelic form as well. And apparently heaven and hell hadn't been separated as long as we'd thought.

"This is not a conversation I want to have with you, human. You're nothing more than a piece of dust."

"Aren't you a great flatterer." I took a step towards the portal. "Aren't you going to close that?"

She staggered forwards a step, her wings still weeping blood. "It'll burn itself out."

"What's Zadok even doing over there?" I stepped closer to the lights, staring up at the tower. It was a literal mirror image of his old home on Babylon. "Letting you run away? I'd have thought he'd want to finish you off, too."

"He did," she said matter-of-factly. "I'm not long for this… world." She sank back down to the Earth.

"You're dying, aren't you?"

She crawled to her knees. "I was dying the moment he cast me out of my own realm."

More like the moment you tried to steal Babylon from Nikolas. And I'd given her Pandemonium, only for her to lose that world to someone she'd deceived.

If she died now, Lythocrax's true name wouldn't spread amongst the demons the way he'd thought it would. Unless *I* told them, but that wouldn't end the war.

"I'll finish Lythocrax off," I said to Abyss, taking my eyes off the portal and looking into hers. Ancient pits of darkness stared back with the weight of centuries. She was old, and tired, and broken. "I swear I will. But I'm going to need help. I can't hurt him with magic, because he's the one who marked me."

"Then take what I have left."

Her magic slammed into my demon mark, filling my body with a fiery light.

21

I blinked awake, confused as to why I lay on a bed, and not a wasteland covered in debris, demon venom and corpses. And the fallen—

"Don't move," said Rachel. "You're in a frightful state, according to Nikolas."

I coughed, blinking around at Nikolas's bedroom. "Why am I here?"

The last thing I remembered was my body shaking with Abyss's power as it filled my demon mark to capacity, and falling onto the demonglass shards besides the glittering portal. My magic must have brought me home. Considering I'd been halfway to losing consciousness, it was damned lucky that I'd ended up on Earth at all.

She looked at me oddly. "What do you think happened? There's been a few demon attacks, but nothing Earth-shattering. Literally."

I rubbed my eyes, relieved to find my hands in working order. "For a start, Nikolas was held captive in a portal around this *house* the last time I checked. And so were you. The fallen… they're gone." They hadn't come with me.

Lythocrax had them now.

Rachel bowed her head. "Yeah, that thing was nasty. Luckily, Fiona's human enough not to have been affected, so I called her, and she got Niko and I out of the demon trap and we took it to pieces. But the portal you went through was gone by then. Niko's been losing his mind—he blamed the guild, for a start. And Javos. He said that an evil thing that looked like you was responsible."

"Shit. I didn't even see where that monster disappeared to. Last I saw, the fallen were attacking her, but Abyss broke through a portal from Pandemonium and interrupted."

Her eyes widened. "She did?"

I took in a deep breath. "She's not the important part. Lythocrax is behind the warlock murders. He's sent this clone who looks like me to cause havoc, but he flew away when Abyss came through. He killed her."

She swore in the demon tongue. "Damn. Really?"

"She gave me a present, though." I twitched my demon marked hand.

"You can use her power?"

"Yep. I can… wow. I can turn into anybody at all."

She raised an eyebrow. "So can I, and I can't think of a way out of this shit show."

"It's more than transformation magic," I said, recalling the false inspector. "I can *become* them—even absorb their memories and mannerisms. Might be helpful. But I only have her magic temporarily, and she was dying when she gave it to me. Don't get any ideas. Aren't you a little worried about how every one of us massively underestimated Zadok? He killed Abyss and drove her out of her own palace without even bringing an army."

Her brow wrinkled. "Wait, *he's* in Pandemonium? I thought you were implying Casthus did it."

"Where's Nikolas? He'd know."

"He's with Javos. There's been a… situation."

Ah. "You're borrowing Nikolas's understatements again."

"Niko decided now was the perfect time to inform Javos that he intends to depose him as leader of the warlocks."

I half sat up. "Seriously? He picks right this minute, while all hell is breaking loose?"

"I don't think it was planned. He was incredibly pissed off at your disappearance and near-death. I think you're driving him out of his mind."

"I don't know, maybe it's the fact that his brother just staged a massive coup and took over a city meant for an arch-demon, too?"

"I didn't think he knew," she said. "I certainly didn't. Seven hells. You can tell him. I've had enough of my family attacking one another as it is." Her tone edged into uncharacteristic prickliness. I didn't blame her. She'd had to ditch Javos, and her monstrous adoptive brother had taken over her former home.

I sat up properly, swinging my legs over the bed's side. "Sorry, Rachel."

She shrugged one shoulder with an attempt at her usual casual attitude. "It's not your fault. The only one of the culprits you have any control over is Niko, and he must have known you'd be fine. But you should probably go and tell him you're alive."

"I'm in his house," I pointed out. "Is Fiona okay?"

"Yeah, I sent her home in case this place was attacked again. She's fine. Do you feel up to walking?"

"Now you mention it… yes." The aches of the battle hadn't faded, but if anything, I felt energised. Because Abyss had given me her magic. She'd chosen to give me her power. To kill Lythocrax.

And I'll kill that Devi clone along with him.

I got to my feet, and drank from the glass of water

someone had left on the bedside table. "Nikolas is at Javos's place?"

"Yep. He's been there a good ten minutes. I can't get through to his phone, so I left a message saying you came back here."

"Good. Javos isn't going to be happy I let the killer slip through my fingers again."

"And now he's losing his title," said Rachel. "It's pretty clear Niko wants him out of here. I'm not blaming you—it's his own damn fault for forgetting he was dealing with a human. But I think Niko would have reacted the same if you were a warlock, too."

"Yes, I know you all resolve your problems by punching one another," I said. "If Javos was a human, he'd be jailed for nearly strangling me, so he's getting off easy. Lucky for him, I'm more pissed off with Lythocrax."

More like raging mad. Like a sleeping beast inside me, my rage coiled up, waiting to strike and unleash its wrath on the monster who'd wrecked my life. But not yet.

Soon.

Rachel squinted at me. "You look... different."

"I just took in another arch-demon's power," I said evasively. "I'll be fine once I figure out how to use it. Hmm. So I can take any person and *become* them..." Even arch-demons? Maybe.

"Niko said she used to conquer worlds by replacing important diplomats and having them assassinate one another or otherwise bring down their overlords."

"She did have a battle form, but she wasn't that strong," I said. "I assume she didn't actually kill any arch-demons."

"No, just stole from them. Armies, worlds... most wouldn't miss her. But I never expected *Zadok* to replace her. He's always been the weak link."

"I think he played on that," I said. "The real question is—

did he do anything while he was *here?* We thought he was a prisoner. He hid his recovery well."

But if he'd meddled here, surely one of us would have found out. On the other hand, I hadn't believed him capable of conquering an entire city either. *I guess it's on Casthus to decide whether he gets to keep it or not, then.* Or me. Because I was apparently in the business of accidentally causing massive changes in the war between realms.

After changing into a fresh outfit, I walked to the lab to replace my supplies. I'd lost all my weapons and most of my demonglass, too, which wasn't ideal. I didn't have an infinite supply. Even Lythocrax didn't, which struck me as odd considering his—and my—magic was tied to it. But I hadn't seen the entirety of the realm he ruled over.

"I'm not driving there. I think my car's taken enough abuse," I said, holding up a handful of demonglass. "Ready?"

Rachel nodded. "For the record, am I telling Javos about all this? I don't know if Niko told him about the fallen, but he does know the killer worked with Lythocrax and you went after him."

"Honestly, it's not Lythocrax pulling the strings. He's with… heaven, kind of. He fell on purpose, but he's not the orchestrator."

No… someone else had been responsible for sending me on that mission. A person who'd planted those saphor demon eggs, and by extension, murdered Rory.

Someone at the celestial guild.

But the guild had to wait. Lythocrax had *stolen* the fallen from me, to form his own army, and while I didn't know who was responsible in this realm, I knew the person who'd really laid the trap. I'd been angry with the guild after Rory had died, but I'd never had a real target. I did now.

"He fell on purpose," Rachel repeated. *"Why?"*

"As a spy, I think," I said. "But he couldn't get into any

demon realms until recently. Now his world has been linked with Pandemonium, though, who knows what will happen?"

Only Babylon linked directly to Earth, but his servant had already been running in and out of this realm from Purgatory. I didn't have time to pick a fight with Javos, not when we needed an army of our own to face what was coming. But with one group of allies missing and the other potentially on the enemy's side, the warlocks were a safer bet.

The instant Rachel and I transported ourselves into my lab at the warlocks' guild, shouts erupted from outside the door. The room itself looked much the same as the last time I'd been here, my supplies still strewn everywhere, like nobody had been in the room since I'd quit. But unfamiliar voices came from down the corridor.

"Shit. The other warlocks."

I'd bet Javos had told them he'd found out who the murderer was. *Please say they don't know she looks like me.*

I pushed open the door and walked out into the corridor. A group of warlocks had gathered outside Javos's office—not a room he generally used much, considering he was usually marching around giving orders. My celestial light chose that moment to switch on, and I quickly stuck my left hand deep in my pocket. Better to assess the situation before barging in. Everyone was too fixated on the room beyond to notice Rachel and I slip into the crowd. Inside, Javos was shouting—"Get them out. This is confidential information."

"The hell it is," Nikolas snapped. "You're not qualified to lead the warlocks of this city and it's time for someone else to step in before you do irreversible damage."

"Hear hear," said Rachel.

All eyes turned to us. I gave her an accusing look, then shrugged. "I back Nikolas. For the record. Not sure if I get a vote. Also, fair warning: I think Lythocrax the arch-demon is probably going to attack the city."

"What have you done this time?" Javos demanded.

Nikolas spared me a glance—relief mixed with fury—and then turned back to him. "As I *tried* to tell you, the demon who took Devi is the one who's been killing warlocks."

"Technically, it was someone else giving the orders, but yep," I said, over the warlocks' protests. "The arch-demon Lythocrax created a being, using his creation magic, and it seems to have a type of celestial power. He's been sending it to attack warlocks, to frame the celestials."

"And just how do you claim he's doing this?" Javos asked. "You let those celestials get away with hiding outside the city. Not anymore. I've already sent a team of warlocks after them."

Oh, for the Divinities' sakes. "You idiot," I snapped. "They're hardly the most important thing you should be worried about at the moment. It's Lythocrax who has an army."

Damn. The warlocks here didn't even know about the fallen. But maybe they couldn't be saved now.

"Devi," said Javos, "my brother has those rogues of yours within sight. At one word from me, he will destroy them. And if you think I'm merciless, he makes me look positively mild."

Everyone froze. Power vibrated out from Javos's formidable form, and every warlock in the hallway began to rise into the air. Hands, talons and claws grabbed the walls and floor, some knocking into one another in an attempt to break the spell. Some demons shifted into scarier forms. Auras surged, magic flaring in an burst of lights that nearly sent my demon mark catatonic.

Javos had levitated every warlock in the corridor—and he wasn't about to stop.

"Stop that!" I shouted at him. "Stop it—"

The walls trembled, the bricks shifting. Too late for classical music. The whole place was about to come crashing down.

Nikolas's wings extended, followed by dark-edged lightning. It hit Javos with the force of a truck, sending him flying into the wall. The brick gave way beneath the onslaught of magic, and panic shot through my nerves. I reached out with my demon marked hand, grabbed Javos's magic and pushed. My borrowed telekinetic power smashed into the rapidly collapsing ceiling. *Crap. Didn't mean to do that.* I let a slower trickle of power flow from my palm, and the pieces of falling brick stilled. But I hadn't practised nearly enough to use his magic on the whole house.

"Get out!" I yelled. "If his magic switches off, we're all dead."

Black lightning burst from Nikolas's palms, and the stunned warlocks snapped into action. Some ran for cover away from the teetering walls and ceiling, while others formed shields or deflected the falling debris. The more sensible made for the doors, and a sudden rush of telekinetic power hit the collapsing ceiling. The debris shot out in all directions, leaving the ceiling open to the sky. Dark lightning collided with another blast of telekinetic magic, pushing the house's remains away from the warlocks fleeing for their lives. The moment the last warlock left the building, I ran back to Nikolas, where he and Javos remained in the wrecked office. As I watched, he drew back and punched Javos so hard on the jaw that the warlock left the ground, hitting the debris-strewn earth with a bone-shaking crunch.

Everything stilled. We stood in a circle of debris, in an echoing silence. Javos didn't get up. Out cold, probably.

Nikolas looked up at me.

"Hey," I said. "I got out of hell." I moved closer and hugged him. He hissed in pain, holding his hand at an awkward angle. Ouch. He'd hit Javos so hard he'd broken bones.

"Sorry," I said. "Someone's going to sleep through all the fun."

"Someone's going to wake up and find his leadership position has been revoked." He shook his hand, healed once again. "Let's go."

Lights flashed up and down the street. Portals opening. *Great timing there, Lythocrax.* We were too late to warn anyone—the battle was already here.

"What the hell are those lights?" I asked aloud. "Those can't all be portals—"

"Demonglass," he said.

Someone had left demonglass scattered in the street, and countless demons surged through, along with the fallen.

Lythocrax's army had arrived.

22

"Watch it," I warned the warlocks, some of whom still looked stunned, as though they thought the sudden demon attack was somehow connected with the collapsing building. "They can't be killed. They'll just come back to life."

And they wouldn't stop, not until I'd taken down their creator.

I broke into a sprint. I'd know if the arch-demon was in this realm, but the evil Devi clone was another story.

My demon mark seared my palm, reminding me of the magic within it. Abyss's power. No time for a test run, so I'd be relying on my usual celestial abilities in this fight.

Nikolas took to the sky, his wings beating. Wait a moment. If I turned into a winged demon, I'd be able to fly after Lythocrax no matter where he was hiding.

Way to overlook the obvious, Devi.

"Trap the fallen in pentagrams," I told the warlocks. "The only way to stop them is to contain them. Get props, pentagrams—anything. Hell, grab Javos if he wakes up and strong-arm him into using his telekinetic ability to keep them off the ground. I'm sure he's capable of it. His weakness is classical music, by the way."

I didn't wait for an answer. I ran through the warlocks, yelling the same instructions to everyone who would listen. Nikolas landed beside me, his wings edged in darkness. "Are you ready?"

"To find Lythocrax? Yes. Can I trust you to handle the fort here?"

"It'll have to be Rachel," he said. "Javos sent several warlock allies of ours after those rogue celestials. Someone has to warn them they're heading into a trap."

"Oh *shit*." Like it or not, Nikolas's allegiance was to the warlocks over the fallen. "Okay. Do it. The other warlocks have their instructions."

The Grade Fours were unpredictable and still thought me an ally, but that would change if the warlocks reached them first. I hoped Nikolas would stop them in time.

I took in a breath. "I'm not much use in dealing with the celestials. I'm going after Lythocrax. This is all on him. If I can stop him—"

"You can."

He kissed me full on the mouth, his arms wrapping around me. His wings were still out, his eyes still flickering with golden light. He wasn't just saying goodbye: he was offering a challenge to the other warlocks not to stop me.

Time to make you pay, Lythocrax.

I gripped the demonglass tight in my hand. Light exploded behind my eyes, and flames danced around me. A moment later—

"Not this realm!" I yelled at the demonglass.

"That's not very nice," said Zadok.

He stood edged in darkness on the floor of a room that was an exact replica of his main tower room on Babylon, demonglass wall included. Dark wings extended from his shoulders, and he was clad in dark battle gear not unlike his brother's. Very much unlike Nikolas, however, his eyes were cold and remorseless.

"Neither are you," I said. "Why did my demon magic bring me here?"

"Why indeed. You'll have to ask someone else that question."

Okay... I'd never felt nervous being in the same room as him—no more than any other warlock, anyway. But there was something... off, about his magic. Something darker than before. And on a shadow demon, that was saying something.

"You're acting weirdly," I commented. "Aren't you bothered Abyss is dead?"

"Dead?" he intoned. "Who killed her? You?"

"Lythocrax." Anger sparked to life at the mention of the name... and a memory stirred. Zadok knew about the saphor demon eggs. He'd told me about them. "You have something to answer for as well."

He arched a brow. "Oh?"

"Saphor demon eggs," I said. "You knew what they were before I did. How?"

"I imagine there are a great number of things about the demon realms I knew before you did, Devi."

"You know what I'm talking about. When my demon mark manifested—when Rory died—it was because he touched those demon eggs. Someone planted them at the scene so the two of us would run into them. It was set up so only one of us would survive and walk away with the mark."

"Ah," he said. "I did wonder if you'd ever make the connection."

"You have some nerve offering me information only when it's convenient to you," I said quietly. "You knew Rory died because of whoever planted those demon eggs."

"No, I certainly didn't," he said.

"What's your source? Who told you they even existed?"

"If you must know, it was Themedes. We talked a great deal when he was a prisoner. I thought nothing of it."

He wouldn't. But the eggs themselves came from Pandemonium. The demons had handed the eggs over… because the guild traded with them.

The agents of the guild had murdered Rory. The celestials —for all intents and purposes—were my enemies now.

But the guild's celestials weren't pulling the strings. Even Lythocrax was merely a stand-in. Someone had sent him down from heaven for the purposes of amassing an army against their own fellow Divinities.

Zadok tilted his head. "Did you need him? The human? Wouldn't you rather join with me instead?"

"You're creeping me out," I said. "What in the world happened to you?"

"What happened?" He smiled, a grim smile. "Have you got all day? I think not. Most recently, I acquired a set of enemies to vanquish. I also seem to have gained a city."

"And lost your mind."

His smile was razor sharp. "When did I ever claim to be sane?"

Wait. Now I knew what was off about him. His aura. It'd disappeared. It was dark enough in the room and my arrival had been unexpected enough that I honestly hadn't noticed before. But no demon was without an aura. Right?

I waved a hand. "Is that a new party trick? The aura thing?"

"Aura thing?"

He stepped forwards, revealing his shadowy aura was right there. Like I'd imagined it disappearing. Or my own aura vision was faulty.

"If you're innocent of dealing the demon eggs, you're not

on my hit list, so I'm going after Lythocrax. If you'd like to join me, be my guest, but don't think this means we have any kind of arrangement."

He watched me with a golden tinted gaze. "Revenge seems to be your primary drive, or it will be, once you truly embrace what you are. As for me, the amount *I* could gain might well be infinite. But I have a crusade to fight of my own, so now is the time for me to leave you."

"Wait." I held up a hand. "Are you at all aware of what Lythocrax is doing? He stole the fallen and turned them into his own. He's waging war on Earth as we speak. I'm going after him. You have allies, I assume, if you have all this."

He flashed me a last smile. "I wouldn't do to forget our past arrangements. I consider you an ally, Devi Lawson. But this is not my battle to fight."

No. It's mine. I gripped the demonglass in one hand. "Your choice."

"Until we meet again," he said, and disappeared as the glass swallowed me up, taking me into Lythocrax's realm.

My body crashed into the Devi clone, and I rolled on the ground, narrowly avoiding her blade.

Black lightning sizzled from my fingertips, unrestrained. The shadow demon's power. She dodged two attacks but not the third. The sound of shattering glass came from where my attack struck. I stared at her. I'd blasted a hole into her chest, but while golden blood dripped from the wound, her body was... solid. No internal organs. A living, breathing person, created entirely of glass. No—*demon*glass.

"He's certainly creative," I gasped out. "Get him here. I want to kill him."

The Devi clone reformed her celestial blade, not speaking. The shattered hole in her chest continued to drip golden blood. It wasn't healing, but she wasn't dying. She must have a weakness… and I had a way to block her from killing me while I figured it out.

I reached for the new, unfamiliar demon magic Abyss had given me. Then I focused all my will on the clone's glass-like form, willing myself to become her—to become unbreakable glass, immune to her celestial touch.

I didn't really think it would work—but when I looked down at my hand, it'd turned glassy, see-through.

She lunged at me, intending to push celestial power into my demon mark again—and I caught her hand in mine and shoved her off balance. I couldn't imitate magic, but our magic was one and the same anyway.

Except unlike me, she didn't have demonic power.

Her thoughts seeped into mine. *I am a weapon. I am the gods'.*

I live for them. I kill only for them. I am nothing. I will be nothing. I fear nothing…

I shook off her thoughts, alarmed at how quickly they'd replaced mine. No wonder Abyss walked around in her human-like disguise rather than pretending to be other people all the time. In the end, the clones of Damian Greenwood and the inspector had seemed so much like their real-life counterparts that nobody had been able to tell the difference.

In her mind, there are answers about how to kill her. And him.

I deflected her attack, digging deep within my mind for her weaknesses. She'd been forged as a weapon… turned from nothing, from dust, into something to be feared… I did my best to ignore her other thoughts and dived deeper in search of what I needed.

Then I stopped. I was her weakness. She had no defence against her own reflection.

I drove my newly glass-formed fists into her shattered chest, and she screamed in rage. I'd already overpowered her.

Golden blood dripped from the gaping hole. The wound wasn't healing. Unlike me, she couldn't use regenerative magic.

Black lightning sprang to my fingertips for the last time. My hand over her heart, I drew out the last of the shadow demon's power—and let go.

She shattered beneath me, pieces of demonglass crumbling to the ground. I stepped back, her thoughts whirling around my head.

Only when the armies of heaven and hell are brought to their breaking point—then, it will end.

The thought shocked me back into my real mind. I'd been a damned fool. Lythocrax was already on his way to Earth. Never mind the bridge—an arch-demon could level the city.

Shattered pieces of demonglass lay all around me on the barren wasteland, the broken remains of the Devi clone reduced to rubble thanks to the demonic magic I'd unleashed. I'd taken all that remained of Abyss's power, and I could even become an arch-demon if wanted to.

I just hope his hate doesn't bury me alive.

My own rage burned like a furnace. It would have to be enough.

Lythocrax's demonic form wrapped around me. Power rang through my bones and shook the ground beneath my feet. I towered, the whole world seeming to shrink before my first step. Strength hummed within me. I'd created this world. It was mine…

No. the real arch-demon is on his way to Earth, and I'm going to kill him before he gets there.

Wings unfurled behind my shoulders, and I took to the skies.

23

I flew, honing in on the demon whose form I'd taken. He'd had his Devi clone send the fallen through to Earth using her own magic, but he hadn't followed them. Abyss, in her desperation, had forged a link between the two realms. It required a huge surge of energy for an arch-demon to cross between realms, but he could create anything. That was his power.

Being him—flying as him—made part of me want to vomit at the thought of spending another second in his head, but I crushed my human emotions beneath the demon raging inside me. Rage alone kept me flying on. Strength and power, magic and explosive force—he had it all. *Where are you?*

I probed his memory and recoiled. It was like sticking my finger into oily demon blood. If I dived too deep, I'd drown. I'd need time to tease out his secrets. Time I didn't have, especially a mile up in the air.

Then I saw him, a winged shape—above a glowing pentagram of fire.

No.

I flew at him, collided with his huge demonic body, and we crashed through the portal.

Earth's cloudy skies surrounded us. From the ground, aerial battles looked fast and brutal. Up close, I barely had time to recover from one blow before the next landed, our bodies colliding in a clash of steely pain. If I wore my human form, I'd have broken within the first few seconds. I pummelled him with my steel-like fists, taking pleasure in every wound I tore into him. I couldn't use his magic, only my own, but it didn't matter. Blood dripped from my own wounds. He hit *hard,* more vicious than I'd have expected from an arch-demon I'd assumed until today was all talk. I hadn't used his name, but his caution and hesitation to strike me directly was entirely gone.

Wait a moment. He hadn't actually seen Abyss die… so he must think I was her.

Lythocrax pummelled me with his steel fists, knocking the breath from my lungs and tearing into my skin. There'd be a limit to how much abuse this body could take—especially as I had less regenerative power than he did. Abyss had been on her last legs, after all.

His fist slammed into my skull, momentarily blanking out my vision.

Memories exploded behind my eyes, too fast to make much sense of. I was falling, and darkness rushed in.

Memories of a cave viewed through fog… of shapes too dazzling to look upon directly. Winged shapes. Angels. His memories.

Lythocrax's emotions tore through me like a tidal wave. *Anger at being manipulated, at being shoved into helping this ungrateful human girl.*

Pleasure when I realised I could finally be rid of her, and use my other pawn to take away her power.

Rage when she slithered out of his grip, and found her way to my realm anyway.

Fury when she used my name against me.

So much fury. I was drowning in it.

Then I saw a face I knew. Rory.

My own anger pushed back against Lythocrax's, and I came back to awareness—to Devi—as the two of us crashed into the ground of Lythocrax's own realm. We must have passed through the still-open portal. Blood dripped into my eyes from a cut on my forehead, and more cuts laced my body. He fought mean and dirty, but he bore as many wounds as I did. I might not have his magic, but I *had* borrowed his freakish strength.

"I'm surprised," I coughed. "I thought you were all talk, Altheare."

The echo of his anger momentarily overwhelmed my own emotions. Had I accidentally made our connection deeper by becoming him? I'd never have guessed that if I took on someone's form, I'd experience their emotions in real-time.

"Don't say the name, tainted one." He spat blood onto the ground.

"You're one to talk." I coughed again. My voice had turned back to my own, and I felt his form slipping away as exhaustion threatened to claim me.

"Devina," he growled. "She gave you her magic?"

"Yep. Now I know all your dirty little secrets."

"Lies. The truth would break you."

I spat out a mouthful of blood. "Wow. You have issues. And for the record, you picked *me*, so it's not my problem if it went badly for you, Altheare."

"I can break you in this form."

"You can try, Altheare. Alternatively, you can fuck off and

die." As I spoke, I drew his form around me again and probed into his mind, but it seemed as depthless as ever.

"You're built to fall, Devi. Like all of us. Accept it. Embrace it. Or give in and face your true end at my hands. I'll even make it quick."

"Why?" I asked. "Why did Rory have to do so I could live? Says who?"

Nobody questions the Divine Agents.

The term was unfamiliar, but came directly from his thoughts as I became him once again. His emotions rippled under the surface, but my own curiosity pervaded.

"Who are the Divine Agents?" I asked, aloud.

The ground shook as he rose to his full height, blood seeping from his wounds. "How dare you steal my thoughts, mortal scum."

"I can do worse, Altheare." While part of me remained nauseated at the idea of being connected with him, I couldn't deny a sense of satisfaction at his fury. He'd be trying to guard his innermost thoughts—and if you tried hard not to think about something, it'd likely be the first thing to come to mind.

Let's see what he's hiding.

More images flashed. I coughed blood again. I needed to regenerate, but—

The Divine Agents were angels. They gave him the orders.

Lythocrax's huge fist hit out. I took the blow, clinging onto his form, his thoughts slipping through my fingers—

"The Divine Agents… told you to mark me," I ground out. "What did they give you in return?"

"Power," he said, landing beside me. "I would be the first demon to retain my divine magic. I would bless you with my mark. And you were ungrateful enough to turn against me."

"Because you tried to destroy everything I cared about. If

you'd wanted someone who didn't give a damn, you should have marked another demon."

"You know why you had to be human." His fist clenched. "And I will beat you into that form again."

I barely had chance to take to the air before he slammed into me, bearing us both through the portal again. Below the churning clouds, Haven City sprawled. My home. I flipped him over and managed to deflect his attack before he knocked me out of the air.

"You *won't* destroy them," I screamed. My body—his body —was broken and bleeding. Blood rained onto the city below. The poor people below were going to have a barrel of fun cleaning up the aftermath.

Regenerate...

Lythocrax's heavy body tackled me again, and this time, we missed the portal and continued to fall.

Shit. This is gonna hurt.

We crashed into an unfamiliar street, narrowly missing the nearby houses. Screams surrounded us, along with the noise of the warlocks fighting against the still-spawning demon army. I spotted Nikolas's winged form in the air, too, but had no time to take any of it in. Lythocrax gripped my head and slammed it into the pavement, triggering a small earthquake. I rolled out of the way, my head ringing, my body crying out a warning that I was about to run out of regenerative power. The houses continued to tremble as the earth shook, and I grabbed a nearby lamp post with bleeding hands—

Human hands. Shit.

He drew back for the killing blow, and a mass of bodies swarmed him, clawing, screaming.

The fallen were defending me. They hadn't forgotten I'd claimed them.

Lythocrax roared and flailed his massive arms. In a single

blow, he threw several fallen aside, but he'd given me a moment's reprieve. Nikolas's regenerative magic flooded my demon mark and I sensed him behind me, but he didn't intervene. He knew I wanted to finish this myself.

"You didn't claim them, I growled, summoning my celestial blade. Demon power rippled along to the hilt, the remnants of Abyss's magic coupled with Nikolas's lightning. I felt him feeding the power into me from a distance—enough to end this.

I grabbed a handful of demonglass. Shattered glass burned my hand, in my blood. The source of my power, binding me to this realm. Earth.

Every hit I'd taken, I'd held the demonglass as a shield. Magic poured into my demon mark once more, and I lunged forwards with celestial speed—

And slammed the shards into Lythocrax's throat.

Blood poured out. He writhed, but the fallen held him down. Their claws tore into him, ripping his tough demon skin. Not enough. I needed to become him again.

I drew on Abyss's power, transformed into him, and *pushed* deep down into his mind. Like glass shattering, memories burst before my eyes.

Arch-demons' weaknesses came about when they fell…

When they spurned the gods. But he'd fallen on purpose. And he'd chosen his weakness.

His weakness was his own power.

A wave of rippling light passed through his eyes. Demonglass. His power source… blindingly bright, but not unbreakable.

The arch-demon screamed.

"Altheare," I told him. "Die."

The demonglass glowed in my hand, fusing into a single weapon, and I drew it across his throat. His head hit the ground, and his body stopped struggling. The fallen continued to hold him down, even as his blood soaked into the road, and the roars of the battle raged around us.

I looked into his empty eyes, felt his emotions inside me flicker and die. The noise in my head ceased as I let the magic go, felt the demon's form slip away, and became human again.

2 4

The fallen crawled off his broken body, leaving his huge form in the road. The demonglass weapon in my hands trembled as I lowered it. *Whose power did that? Mine, or his?*

Maybe both. His thoughts continued to burn at the back of my mind, though now disconnected and indecipherable. It'd be a long time before I was rid of their taint.

The nearby houses were a wreck, several missing windows and garden walls, and the street had taken a hell of a beating from the two arch-demons pummelling each other into the road. Abyss's magic… I didn't know if I had any left. But I'd done it.

I'd killed the demon who'd ordered Rory's death.

So why did I feel so empty?

Nikolas landed beside me, and rested his hand on my shoulder. "Devi?"

I took a step backwards, my celestial hand lighting up. "I'm going to burn him to ashes. And then we'll clean this up."

The fallen stared ahead blankly, no longer bound to Lythocrax. I needed to figure out what in hell to do with them, but exhaustion masked my thoughts, and weird disconnected emotions kept jolting through me. Lythocrax was thoroughly dead, so it must be a side effect of Abyss's magic.

"He killed… Rory," I said quietly to Nikolas. "Not directly. Someone at the guild did. There was an agent there. When I read his mind—he was taking direct orders from heaven. From a Divine Agent. I think there's a faction of angels trying to infiltrate hell, and he got himself kicked out of heaven on their orders. I don't know how far he got into infiltrating the demon realms. I didn't read enough of his memories to be sure. But he was definitely sent here for that reason. And he marked me, with the help of someone at the guild."

Nikolas didn't say anything for a moment. "Devi… I don't want to push you, but you killed an arch-demon. It's only a matter of time before the others find out. Casthus will find out. He… might see you as a direct threat."

He was right. Worse, Zadok would tell me to hunt down those guild bastards without a second's thought. Revenge was *his* thing. He and his brother were like… okay, not like the angel and devil. More like the devil and the slightly more evil devil.

"Your brother," I said. "He's… he's acting seriously weird. He took over that tower and drove out Abyss. I know he knew her weakness, but he caved to her once before and I didn't think he had that much power even before Casthus tried to have him killed. Why is he so confident he'll get to keep it?"

"I don't know," he said. "I seem to have missed a few things where my brother is concerned. I certainly underestimated his tenacity."

"He did grow up on a demon realm," I pointed out. "And

he's spent the last few days stewing in his own drive for revenge while secretly gaining power, apparently."

"No." He looked irritated. "The reason I felt secure leaving him on Babylon in the first place was because I knew I could overpower him easily, if it came down to it. If he's done anything, it's recent."

"You mean, made a deal with another arch-demon. Because that's what we really need right now."

Never mind the war between heaven and hell. Shadow demons against shadow demons, on a realm that was still linked to Earth? What else had he been plotting?

"We'll deal with that later. What about the fallen?"

He stiffened. "There's a portal."

I turned around to where he was looking. Shards of demon-glass lay where we'd been fighting—the same portals the fallen had originally come from. Several of them had begun to move in that direction. "There's nothing on that realm left. Hang on."

I pointed my celestial hand at the rippling portal. The lights expanded, showing a wasteland—and a distant city. Not a city I knew. Lythocrax's last creation.

The fallen moved forwards, eyeing the portal. Inspiration struck.

"I don't know what there is on that realm," I said to them. "It has no leader. It might be dangerous, but it's probably the safest demon realm there is."

An offshoot of heaven, if I believed Lythocrax. Despite his demons, the fallen would be able to survive in a place like that. And it looked like he'd been busy creating more new life, too.

"You want to go through?" I asked.

Several of the fallen nodded, while others moved slowly in that direction.

"I sense them," one of them said slowly. "The Divinities."

My heart sank. "That might not be a good thing. Have you ever heard of the Divine Agents?"

The fallen shook his head. Worth a try. Maybe the guild knew. From Lythocrax's thoughts, it sounded like the Divine Agents were an offshoot of heaven, independent of the ruling Divinities—but still against hell. For what it was worth. Since they'd had Lythocrax kill the angels on Purgatory, they sure as hell weren't the same Divinities I'd thought I knew.

Speaking of Purgatory—I never did find out if the inspector had survived, but if the angels hadn't, I doubted he had.

I nodded to the fallen. "If you're sure, you're welcome to go through. The shadow demon will never find you there." That much, I could count on.

The fallen moved towards the portal with jerky movements, murmuring thanks. It took all my energy to stay on my feet, to stop my thoughts from spinning back to Lythocrax's—to the information I hadn't had the chance to process yet.

"The celestial rogues?" I asked Nikolas. "Did you reach them in time?"

"The demons came through into this realm before the warlocks mounted their attack. But we're going to have to make sure to deal with them, and fast."

Before Javos took matters into his own hands. "I killed the Devi clone," I told him. "The murderer is dead."

Not that those rogue celestials were exactly a stable element, either. And I doubted Javos would give up so easily.

The last of the fallen passed through the portal. I hoped they'd find peace in that realm, or as close as possible on a newly formed demon world. They'd made their choice, and I'd respect it. That realm was far from perfect, but with no arch-demon raining hell down on them, they should be able to survive.

Nothing was certain. Evil created, good destroyed. And the enemy was still unknown.

I turned to Nikolas. "I take it Javos is deposed now? Does that mean you're stepping in?"

"Since nobody else will? Yes. It's going to be difficult, but I think I can get the warlocks to rally around me. We'll need unity, with what's coming."

"The war between heaven and hell?"

"The war between father and son." He paused. "I checked in on Babylon, and apparently my father received a gift from his son. The skin of his former fire demon servant."

"Zadok did that?"

"I think he believed it would be sufficient enough to prove his intentions."

I grimaced. "He's going to get killed for real this time."

And yet he wasn't the worst of it. I'd stolen the fallen out from under the shadow demon's nose, and while he'd let me do so, I suspected he was planning to retaliate. Especially now I'd permanently moved them out of his way.

Yet he wasn't foremost on my mind. The people who'd killed Rory were still out there—still at the celestial guild, for all I knew. Maybe revenge shouldn't be my first priority, but it was definitely high on the list. Underneath 'stop the demons from destroying the Earth and declaring war on everyone I care about'.

I watched the portal's lights die out. "Let's find the others. Fiona... crap, she's probably at home, if she didn't join in the fighting."

I began to walk away, with Nikolas right behind me. My energy levels were utterly depleted, and I'd feel like crap when the adrenaline wore off. I hadn't seen Fiona's fire magic in the battle, but I doubted she'd stayed out of the fighting.

My celestial hand glowed, burning every dead demon I

came across, as I walked. Demon battles left one hell of a mess. Spotting a tangle of venos demon corpses, I made to blast them to ashes—but another celestial light flared past my face, close enough to make my skin tingle.

I spun around. "Who—?"

"Devi!" Fiona shouted at me from the roadside. She wasn't alone. A person—female, I guessed—stood beside a motorcycle parked nearby, a helmet covering her face.

"Fiona!" I gasped out. "I'm glad you're okay."

She grinned at me. "You're going to have to fill me in, but there's someone here who really wants to meet you."

"Oh?" I said warily.

"I made a friend."

The girl standing against the motorcycle removed her helmet, her dark hair streaming loose, her ripped jeans stained with demon blood. And her wrists bore similar cuffs to mine.

She looked up at me. "Hey, Devi. I've heard a lot about you."

"This is Faye Carruthers," said Fiona. "The creator of DivinityWatch."

ABOUT THE AUTHOR

Emma is the New York Times and USA Today Bestselling author of the Changeling Chronicles urban fantasy series.

Emma spent her childhood creating imaginary worlds to compensate for a disappointingly average reality, so it was probably inevitable that she ended up writing fantasy novels. When she's not immersed in her own fictional universes, Emma can be found with her head in a book or wandering around the world in search of adventure.

Find out more about Emma's books at www.emmaladams.com.